MW00422742

An Outlawed Heiress & Her Duke

Denise Daye

DEDICATION

For the Confederated Tribes of Grand Ronde

I loved working for you! Thank you for being nothing but kind to me and for teaching me about your beautiful culture…

TABLE OF CONTENTS

CHAPTER 1

D eath is never easy. Whether it happens for the first, or the thousandth time. Death is death, and it is painful every single time for the ones who are left behind. For Esther, this was the second painful death in her life. Both of her parents were now gone, forever.

She grasped her father's cold hand against her soft, wet cheek as if it would bring back the warmth into him. Her tears were now gentle, a strong contrast to hours ago, when they ran down her cheeks like an angry thunderstorm full of despair that had lost all hope.

"Come now child, let him go with God," she heard Father Pilgram say in a kind voice.

But Esther couldn't. *Just a little longer*, she said to herself. *Let me hold him just a little longer*. It broke her heart, more than it had when her mother passed away. Not because she didn't love her mother as much; she probably loved her even more, but she was still so young when she'd

1

passed away. All she had left of her were a few memories.

Her father had tried hard to make up for the loss of a mother at such a young age. He spent every moment he could with Esther. No dollar was ever spared when it came down to his little pumpkin. No man could have spoiled or loved a child more dearly than Cliff Silverton had loved his little girl. And now he was no more. If it wasn't for the doctor announcing his death shortly before midnight, Esther could almost make herself believe that he was in fact just resting. He looked so peaceful — as if he was just taking a nap, like he did so often after a tiring work trip.

"Esther, Father Pilgram is right. It's time," Morris said in a supposedly intended sad tone, resting a hand on her shoulder.

She jerked up, almost furious, shaking it off. If it wasn't for the presence of the doctor and Father Pilgram, she would have swatted it off like a fly. How dare he play the grieving friend now! She had sent for him yesterday evening, just as her father had wished, but Morris didn't grace her dying father with his presence until long after he had already passed, his disproportionate, portly body stinking of cheap parfum and whiskey.

The doctor, an older man with a long, gaunt face and small glasses, exchanged confused looks with Father Pilgram. But Esther didn't care and threw Morris another hateful glare with her fiery eyes. If it was up to her, she would have asked Morris to leave, get out, to never come back… But this was her father's deathbed, not the place to make a scene, no matter how much she hated him.

"Yes, Morris, thank you." Her voice trembled, despite her trying to sound as calm as possible.

And like so often in her tragic life full of death, Esther Silverton gathered all her strength once more and let go of her father's hand, gently placing it back onto the silk cover next to his chest with a faint smile on her lips that said nothing short of goodbye, from the bottom of her heart, with all the love she had.

"Why don't you go rest some now, *Pumpkin.* I shall arrange everything from here on," Morris said, trying to provoke her. He knew how much she hated it when he called her by the name her beloved father had given her when she was still knee high to a bumblebee. She ignored him, turned her gaze back to her father. At least that way she didn't have to look at the despicable man who in his heart had been waiting for this very moment every morning when he opened his eyes to greet the world.

Morris was her father's business partner who had been at his side since before she was even born. And if it wasn't for his gambling problems and terrible ways with money, Esther might count herself lucky to have a friend like him in times like these. But Morris was no man to count on. He was no friend in times like these. Every dime Morris would make at her father's side went into whoring, gambling, drinking and every other despicable activity a man could possibly find in New York—and there were plenty. Her father was too kindhearted to see Morris for what he truly was. *'He will find his way,'* he would always tell Esther after paying another gambling debt for Morris, fondly thinking back to the time when the two of them, barely old enough to grow a beard, had spent every cent they owned to buy a run-down cattle farm in Texas. The deal was too good to be true, and that is what it was, too good to be true.

The hundreds of acres of land they bought were known to every person in town as dead valley. Nothing ever grew on that land, and nothing ever would. But what at first seemed like the biggest scam in local history had turned out to be a fairytale. This dirt-dry piece of land that some said they wouldn't even take for free turned out to sit on the biggest oil deposit in the state of Texas. Overnight, her father and Morris became wealthy beyond belief. Her father, who was too poor to buy his childhood sweetheart a coach ticket to join him in Texas, was now rich enough to build his own railroad right into the town that was now renamed Oilton. But unlike Morris, her honorable father was no man who would throw himself into expensive clothes, women, and houses. No, he re-invested his money, married the love of his life, and lived a quiet and peaceful life. This American dream unfortunately never came to life for Morris, who changed from a humble country boy into a despicable monster.

Esther shook her head in disbelief. Her beloved father was really gone now. For months he had suffered from a chronic, mild case of the new disease called appendicitis, so he'd decided to send for a famous English surgeon from London. But like countless times before, the Silverton curse struck again, and what was a mild case for months turned into acute appendicitis just at the moment they'd received a letter from the famous surgeon, Dr. Tait, saying that he would accept the ridiculously generous amount of money offered to him by Cliff and was already on his way to America.

"Miss Esther," the familiar voice of Ginny whispered from behind the door, as if she knew it was bad timing but thought it was still important enough to knock.

"What is it, Ginny?" Morris hissed at her, swinging the door open. "Can't you spare us your insufferable impertinence even in the face of death?"

Ginny was close to bursting into tears when Esther rushed to her rescue, but too late: the tears started rolling. She shoved Morris aside and took over control of the door. Ginny glanced quickly over to the bed where Cliff lay and shook her head, frantically wiping her tears away.

"I'm sorry Miss… I-I'm sorry for being dull-witted again…"

Esther gently placed her hand on Ginny's shoulder. Ashamed of how Morris mistreated the poor servants at every chance he got, she tried to control the damage as well as she could. "Ginny, don't say such things. My father cared deeply for you and he would not approve of you or anybody else calling you such." Esther threw Morris a condescending glance before drawing her eyes back to Ginny, who still couldn't get a hold of her tears and made a pitiful attempt to nod. It was obvious how much she and the other staff had cared for Cliff Silverton, a man whose kindness made them feel like they were part of the family.

She used her maid's apron to wipe her face dry. "It's the doctor. Lawson Tait. He just arrived, asking for the master of the house."

Esther nodded with a sad smile on her face. Once again, her mind was drawn back into thoughts about the Silverton curse. Her father was barely cold when his last and only hope had arrived all the way from London.

Esther shook her head, pulling her thoughts back to face the tormenting world she now had to call reality. "Of course. Please tell him to wait in the drawing room."

She'd barely got the words out when Morris squeezed past her and stepped out into the hallway next to Ginny. "I will take care of —"

"No need." Esther interrupted him. If he thought he would take over the house, he was wrong. For a second, just long enough to notice, Morris clenched his jaw in anger before instantly fading into a fake smile once more.

"I will take care of the announcement then. The company has to be notified." He straightened his vest and disappeared before Esther could say another word.

Ginny followed him with wary eyes before redirecting them carefully back to Esther, not sure what to make of this.

"It's alright, Ginny. Go now and inform Dr. Tait that I will be right with him."

Ginny gave a curious nod before hastening over the red rugs downstairs.

Esther re-entered her father's bedroom. The heavy curtains were drawn shut, letting in only the slightest amount of daylight to witness her father sleep forever. The gas lamps mounted on the walls gave the room a suffocating, gloomy feel. Esther looked over to her father, sensing that painful knot in her throat again that would turn her legs into a puddle. She clenched her fists as hard as she could as the blood between her palms turned warm, to avoid the storm of tears that would otherwise run down her cheeks. It worked, barely, and she was able to face Father Pilgram without having another breakdown. He walked up to her the moment their eyes met.

"My dear child, I will make the necessary preparations." He gently caressed her hand. Were those tears she saw in his eyes? "Your father was a dear friend and it would be an honor for me to organize his last farewell."

Esther nodded. Neither her father nor Esther were deeply religious, but Father Pilgram was the man who had baptized her and had been there for her family through every occurrence of death — and there were plenty if you counted grandparents and aunts. Father Pilgram squeezed her hand for one last time, before signaling the doctor to leave.

For the first time in hours, she was alone with her father. Esther wanted to walk over to him, to hold his hand, to whisper her last words into his ear, that it mayhap wake him from his slumber after all, to tell him that she loved him and always would, when she heard Ginny's distressed voice shout from below.

"But the miss said she would —"

"Mind your place, woman!" Morris yelled back at her in rage.

That painful knot in her throat turned to anger. There would be no time to say goodbye to her father. Morris would not allow it. And if she knew this man as well as she was certain she did, shouting at servants and pretending to be in charge of the house would be the least that Esther had to fear from him. There was an oil empire to inherit and although her father's will was as clear as crystal broth, Morris would never get a better shot at taking over the company as he would now. And to give her even more of a headache, her family's longtime friend and lawyer Douglas Jones was away on some urgent matters somewhere in New Mexico. He had agreed to lead talks between the Jicarilla Apache Natives and the US government regarding their lands. It was supposed to be four weeks at the most but had now turned into months. He might not even have received her last letter informing him about the horrible condition his longtime friend had had to endure.

Taking a deep breath, she faced the mirror that stood next to her father's dresser. She looked awful. Her chestnut brown hair that was supposed to be combed into a tight bun hung loosely next to her face. Her usually passionate caramel brown eyes looked dull and swollen from crying. And her fine nose that made her the beauty she was famous for, was red with snot running down from it. At least her lips were as red as crimson from biting them too much, making them look as if she wore lipstick. Tying her hair back into a tight bun, she caught a glimpse of her father's bed in the mirror. The burning sensation of tears was creeping up again when she heard Morris's insufferable voice from the distance again.

"Ah, Doctor Tait! What an honor," he touted, acting as if it was his house.

Anger replaced the tears that were about to roll down her face. She slapped both cheeks gently as an encouragement to get ready for battle. Morris's antics needed to end now.

"Don't worry about me, father, I'm a Silverton," she whispered loud enough for her father to hear.

Robbed of the tender last moments she wanted to spend with him, she firmly closed the door behind herself, a mixture of sadness, anger, and determination written all over her face. If Morris thought that the death he had prayed for so many years would finally place the Silverton company into his hands, then she would not only prove this man wrong, but she would also do so with a bang as loud as cannon fire. It was time to set things straight. It was time to take her place as the last remaining Silverton and make her father proud, from wherever he was watching.

With long, confident strides, she descended the stairs and made her way through the enormous entrance hall that led to the drawing room, passing a few servants whispering at each other in excited anticipation of what was to come. The marble under her feet trembled, echoing after every step as if to scream out her anger in her stead. Ginny was about to carry in a tray of tea and cake when Esther gestured her to take it back. She understood instantly and threw Esther a proud smile that said, *this is your home, go show him.*

Esther swung open the door to the drawing room, almost banging it against the wall. Morris, and a chubby, dark-haired man in his thirties, jerked toward her in surprise. Both men stood next to the marble fireplace in between two golden painted silk couches that glistened under the warm dancing flames of the fire. Wide overarching crystal chandeliers hung from the ceilings, flickering like stars. Rich and long draperies covered towering windows that overlooked the estate—the biggest in New York City. Nothing in this house was less than the best and finest, a habit Cliff Silverton had acquired after the death of his beloved wife to spoil his daughter, who surprisingly had turned out kindhearted and selfless and, to his dismay, did not care for such things at all. Not even moving her from her childhood ranch in Texas to the high society of New York could change that, and at some point, he finally gave up and let her be the independent, strong-willed woman she wanted to be.

"Doctor Tait! Thank you for making the long and tiring journey all the way from England. Welcome to my home," she said confidently, walking toward him with her hand outstretched for a handshake. Doctor Tait glanced over to Morris for a brief, lost moment but then walked toward Esther to meet her in the middle of the room.

"Miss Silverton, I've just heard. My deepest condolences," Dr. Tait said, taking her hand into his instead of shaking it. He squeezed it with the strong touch of honest sympathy. "I did not waste any time after I received your father's letter, but as it seems, I am too late…" He stared down at the floor, almost as if he felt ashamed.

"Please, don't apologize. I thank you for coming," Esther said, slowly letting go of his hand.

Dr. Tait shook his head, still avoiding eye contact. "Of course, I shall not charge for this journey."

Esther was about to say something, but Morris now stepped closer, nodding in agreement.

"How very honorable of you," he said, crossing his arms. And there it was. Morris's first public outing of handling the Silverton fortune as if it were his now. What made him think he had any say in how and where her money would be spent?

"Honorable indeed, but my father would have wanted you to receive every penny of what was promised. You crossed an ocean for the Silvertons, and a Silverton always keeps his—" Esther paused, feeling the weight of her words. It wasn't *his* word any longer. It fell on her now to continue the family's honor. "A Silverton always keeps her word," she said, throwing Morris a quick sidelong glance. Was he biting his lip in anger? Good.

Dr. Tait seemed to be thinking about her generous offer, then grabbed her hand and shook it strongly as a sign of gratefulness.

"I thank you deeply. The money would be greatly needed at our hospital to continue the study of this terrible disease that has claimed so many lives." For the first time that day, Esther was able to feel the slightest bit of joy. To think of the money having such a purpose filled her with a feeling of deep satisfaction.

"How very fitting for this sad occasion," she said, squeezing the doctor's hand for a last time. "Well, why not double it?" She added with a smile. She heard Morris gasp from the corner.

"Are you certain? The amount would be...unheard of!" Dr. Tait asked with wide-opened eyes.

"It would be my honor," Esther said to confirm that her offer was genuine. The doctor's face sparkled with gratitude as he bowed deeply in front of her.

"Miss." Ginny knocked at the door, opening it carefully. "Sorry for the intrusion, but there's a gentleman here."

Esther turned to Ginny, her brows closely drawn together. "Who is it?"

Ginny shook her head. "Not sure, Miss, but he says he is a lawyer and here on urgent business."

"Jones!" She felt her heart skip a beat. Talking about family friends when they are needed. Jones had been the Silvertons' lawyer for as long as Esther could remember. He was as loyal as he was smart. There was no doubt in her mind that he would help her remove Morris from her home and make certain that he would never see a penny of the Silverton fortune ever again. Jones hated Morris as much as she did, if not more. But just like Esther, he was never able to get through to her good-hearted father who always saw the best in Morris, and to her dismay, never the worst, even though it was glaringly obvious.

She turned toward Dr. Tait. "I am terribly sorry, but would you please excuse me? You can leave your contact information with Ginny and I shall arrange for your payment shortly."

Dr. Tait seemed more than understanding of the whole situation. "Of course. I shall be staying in New York for several weeks to give lectures. Do not concern yourself with me. Again, I am so terribly sorry." He gave a courtesy bow before passing Ginny and Morris on his way out, nodding a polite goodbye to both of them.

Esther studied Morris's face. Now that Jones was here, was he worried? But much to her surprise, she did not find the anticipated anxiety in it. Far from it. For a man who was about to get cut off, he seemed oddly calm. Did he possess the slightest bit of dignity after all? Accept that he would have to work for money now? Esther was about to compliment him on his surprising ability to show class in times like these when the door opened wide, revealing a tall, skinny man she had never seen before. Like Morris, he was in his late fifties and dressed in that typical, black day suit of a lawyer.

"Ah, Morris my dear friend." He walked over to a now smirking Morris to shake his hand enthusiastically before turning to face Esther. "Miss Silverton, what a pleasure to finally meet you," he said in a suspiciously overfriendly tone, grinning so wide his round glasses almost fell off, which he caught just in time before stretching out a hand toward her.

Something was not right. To this day Esther struggled with reading folks of society. Her upbringing on a ranch in Texas had left deep roots, but it had also taught her to trust her gut. And this guy made it twitch and turn just as much as Morris did. She crossed her arms, refusing to return the gesture of a handshake, which caused the man to throw Morris a quick, concerned look.

"And you are...?" she asked in a clear, unwelcoming tone. Ginny, reading the growing, uncomfortable atmosphere, rushed out to get tea.

"This is Mr. Gorsh," Morris said, signaling the lawyer to take a seat on one of the two silk couches. He complied and placed his leather handbag on his lap.

Esther took a step closer. "And who is Mr. Gorsh, if I may ask, and what is he doing in *my* house?" Her annoyance grew thicker by the second. Father Pilgram would return soon to collect the body of her father for keeping. She still hoped to say her final goodbyes, properly and undisturbed, which Morris had already ruined once this morning.

Morris was about to speak when Mr. Gorsh held up a hand to signal him that he would take care of the talking. Surprisingly, Morris, who was known for his temper and arrogance, did not seem to mind this gesture. Quite the opposite. He stared at Esther in excited anticipation, as if he couldn't wait for what Mr. Gorsh had to say.

"My dear child, I am the lawyer your father hired in case something should happen to him."

Esther chuckled, waving her hand in dismissal. "Nonsense. Jones has been our lawyer for years. My father would never have replaced him behind my back."

Mr. Gorsh nodded, seemingly well prepared for this type of argument.

"Yes, indeed. Douglas Jones is in fact still your family's lawyer."

Esther narrowed her eyes as to why the hell this guy was still sitting on her couch then.

"However." He continued, opening his black leather bag and pulling out a piece of parchment. "As you know, Mr. Jones has been away for weeks to deal with this silly Apache business." He shook his head in disapproval. "What he hopes to accomplish by dealing with these worthless *savages* I am not certain, but to each his own, I guess."

Worthless Savages?! His words burned through her skin, crawling into her chest. Esther didn't know much about the legal situation Jones had been asked to attend as the government was very secretive about it. However, if one would bluntly speak the truth, then all the land they were so proud to stand on did in fact belong to the natives. And to call them savages, to her face... Did this idiot not know, or was he simply speaking blindly? Esther clenched a fist.

"Jones will have more success dealing with the *savages* out there than you will ever have dealing with the *savage* on whose couch your despicable persona is sitting!" Esther condemned Gorsh as calmly as she possibly could, so that her father's soul might leave this house in peace, not hearing yells and screams. But on the inside, she was boiling, trembling with rage.

The shock of the information she had just shared hit Mr. Gorsh so hard, his mouth fell wide open as the document in his fingers slipped from his grip and ruffled onto the floor. He jerked his gaze over to a frowning Morris who cleared his throat to control the damage.

"The late Mrs. Silverton…was…Cherokee." He educated Mr. Gorsh, rubbing his neck.

"I-I had no idea!" Mr. Gorsh mumbled, flabbergasted. "But-but wasn't Mrs. Silverton—" Mr. Gorsh began to stutter, which was unbecoming of a lawyer. Morris interrupted him, an attempt to ease the situation before things got out of hand.

"The late Mrs. Silverton was an honorable Christian adopted and raised by god-fearing Americans."

A dismissive laugh escaped Esther as she walked over to the document to pick it up. "It would be more accurate to say that my mother was a slave on some white folks' ranch after her parents were murdered for the very land she had to farm until my father rescued her, honored her, and loved her until her dying breath. You see, not all white men are inhuman thieves like—"

"Esther, that is enough," Morris scolded her before she could finish that sentence.

"For once I agree with you, Morris. It is quite enough. My father is barely cold, and you dare to bring this worm into my home, not only with the audacity to present this fake will but also to insult my deceased mother?"

Mr. Gorsh lifted his hands as if someone had just pointed a gun. "I am truly sorry for this misunderstanding…"

Esther didn't respond but held the paper that was supposedly her father's last wish close to her face to take a closer look at what these snakes were fighting over. It stood out right away that the signature on this document did indeed look like her father's. *They certainly did not spare any efforts to make this fake document look real.* She shook her head in disgust.

"So, let me guess. The whole Silverton fortune goes to Morris?" she said unfazed, as if she had absolutely no worry that this document would be exposed for the forgery it was. Nothing more than a pathetic attempt by a despicable man to seize another's fortune. But both men grinned as if what she said was incredibly silly.

"Of course not." Morris sniggered at her. "Don't be absurd."

A mix of growing impatience, mistrust and confusion slowly swallowed her mind. She focused her gaze on the parchment again, scanning through every word while ignoring those insufferable men in front of her. The will indeed did say that all assets, the estate, and the entire company would be transferred to Esther and her alone. She stopped reading, hesitantly turning toward Mr. Gorsh to catch a glimpse of his face, and then to Morris. Why was Morris so happy then? Surely, he wouldn't just do the right thing and step aside, removing himself from this home and its fortune forever?

"So, what's the catch? I am not foolish enough to assume that this whole charade of going behind my lawyer's back was all for nothing?"

Both men pretended to be hurt by her accusations.

"My dear child, there is no catch. The fortune and the company of course shall be yours, just as your father had wanted it." Esther crossed her arms, signaling that she did not trust either of these men farther than she could spit—which wasn't very far.

"However…"

"Here we go." She rolled her eyes and sighed, almost in relief that he finally got to the point.

"Your dear father…" Morris announced with a pathetic attempt to look sad, making Esther nauseous, "…God rest his soul. He was worried about you getting taken advantage of." He placed his hand on his heart. "And rightfully so…"

"Rightfully so," Mr. Gorsh parroted while Morris nodded his head.

"So…" Morris walked over to the little tray next to the fireplace that had a bottle of whiskey on it and poured himself a glass. "So, he thought it best to name me your guardian until you are of age."

Esther almost dropped the parchment as she felt an icy shiver run down her spine, a burning sensation that almost caused her to burst out in scorching outrage. Did she really just hear him say *guardian*?

"I'm twenty!" she heard herself shout with a strange voice that didn't sound like her own. "Guardianship is out of the question!" She added, clenching her fists in fury, unaware that the parchment had wrinkled under her tight grasp.

Morris slugged down the whiskey before walking over to her. He pried the will out of her fist and showed her the section she'd failed to read.

"Here," he said, tapping his finger on it before handing it back to her. Esther glued her eyes on the piece of parchment that might doom her for years to come.

Furthermore, I hereby appoint my entrusted friend and partner, Ben Morris, to be my daughter's legal guardian until her 25th birthday or she is to marry, whichever is to come first.

"Twenty-fifth birthday?!" Esther cried out loud, reading it again to make sure she wasn't totally going insane. But the words remained the same.

Something wasn't right here. Her father would have never done such a thing behind her back. There is a drastic difference between paying a troubled friend's gambling debts and giving him his only child.

"Absurd…" she mumbled to herself as she read the part once more as if it would wake her up from this momentary nightmare. Mr. Gorsh stood up and waddled toward Morris who was busy pouring himself another shot from her father's best kept whiskey.

"I have to say, child," he declared in an arrogant tone, signaling to Morris that he would like a glass as well. "You could show a little more appreciation for Mr. Morris to take on such a heavy burden." He took a long whiff before tasting the whiskey that brought a shimmer into his eyes. He smiled in fascinated approval. "Exquisite." It escaped his lips before he could realize how inappropriate he was.

"The best in the nation," Morris said with pride as if it were his, before also realizing how inappropriate he was as well. This was it. For her dead father's sake, Esther had tried to stay calm to honor the day of his passing, but this was too much. Closing her eyes, she felt the burning sensation creeping from her lungs and up to her throat until she could no longer hold down the flames that scorched her, begging to be freed in an angry roar.

"Get out!" she shouted into the room, pointing toward the door. Morris and Mr. Gorsh looked at each other in a mixture of fear and shock. "I—said—GET—OOOOOOUT!" she yelled once more, throwing the crumpled parchment that Morris insisted was her father's wish onto the floor as if it was cursed. Ginny stormed in to see if everything was all right. Esther tried to calm herself, her whole body still shaking.

"Ginny, please escort Morris and his snake out. They are not welcome here," Esther growled in a more controlled voice that was still witness to her anger. Mr. Gorsh hastily put his glass down to grab his bag from the couch, almost tripping over the rug. Morris on the other hand just stood there, not moving an inch. His eyes were locked on Esther, taking a calm sip of his whiskey. She felt that cold shiver again as she found his gaze. His eyes were filled with nothing but hatred. No, this man was not done yet. He would do everything to claim the Silverton fortune, and his eyes were telling her that, right here in this room. And it was in this very moment that Esther realized that they had gravely underestimated the man she always thought she knew. Morris was not only the pathetic, gambling drunk she thought him to be. No. Those were the eyes of a man who was willing to do whatever was needed to get what he wanted. No rules, no limits, no regrets.

How long Esther had stared into those dark eyes she could not tell, but voices from the hallway tore her back into the present.

"Be careful with the dear Mr. Silverton." She heard Father Pilgram's voice from the hallway before catching a glimpse of a coffin passing by the opened door.

"Papa!"

Without wasting another second, she ran out to find Father Pilgram and three young men escorting a coffin out the front door.

"Wait!" she cried after them, feeling the scorching sun on her head as her feet carried her over the dust riddled path, wailing and begging desperately to be heard. They all stopped and turned.

Father Pilgram mumbled something to the men before walking up to her, his forehead wrinkled in confusion. "My dear child, I thought you were resting. Did you not say your goodbyes yet?"

Esther's legs almost gave in seeing the shiny, black coffin that carried the remains of what was most precious to her, enclosed in a dark casket never to see the light again.

But what was she supposed to do now — ask them to carry him back upstairs? To take him back out and lay him onto his bed again so she could spend a few more moments with him alone? Father Pilgram caught her just in time as her legs buckled, almost dragging the good Father along with her. Her knees harshly hit the ground before he managed to lift her back up and hold her in place. Suddenly she saw Morris and Mr. Gorsh walking around her father's coffin, not even looking at it once, as though it was just an inconvenience in their paths and nothing more. Her heart that had barely known anger before was now filled with hate. This emotion was as new to her as the loneliness she would feel from here on out, but by God, and if it would be the last thing she would do, she would not let her father's legacy and fortune be destroyed by this monster that dared to call himself his friend — and supposedly her guardian.

"Esther?" she heard Father Pilgram's gentle voice tear her back from the parts of her mind she had disappeared into for the promise she'd just made.

"It's all right, Father. Please continue."

Those were her last trembling words before they carried Cliff Silverton out of her sight. She didn't know it then, but life had it that this would be her last moment with the man she loved so pure and dearly—the last Silverton besides herself.

CHAPTER 2

Mr. Bend lit his cigar then shook the match until the fire wisped away. He was a short, older man with a huge double chin that made his face look completely round, reminding Esther of a frog. His clothes, however, were those of a well-to-do gentleman, which was to be expected for one of the best lawyers in the nation. He was the fifth lawyer Esther was consulting and was rumored to be 'the man who gets results.' *He'd better,* Esther thought to herself, placing her father's will along with a substantial amount of bank notes on the enormous solid wood desk he was sitting behind. He raised an eyebrow as if to ask why the paper looked like it had been torn out of a tiger's mouth. Esther innocently shrugged, paired with a hopeful smile.

It was of no question that she was of fine origin. She wore one of her finest gowns, a dark blue Parisian silk dress with a heavily decorated train in the back. Her hat was the latest in fashion too, a large Gainsborough with one side turned up, beautifully decorated with a large bow made of the finest silk.

"My condolences, Miss Silverton." He picked up the document, making his head disappear behind.

"Thank you," she sniffled, moving her body to the side to catch a glimpse of his face. He wrinkled his forehead; was that a bad sign?

"So, you suspect this document to be a forgery?" he said, still holding it close to his face.

"I have reason to believe so."

He placed the will back onto his desk and took a deep puff of his cigar. Its slowly creeping stench clouded the room into a fog. She leaned back, twitching her nose and waving the smoke away from her face in an attempt to escape — to no avail.

"I wouldn't be surprised, considering Douglas Morris is involved in this." He shook his head in disapproval. "I played cards with him at the club once. He tried to cheat, but someone exposed him." That *truly* sounded like Morris. "But of course, nothing came of it and we all went on as if nothing had happened."

"Why is that?" Esther wondered.

His eyebrows lowered and pinched together. "Because you don't cross Cliff Silverton."

Esther wanted to frown, confused by what he was trying to imply, but kept her mouth shut.

"Morris was the partner, and more importantly *friend*, of one of the most influential men in town. You don't mess with the guys above."

This bit of information was surprising to her indeed. After Esther had become of age, her father had moved to New York to provide her with a life of fine dresses, parties in elegant parlors, and a rank in the country's finest society—far away from the dust of the West. But soon after they'd moved, it turned out that none of these things mattered to his daughter and Esther ended up spending all her time at University lectures and charity events. Away from the gossip of New York's finest, she had no idea that her father was this influential.

But now, with her father gone, shouldn't that mean that Morris was stripped of her father's shield like a peacock of its shiny feathers?

"Does my father's passing mean we have a chance of exposing Morris and overturning this will? People seem to be aware of his low moral character."

She couldn't tell if she sounded hopeful or desperate. Mr. Bend put his cigar in a silver ashtray and leaned forward. His lips frowned downward as if he was sorry for what was to come.

"No. I'm sorry. I really am, but cheating at cards is not the sort of evidence we would need to challenge this document in court. It would be a waste of your time and money. Which—" He paused for a second, picking up his cigar. "Which you won't have access to any longer until your 25th birthday."

Esther tipped her head to look heavenwards. The desperation squeezed her already fragile chest as she choked on the memory of her father's final days. Mr. Bend was watching her in sympathy.

"I was wondering," she said, sounding hopeful, "does the signature seem authentic? Would it match if we compare it to other documents?"

For a moment, there was a heavy silence in the room. Then Esther nodded.

"It might be genuine then," Mr. Bend finally said. "I can only imagine the magical words Morris must have chanted into your sick father's ear to make this happen, but your father might have signed this will in good faith, believing it would be best for you."

Esther's head flopped forward as her mind sunk further into murky thoughts. Never in her life before had she thought her father a fool. But sitting here listening to Mr. Bend's words was as painful as pieces of glass shattering in her ears, even if they might be the truth.

She felt no anger nor hatred toward her kind father, and even the word fool was more said in sadness than anything else. To his last breath, he seemed unable to see Morris for the great hoax he was. Instead, her father cherished him as the childhood friend he'd chased snakes with and covered for when one of them got in trouble. It was obvious to everyone else that her father's innocent, cheerful Morris from his childhood was long gone. And in front of her was the price she would now have to pay.

"Mr. Jones…" She heard Mr. Bend tear her out of her miserable thoughts. "Is he truly not to be reached? If anybody could be of help, it would be him. I am certain he has or at least knows of a previous will. With that in hand, we might stand a chance."

Another cloud of cigar smoke crept its way toward Esther, but this time she didn't care and allowed it to swallow her whole.

Another knot formed in her already painfully burning throat. *Where was Mr. Jones?* Was he even still alive? Esther had paid his wife a visit this morning to see if she knew how to contact him, but instead of finding information, she discovered a desperate Sylvia tearfully blaming the government for sending her husband into the 'Wilds of the West' where 'he might have been eaten by coyotes by now' for all she knew.

"Unfortunately, nobody has heard from Mr. Jones in weeks, maybe months. He was sent to New Mexico to assist the government in peace talks of some sort. According to his wife, the government kept reassuring her that he is in good health but none of the letters addressed to him have been answered in weeks."

In disbelief, Mr. Bend slammed his huge hand onto his knee that made a ringing sound that echoed around the room.

"Unacceptable," he almost shouted. "Mr. Jones was a friend of mine. I shall make my own inquiries. The government is as trustworthy right now as a pair of shoes without soles." He was shaking his head in disgust. "That business with the natives down there—despicable."

"Indeed," she mumbled, still in shock over her own situation.

She slowly pushed herself up from her chair a few inches, worried that her legs were about to give up on her again. The thought of Morris in charge of her family's wealth, home, business, and even worse, her every decision, made her dizzy enough to almost faint. The room seemed to have darkened, the ceiling too high and the floor too wide.

"Miss Silverton." Mr. Bend's voice broke through, sounding almost afraid. Her heart pounded in fear of what more news could be worse than the last twenty minutes of their conversation.

"I'm afraid I cannot just let you leave without telling you something you should know."

Esther took a deep breath to prepare herself.

"Father, you fool," she whispered in a loving voice.

"If this is about Morris's spending habits, I am well aware that he might spend my name into ruin before I can claim my inheritance."

Mr. Bend shook his head. "I'm afraid it's worse than that..." He stood up and rushed around his desk. His voice made her freeze, her body rooted to the spot.

"What...what is it?" she barely managed to ask.

Mr. Bend closed his eyes and let out a sigh of worry. "A few years back, it was rumored that your father and Morris had a fight."

"A fight?" she echoed his words.

"Yes. Those are rumors, but still. It was said that Morris impregnated a young prostitute, barely fifteen. He refused to care for her or the baby. When your father heard of this incident, he confronted Morris, demanding he do the right thing." Mr. Bend stopped for a moment as if he were trying to gather strength.

"What came of it?" Esther asked, unable to wait, but also afraid to hear the answer.

"Morris insisted it was all lies. Rumors spread by a rival company. He swore he had done no wrong and challenged this woman to face him in court."

"So, did he win or lose?" Esther inquired, hanging on his words. Mr. Bend stared at the floor for a moment. "In court, I mean." She clarified for him.

"Neither. The woman was never heard of again."

Esther's hand shot up to her mouth.

"But…but how could that be? How could he get away with this?"

Mr. Bend shook his head in shame for his own profession. "With what? Those were rumors and according to Morris, the woman fled due to her worries of being exposed."

"Nonsense. He must have done something horrid to that poor woman!"

Mr. Bend frowned. "Not in the eyes of the law. Not without evidence."

The meaning of the lawyer's words started to settle in, leaving a bitter taste in her mouth. Was she in danger now?

"Would he stand a chance to get the inheritance in case of my death? It doesn't say that in the will."

Mr. Bend let out a deep breath.

"Well, not black on white, but it does mention that the inheritance shall go back into the company in case there should be no heir. And as Morris is the only partner in the company, he would become the full owner in case of your death. Morris would get everything through the Silverton business dealings."

Esther struggled for words. So now, on top of everything, she also had to fear for her life?! As if it weren't enough that she had watched everyone she had ever loved slip through her fingers like sand.

Did life really think she was ready for another heap of misery just yet?

She stumbled backwards a few feet, unnerved and stammering, when Mr. Bend grabbed her by the arm. She was such a strong independent woman, but this was the second time within the day that someone had had to grab her to save her from falling out of despair.

"What am I supposed to do now?"

She let go of his arm in a sad attempt to show she could stand on her own. Her big, teary eyes met with the serious, sympathetic eyes of Mr. Bend's. For a moment he stared at her, unsure what to say, finally breaking the silence by shaking his head in a way that indicated he'd made up his mind about something.

"Now you listen carefully, as I cannot repeat my words nor explain them in more detail," he said, walking back to his desk and grabbing the will and the money Esther had left there for him. "These wills can only be executed if all parties are present. If, for some reason, the main heir was to disappear shortly after a guardian has been named or identified, there is a chance that all funds might be frozen until the matter can be cleared up."

Her heart pounded like a hundred stallions eager to escape, their hooves thumping through her chest that for a moment seemed ready to explode. Had she just heard this right. Disappear? But how?

"And to where?" she asked not realizing she'd said those words out loud.

"Nobody, and I mean *nobody*, should know about such details."

Mr. Bend handed her back the will. She reached for it slowly, feeling the weight of such a weightless piece of parchment filled with nothing but ink.

"For how long would an heir have to vanish?"

"I'm not certain for how long, and whether this would even work, but considering it's about the Silverton inheritance, I would be very surprised if authorities wouldn't launch an investigation thinking they might be able to get their own hands on it."

Esther let out a discouraged breath.

"I'm only twenty. How could I possibly hide for five years?"

Mr. Bend tilted his head. "Technically, you would only have to hide until you are of legal age."

Her gaze shot in a daze. "What do you mean?"

"Twenty-one. At that age, you are free to marry. Remember, it's either twenty-five or marriage."

Her mind trailed off into thought. Indeed, it did say that. But marriage... With whom? And with a fortune like that, she ran an exceptionally high risk of attracting every Morris on this planet. Some might not even be as blunt about their despicable traits as Morris was, luring her in with sweet words and laughter, only to steal her money and mistreat her by the end of each and every day. All things considered, her wealth seemed more like a curse.

She stared down into her hand which unknowingly held Mr. Bend's payment in it, then shot her gaze toward him.

"I couldn't," he said in a caring voice.

"But—"

"Use it wisely and make it last," he said, giving her hand a light squeeze of encouragement. This was the first kind act she had come across in a long time. She would always remember his generosity.

"From the bottom of my heart, thank you."

She placed the money back into her purse, stunned by this newly emerging feeling that from now on, money, unlike before in her life, would not last forever.

Mr. Bend opened the door for her, then waved his secretary to stay seated, as he walked Esther out himself.

"You take care now, Miss Silverton. And who knows, maybe a nice chap is waiting just around the corner to sweep you off your feet and put an end to all of this nonsense."

With a sad smile, Mr. Bend closed the front door of his office, leaving Esther in the busy streets of New York on a sunny but freezing November day.

For a moment Esther just stood there, confused, scared, and full of uncertainty. She stared at the door as if she were waiting for somebody to open it once more.

Carriages and pedestrians passed by, going about their business as if it were a normal day like any other—which for them it was.

But not for Esther. Overnight, her life had changed forever, from the once-American dream to everyone's worst nightmare. Morris was probably in his office right now, gathering an army of lawyers and notary publics to officially have the will read at her home later this day. Doubts started to creep into her flooded mind, drowning her already muddled senses. Maybe she should just let Morris have it all, run headlong home to officially step down, crawl back on all fours and watch Morris ruin her father's empire and good name.

But right there and then, the thought of her mother eased into her mind. An inspirational Cherokee woman who had lost her parents. A woman who had served as a slave to the thieves who took her land. A woman who had slowly watched her life getting eaten away by the cancer. A woman who never gave up—strong, caring, and full of honor until her last breath…

Esther shook her head, slapped herself out of it. How dare she think of retreat before the battle had even started? How dare she give it all to Morris and act like the coward she saw in him and hated so much? How dare she let her parents look down on her from wherever they were now, seeing nothing but a quitter. No, she would fight. There was hope and she would rather go down with a big firework than crying like a helpless wench in a corner of a house that wouldn't even be hers any longer. For the first time in days she had clarity.

"All right," she said in a determined voice, turning around, finally ready to face the world.

"I'll show you what a Silverton is made of." And at that moment, the most marvelous idea crossed her mind and put the first honest smile of the day on her face.

If she were to disappear, she would do so with a parting gift to the very man who might not only be after her money, but her very life.

The carriage pulled in front of the Silverton building on Silverton street, bustling with people moving about, plenty of whom saw her and recognized her at first glance — all of which would serve her well soon enough. Her father's property stood a staggering height, made of granite walls that shimmered just like the sun from the morning rays all the way to the afternoon. As one of the most modern and tallest buildings in New York, it stood as a symbol of hope and progress in a city that had been no more than wasteland not too long ago. From here, her father used to manage his legacy, which involved investments in everything the mind could possibly imagine: from shoes to furniture, threads to needles, books to fine prints, even to mustard and ketchup, the Silvertons had a stake in it.

Esther alighted from the carriage and lifted her head up to take a better look at the very reason she was in this predicament in the first place. She knew every aspect of the business. Her father had made sure of it by letting her attend important meetings and taking her on business trips with him. But she never felt like her heart was in it. To her, nothing was more exciting than experiencing a new discovery in the fine arts or sciences. After all, she was a woman dedicated to the modern world, inventions, and progress.

Her father's idea of moving her to New York to mingle with high society could not have gone more wrong. Day in and day out, she attended different lectures, enrolling in various classes, and even decided to attend university to major in physics. And yet, all that was gone now. As things stood, she had to major in the arts of survival, attending the school called reality.

She took a few steps toward the Silverton building. This was it; she thought everything through. Would it work? What if she got caught? But there was no time for doubt. She calmed herself down before turning around to the carriage driver.

"I am to visit Mr. Morris. Please wait for me here."

"Yes, miss." The carriage driver nodded, loosening the tension on the horses' reins to signal them to relax, which they ultimately did. Esther did her best to cause her body to intentionally tremble, tightening her muscles hard enough that she almost felt her bones buckling under her skin. The carriage driver noticed with a worried stare. "Miss, is everything all right?"

Esther blinked back at him, clacking her teeth under tight lips like she felt cold in the dead of winter, under the scorching sun.

"Yes. It's just—if I'm not back within the hour, please go straight to the police."

The carriage driver drew his brows as he leaned closer as if to whisper. "Miss, are you in danger?"

Esther shook her head in a deliberate failed attempt to diminish his worry. "It's probably nothing. Please excuse my weak nerves."

She forced a fake smile. But before the carriage driver could say another word, she handed him a dollar bill and turned on her heels, distancing herself with wide abrupt steps. She didn't have to peek over her shoulder to know that the carriage driver was still following her every step.

Perfect, she applauded herself for that little performance, thinking maybe she could have probably done well in the theater arts as well. The footmen instantly recognized her as soon as she was within a few feet from the grand, golden entrance doors.

"Miss Silverton." They saluted, tearing the doors wide open for her.

"Good day to you. Is Mr. Morris in?" she asked them, well aware of the fact that no one knew better who entered and left the building than the footmen.

"Yes, miss. He is," the older one answered, taking off his hat and bowing slightly. Their dark blue outfits with white colored branches and golden buttons always reminded her of the army.

"Thank you." She nodded back, walking through the doors.

"Should we run ahead and give notice of your arrival?" the younger footman shouted after her.

"No, that won't be necessary," she shouted back without turning around. A few employees going about their business in the enormous entrance hall turned toward her. *Very good, more people who saw me here.*

Esther made her way up the golden stairs to the first floor where her father and Morris's offices were located. She wouldn't be surprised if Morris had already moved into her father's office to demonstrate his power at the company.

Mr. Gideon, an accountant working for the company, passed her on the stairs and wanted to engage in a conversation, but she ignored him, staring a long, drawn out gaze as she kept walking.

For what she had planned, she couldn't run the risk of Morris coming out of his office and finding her here.

She tiptoed down the first floor's hallway and stopped in front of an enormous painting of New York, right next to her father's office which had Morris's name plastered on its bold maple doors. He had already claimed it.

She could see his silhouette moving behind the frosted glass. What would she give to tear that door open and throw him out of her father's office? Maybe even out the window if she could manage it. Esther cursed, biting her lip with her eyes almost glaring fire through the glass. Suddenly Morris's silhouette moved toward her. She froze. Had he seen her? But just when it seemed as if he would open the door to expose her, he stopped at the whiskey tray next to the door to pour himself a glass of her father's fine whiskey. Hopefully, he would choke on it. Maybe she could help a little?

No, she had to be more clever than giving in to a temporary feeling of satisfaction. Sure, it would feel great to have him yanked out of the office. But for how long would that last?

It was far beyond doubt that he was planning on having the will read in front of witnesses, claiming everything that was hers.

She focused her attention back to the enormous painting of New York and reached behind and under it, keeping one eye closely on the shadow that loomed behind the door. Her fingers snaked their way around it as the shadow of Morris grew larger and larger until it consumed the entire door. Her breath stuck in her throat: the sound of clacking, followed by the slow turning of the door handle when she finally found the secret hatch, pulling the painting open, exposing an entrance to a small staircase. She threw herself in, shutting the painted doorway. Had he seen her? She froze at the sound of footsteps from the other side, waiting, until they faded out of earshot. She let another minute pass before finally allowing herself to breathe.

She straightened herself, wiping the sweat from her forehead.

Her father had had these stairs built to have a private way in and out in case he did not want to run into people in the waiting area downstairs in the entrance hall. Nobody but him and Morris used it, besides that one time when she begged her father to play hide and seek with her when she was younger. The memory of it placed a warm smile on her lips and lightened her face in this drafty corridor leading downward.

She could barely remember this place, surprised at how dark the staircase was. If not for a little bit of light that came from a small window below, it would have been pitch black.

Esther slowly made her way downstairs toward the light of that window filled with thick dust and riddled with spider webs, almost making the door beside it unnoticeable. She reached out to open the door, and the staircase was instantly flooded by the bright daylight of an alley right behind the Silverton building.

Taking one final breath and one final glimpse of her father's memory, she hastened out of the alley and onto the busy street to fade into the hustle and bustle of the pedestrian crowd of downtown New York, leaving nothing behind but a little surprise for Morris.

The trail of her disappearance would lead straight to him, making him the last person to have had contact with her — supposedly that was.

CHAPTER 3

The cold wind hit Esther in the face like an iron whip. She had wandered around for hours, unsure where she could stay without being recognized. The initial warmth she had felt in making Morris a main murder suspect had worn off by now, thanks to the icy cold temperatures. It was the coldest November on record, and folk were saying that 1881 would be the coldest winter in the history of New York. Considering Esther's luck so far, she thought it was just another little blow life had in store for her.

She had enough money in her purse to last several months—if she lowered her standards drastically, that was, and stayed in some of the shadier parts of town. At the very least, that would buy her time to come up with another plan. Who knew, maybe she would find a nice chap whom she could marry just for the sake of getting her fortune back. In a few months' time she would be twenty-one, and if Morris didn't get a hold of her before that, she had a good chance in winning the overall war.

Esther turned into the Italian quarters, a part of New York that was one of its poorest. The streets were caked with mud, filled with vendors on every corner whistling at every passerby that swarmed and swallowed the place. From what she had heard, it was safer here than the Irish quarters.

The sun was fading, leaving a wide, overarching streak of red and orange lights. It was getting late. She had to find a place to stay or she could freeze to death or be robbed. Fighting off another cold breeze by squeezing her fine wool coat tighter around the neck, she spotted a fairly decent-looking pub with enough of a crowd to hopefully let herself slip unnoticed.

Loud laughter and the sounds of cheerful, Italian singing had subconsciously attracted her to it. Esther was about to open the door when a man stumbled through it, blackout drunk. He fell onto the street right in front of her feet, grabbing her coat in a last, desperate attempt to avoid the fall. Shuffling her feet to regain balance and not go down with him, she swatted at the drunk man's hand to release her.

"Let go of me, and I will help you back up!" she huffed at him, without avail. He was now sitting up, tugging at her coat once more with a grip so tight, it seemed as if his life depended on it.

"Beeeeelllllllaaaaa," he mumbled in a drunk voice with an Italian accent. He was grabbing his melon hat and tried to put it on, but he was so drunk he didn't place it over his head but several feet next to it instead, so it fell right back onto the pavement again. Esther let out a sharp breath in annoyance as she was at a loss what to do. She wasn't foolish enough to have left the house without her Derringer, a small pistol with an artfully decorated handle that her father had made for her back when they were still living in Texas. It could hold two bullets at a time; not as much as the latest revolvers, but it was a luxury nonetheless to the widely popular flintlock pistols that could hold only one. And as a former ranch girl, she darn well knew how to use it. But she did not feel that this man was a threat. He was more of a nuisance.

Esther tried another pull of her coat, which triggered an uncontrollable outburst of laughter from the drunk man who obviously thought it funny that she was unable to rid herself of him.

"Could you at least point me in the direction of a reputable boarding house?" she asked in an angry voice, using the fingertips to rub her temples as if to ward off a headache.

Suddenly another man in his thirties came out of the pub. He was dressed in a nice day suit and elegantly put on his top hat. His face had all the charming features of an Italian man of the ladies, which was instantly confirmed by his big grin that exposed his beautiful, white teeth.

"No no no no, Luigi…" He scolded the drunk man in a thick Italian accent. He aggressively stomped his foot onto drunk Luigi's arm, forcing him to release Esther's coat. Luigi let out a scream of pain, which Esther didn't like at all.

"Thank you. I've got it from here," she said in the hope that the slick beauty would stop hurting the drunk man on the floor. He did a little courtesy bow and removed his foot from Luigi's arm.

"De lady's wish is-a Luigi's command-a," the apparently second Luigi she had met in less than five minutes said. Drunk Luigi rubbed his arm where the painful foot had been moments ago. Esther drew her brows together in suspicion.

"Luigi? Your name is Luigi too?"

The man shrugged his shoulders in innocence.

"Si. It's-a, a very, ow can I say, oosooal name arrround ere."

Esther was still not convinced so Luigi added: "You arrre not from arround ere?"

A charming smile tried to lure her in.

Esther shook her head. As odd as all of this was, maybe he could point her in the right direction of a reputable but affordable boarding facility.

"No. I'm from out of town. Would you awfully mind directing me toward a reputable boarding house or hotel?"

Luigi clapped his hands together. It was quite admirable that he seemed to say and do everything with a big, energetic smile on his face.

"Of course. Tis is-a Luigi's town. Joost follow a-me."

Esther was not convinced to follow a man she had just met like that. But all of a sudden, the other Luigi, still sitting on the floor, launched toward her, trying to grab her coat again.

"E Pericoloso!" he screamed trying to grab her coat again. But Esther was able to step back just in time, so instead of getting a hold of her again, Luigi fell forward onto the street.

"A fanabla," charming Luigi yelled angrily and stepped on drunk Luigi's hand, who screamed out in pain. Esther had to put an end to this.

"Well, maybe you could just walk me down the street and direct me from there," she said in the hope of stopping poor drunk Luigi's abuse. He was a nuisance, but by no means did he frighten her. Too many times had she encountered harmless, drunk cowboys on her ranch and therefore knew the difference between a dangerous man and a mindless drunk.

Charming Luigi immediately smiled again, offering her his arm. Esther took it with hesitation. She did not like this man at all, and something was odd here, but for the poor drunk guy, she thought it better to walk this man away from the situation. A few steps down a street still filled with people and vendors was surely something she could manage.

Luigi walked her down Mulberry Street to some sort of big street curve with tall buildings. He pointed at the curve. "Tis oosed to be Moolboirrry Bend-a, boot now it is-a safe." He grinned.

Esther had heard of the terrible Mulberry slums that Charles Dickens had so bluntly described as "reeking everywhere with dirt and filth," but as Luigi had said, the city had cleaned up those parts aggressively—at least to her knowledge.

Luigi turned into a smaller street that was packed with shops and carts on both sides of the road, making it almost impossible to walk on the sidewalk. People were pushing for space and shouting in different languages. Esther was truly fascinated by this side of New York which she got to see for the first time in her life. So many faces at once, all with different shades of colors hidden by the dust and mud of the fading day. They glittered like stained marbles, unwashed and squeezed in a tight box, but gleaming, nonetheless. She turned left and right, unable to soak it all in.

"Newspaper, miss?"

A dirty boy jumped in front of her, his whole body visibly shivering from the bitter cold. It was almost impossible to tell his hair color as his head was covered in dust and coal stains. Blonde? He wore nothing but thin brown pants and a wool sweater that had holes all over. In this cold that was nothing short of torture. It took a while for Esther to notice that he was wearing two different sized shoes. One way too large black one, and one Esther guessed to be a way too small brown one. Luigi grabbed the boy by the neck and pushed him out of the way.

"Che cazzo," he cursed at the boy, which made Esther flinch in dismay as she stepped in between them.

"That is enough," she growled at Luigi, taking the boy behind her. For a moment, Luigi's face changed into something disfigured and discomforting before throwing his hands up, mumbling something she couldn't make out.

Esther turned around to the boy and opened her purse. Considering this was all the money she had to survive on for God knows how long, this was probably not a very smart move, but she would rather starve than let this poor soul walk away with nothing. She pulled out a twenty dollar note. The boy shook his head in disbelief while Luigi cussed in the background.

"But...that's a twenty, miss..." His little voice trembled. Esther bent over to level herself with the boy. She guessed his age to be twelve or so.

"What's your name?" Her voice was warm and kind.

"Milton, m-miss," he stuttered. Esther reached out to grab his hand, but Milton instinctively stepped back, as if his body was trained to dodge a beating.

"I won't hurt you," Esther said, stretching for his hand again. This time he let it happen. She placed the twenty dollar note in there and tightly closed his fist.

"Now you promise me that you will buy clothes for you and your family before you make your way to the chocolate store," she commanded gently with a smile.

The boy nodded his head, still in disbelief about her kindness. Esther turned to Luigi who was suspiciously staring at her purse.

"Thank you for walking me this far. I shall manage from here on," she said in a dismissive tone. Luigi put a wide overdrawn smile onto his face which seemed nothing but fake.

"No problemo. Bot de otel is-a rrright at tis corrrna." He pointed toward the end of the street. Esther's gaze followed his arm all the way to his fingertip.

"Right over there?" she asked, a bit skeptical.

"Si, si. Right-a dere. Twenty more meters." Esther tilted her head to the side. The street was still busy, so he surely wasn't planning anything, she convinced herself cautiously.

"Twenty more meters?" She inquired once more.

"Si." Luigi nodded confidently. Esther noticed that the sun was already disappearing behind the buildings. At this point she had not much of a choice but to give this incredibly dubious man a shot at his word.

"Ok, let's go," she said, holding her purse with her money tight to her body, her pistol even closer. Luigi did a courtesy bow again and led the way. Esther joined him, barely making it a few feet when she felt something cold grabbing her by the wrist, pulling her to a halt. Milton gazed at her with his bulging eyes, his brows squished together in anger and fear. He shook his head wildly from side to side, signaling a terrifying no. Esther didn't need to ask what was going on, because deep down her gut had told her from the moment she first met Luigi that he was trouble and she wished she would have listened to it. She felt her leg muscles tightening as a cold shiver ran down her spine. But before she could even say a word, Luigi jumped right next to her, grabbing her by her upper arm so tightly it hurt. His cheerful eyes had turned darkly grotesque, sending out a non-verbal threat to her and Milton.

"No sound-a. Inteso?" he whispered in a low, growling voice pulling out a knife for a short moment before making it disappear again. Things went so fast from here on. Out of nowhere, Milton leaped toward them, biting Luigi into his arm so hard he screamed out in a high-pitched roar.

"Ruuuun!" Milton shouted before turning around to escape through the busy crowd, dragging Esther behind him by her hand. Dodging merchants and carriages, she had a bit of a hard time keeping up with Milton's incredibly swift body movements. She dared to look over her shoulder, scouting Luigi scampering behind them. Her steps were trudging through thick mud pulling her down, but those small, cold hands pulled her back out over and over again. Like a weasel, he seemed to know exactly when to shift, finding holes and routes in a crowd of people like he was parting the sea or commanding the streets.

Finally making it out of the busy street and into an abandoned small alley, Esther stopped to catch her breath. Milton didn't and ran all the way down to the end of the alley that was blocked off by a tall brick wall. But before she could worry about how to climb that wall with noodle legs that could barely take another step, Milton kneeled next to a box in the left corner and pushed it aside to reveal a small hole in the wall. He turned around to Esther.

"Hurry, miss!" He frantically waved her over. She obeyed and was about to run over when she heard footsteps behind her.

"Figlio di puttana!" Luigi shouted in rage, pulling out his knife. Milton could have left without Esther, but much to her surprise, he didn't. Quite the opposite. He stood back up and rushed over to her as if he were willing to fight by her side until his last breath. Esther stepped in front of Milton in a protective gesture, her adrenaline racing through her veins, almost making her feel intoxicated. She took a deep breath to calm herself.

"Nobody needs to get hurt," she said holding up her hand to signal Luigi to stop and not come any closer. Milton now clenched his little hands into fists. Esther noticed for the first time that his newspapers were gone. When he must have dropped them, she couldn't tell. Luigi wrinkled his forehead, looking back and forth at both of them, but then busted out in a loud, condescending laughter.

"A whore and-a her little toy." He slapped his leg with the hand that wasn't holding the knife, "I am so a-scarred-a!" He ridiculed them, inching closer.

Esther felt the heat of rage boil in her veins. Her eyes narrowed and locked in on Luigi in an intense, fevered stare.

"Oh." Luigi shot his hand to his chest in laughter, acting as if her gaze was a gun that just shot him.

Esther reached into her purse. "If that's what you want, I can help you with that," she growled.

Luigi now reached out his hand as if he were expecting her to get out the money and place it in it, but he instantly froze to the spot when he saw Esther pull out her pistol instead.

"Getting shot, I mean. I can help you with getting shot," she said in a voice so ice cold it felt like the air around them had dropped in temperature.

Luigi took a few steps back, his brows tightly pressed together in thought. But then he stopped walking backwards.

"A weak womano can't shoot no gun-a," he chuckled, carefully tested his waters, narrowing his eyes, waiting for Esther to respond.

Esther now steadied her arm, pointing the gun right at him. For a moment he seemed to think about what to do, but then must have decided that Esther was *just* a woman as he started to grin and take a step forward. That's all she needed, so she fired. A loud shot echoed down the alleyway, causing Milton to startle all over his little body. Luigi's knife dropped to the floor as he frantically shook his hand in the air as if it were on fire.

"You shot the knife right out of his hand!" Milton hollered in utter disbelief, his voice sounding cheerful as if they were at a fair and Esther had just won him a big teddy bear. Luigi spat on the floor, turned around, and ran for his life.

"Sembra che tu non conosca bene le donne!" Esther shouted after him in perfect Italian.

"What does that mean?" Milton asked.

"Just that he doesn't know women very well." She grinned.

"No, he don't." Milton smiled back at her, but a loud whistle from around the corner brought back the look of worry onto his face. He ran to the whole in the wall. "We have to go; the pigs are coming!"

Esther slowly followed him up to the hole. "Pigs?" she wondered.

"The police," he said, crawling through the hole, turning around on the other side. "If they catch me, they put me away. It's worse than death, believe me!"

He reached out a hand to help Esther crawl through. It was quite small and for a moment she thought she'd got stuck, but thanks to Milton pulling her by both of her hands, they managed to get her through. Once she was on the other side, Milton closed the hole again by pulling the box back in front of it. He waited for a few moments, listening carefully to the other side of the wall before letting out a relieved sigh.

"That was close," he huffed, scratching his head. Esther sat up next to him and scouted the courtyard she found herself in. It was more of a little walled-in space that was formed by several tall brick buildings being built together too closely to allow room for a street or alley, forming a courtyard that was both several feet wide and long.

"I'm truly grateful for your help. I can't believe this Luigi guy deceived me like this." She shook her head in disappointment over her own foolishness.

Years of living in New York's finest comforts seemed to have clouded her sharp senses.

"His name is not Luigi. Luigi is the harmless drunk at Mulberry Bend. This was Snatcher."

Esther felt even more foolish now. "Snatcher?" she asked. Milton nodded.

"He hurts people to take their things. Sometimes they are gone forever after that."

"Good God! And I almost became one of those people... I guess I am not as clever as I thought I was."

Milton put his little hand on hers. "Don't get mad, but you don't look like you know street life very well," Milton said gently, moving his little hand up and down Esther's gloves in strange fascination over its softness. "You didn't know."

Esther let out a sigh. Not only had this little boy saved her, but he was also right about every darn word he just said. Esther might know how to shoot and had a mouth that matched her confidence, but what knowledge did she have about the slums of New York? None whatsoever! How about surviving with little to no means? Nada again!

Esther took her coat off and wrapped Milton's shivering little body in it when she heard giggling from behind her. What she was about to find could not have surprised her more. A little gang of dirty faces poked from the darkness and out of the ground from what seemed to be a lower level in the floor of some sort at the other end of the courtyard. Esther counted three of those little wildlings as far as her eyes could see.

Milton jumped back up on his feet. "Come meet the rest," he said.

"Milton has a girlfriend," a little boy chuckled from across the courtyard, pointing at Esther. The rest of the little gang now tuned in to make a chant of it.

"Milton has a girlfriend, Milton has a girlfriend." They cheerfully teased him, making kissy faces with duck pointed lips, giggling in innocent laughter like only children could.

Milton shook his head in annoyance, but it had an undertone of love in it. It was clear that he cared for those kids dearly.

"When they shut up," he declared in reference to introducing her. He walked over to them, followed by Esther.

The lower level the kids were dancing on turned out to be a heating vent of one of the buildings. It was several feet deep and wide and covered with a blanket which Esther guessed was some sort of makeshift roof, illuminated only by a single small flame that flickered on a tiny candle.

Esther almost dropped her purse at the sight of the little shadows that came closer, their dark faces huddled tight together in the light of a candle that barely had any warmth to give. Behind them were makeshift beds of straw, boards, and dirty blankets. The whole place was littered with tin metal cans scattered about.

"Do you live here?" Esther mumbled, barely able to hold herself together. The little shadows bobbed their heads in response.

Milton jumped down into the vent space, breaking off the awkward conversation. Esther leaned closer as her eyes and lips widened at the sight of the four-year-old actually holding an infant who must have been barely one and was wrapped in a dirty blanket. That Luigi-snatcher-whatshisname may not have harmed her, but the sight of all of this was like a punch in the gut. Looking at all these dirty faces, poorly dressed and with barely any skin on their fragile bones, tore a piece out of Esther's heart.

"That's Miki," Milton said, pointing at the four-year-old who held the infant. Miki was a dark-haired boy with blue eyes and incredibly cute. He grinned at her with a shy, sweet smile.

"Those are the twins, Tom and Jeff." Milton continued the introduction and pointed at two boys that could not have looked more different. One was blonde and awfully skinny while the other one was dark-haired and on the bigger side. Esther looked confused so Milton added: "They are both six and always stick together, so we call them twins. Found them together too. At the shore."

Tom, the blond one, stepped forward and grabbed Esther's hand to shake it.

"Miss," he said with a grin, watching Esther's arm shake wildly in rhythm with his hand, causing the other kids to giggle again.

Milton rolled his eyes. "And this is Arab," Milton said, taking the infant from Miki. Arab was now smiling at Esther and sucking on his thumb. "Found him in the trash at Five Point."

"A-Arab?" Esther heard herself stutter, the first word she was able to get out since this heart-breaking introduction started.

Jeff nodded his head. "Street Arabs is what the people call us," he blurted proudly as if he'd just taught Esther something new, which he had. He seemed to have no idea how awful it was that people called them that and that little Arab was now named after this unethical insult — at least for now.

"How terrible. How can people call you that!" Esther complained, anger clogging up her throat like badly chewed food. The little troop looked at each other as if they had done something wrong. Esther felt ashamed and hastily clarified.

"You have done nothing wrong. I'm not mad at you. I'm mad at this harsh world you were forced to live in."

"We don't name babies until their first birthday. Most of them don't make it out of here." Milton gave a sad smile, gently caressing the little infant he held in his arms.

"Like baby Emily. She's in heaven now," Jeff said as they all went silent with their gaze falling to the floor, seemingly speechless and at the same time clueless of their uncertain future.

"But Arab almost made it, so we started thinking about names," Milton said in a cheerful voice, trying to shoo away the gloomy mood.

Esther didn't think that she would be able to feel any worse than she already did, but meeting this little gang of homeless children was by far the saddest thing that she had ever witnessed. She scanned them, one dirtier and skinnier than the other, living on top of a heat vent with nothing but a wet cover over their heads. How was this possible? She knew about poverty from her charity donations, but she had no idea that it was this bad.

Esther moved closer toward the beds and leaned down to pick up a teddy bear. It was missing a leg and an arm, with barely any stuffing left, but Little Arab immediately stretched his hand out, small fingers squirming their way toward it while making tiny cooing sounds. She hesitated to hand it over as it was straight out filthy.

"Don't you have any family?" she asked with a deeply saddened voice.

"We are a family," Miki said.

Ok, so that meant no adults, Esther guessed.

"What about orphanages?"

All of a sudden, their faces turned pale as if a ghost had just asked the question. Milton's mouth fell wide open as Tom and Jeff ran behind him to hide, holding on to him tightly.

"No, miss, please. Don't put us there!" Tom cried in a squeaking voice.

74

"The men there do bad things to children. Bad, bad things." Milton's voice trembled, more terrified now than when Luigi had threatened them with his knife.

Esther raised both hands in a gesture of peace and surrender. "I won't put you there," she hastily said, worried they might run away at any moment. She had no idea that orphanages were such monstrous places.

"Promise it!" Miki yelled at her with tightly drawn eyebrows and his little fists clenched in anger.

Esther kneeled in front of him and gently placed a hand on his little, tense shoulder. The hard feeling of skin and bones poked her fingers, which felt like another stab into her already shattered heart.

"I promise," she almost whispered, her own voice trembling at the verge of tears.

Milton stared into her eyes, then gave a nod before turning toward his fellow mates.

"She is a good miss. You can trust her," he announced in a strong voice that still squeaked like a child. Little Miki stared at her for a few more seconds before he nodded in relief, bringing the color back into his scrawny face with a faint hint of a smile.

Milton wrapped Esther's coat around Arab. "Are your parents dead too?" he asked, lost in thought as if he was walking his own memory lane of misery.

His words hit Esther deeply, instantly creating a feeling of a deep connection to these children despite all their differences.

"Yes, they are." She tried to sound strong. It was not her place to burden these kids with another sad story.

"Then you can live with us now. It's warm over the vent here," Tom said, grabbing her hand. Esther was about to ask if this was truly where they were living when all of a sudden little Arab started coughing. It turned the group's little happy faces into worry. His cough wasn't just a little cough, but a deep whistling sound as if his lungs were tearing up from the inside. Esther instantly walked over to Milton and placed a hand on little Arab's forehead.

"He's burning!" she gasped anxiously.

"Does that mean he is warm? That's good, right?" little Miki asked innocently.

"No, my little angel," she said, gently rubbing her hand down Miki's little, cold cheek. As street-smart as these children were, they needed help. Her gaze briefly turned toward the hole she'd just crawled through, reminding her of who she was and where she came from, and the little pride she had left that her name carried. She had enough money to survive on *her own* until her 21st birthday if she kept to a minimum. *But you are not on your own any longer,* her heart shouted loud and clear. She took in a deep breath and held it for a few seconds, then forcefully let it out as if that was her invisible signature to seal the deal.

"Where is the closest doctor?" she asked, determined.

"We don't have money," Jeff said, embarrassed.

"Yes, we do." Milton held out the bank note Esther had given him earlier above his head which almost seemed shimmering under the moonlight while the kids stared in awe.

"Are we rich now?" Tom shouted in excitement.

"Far from it." Esther smiled as the gleaming faces looked at her. "This money is for proper winter clothing for all of you."

She reached over to take little Arab out of Milton's arms. To her surprise, the little infant not only held on to her, but instantly buried his face into her neck, craving the touch of a mother-figure like flowers crave the sun. An overwhelming feeling of protective instincts flooded through her whole body like somebody had just opened a dam that was somewhere hidden inside her without her knowledge.

She had no idea how to care for a child. At twenty, she was barely an adult herself... But none of that mattered now. Her bubble of a fantasy to live with endless money and no worries was over. Somehow, she would manage. Somehow, *they* would manage.

"Jeff, can you take us to the doctor?" she asked.

"All of us?" Tom clarified.

"Yes, all of us. And after the doctor we won't come back here. We will stay in a real house."

Tom, Jeff, and Miki excitedly jumped into the air. "A real house!" they shouted.

"But where?" Milton wondered. Esther tilted her head, pressing little Arab closer to her body.

"Is there a cheap but clean place any of you know of?"

They all stopped jumping to start thinking, scratching their little heads and biting their little lips in deep thoughts.

"What about Beth's?" Miki suggested to Milton. He seemed to think about it for a moment, but then started nodding.

"Yes, Beth is trustworthy. She always buys newspapers from me although she can't read."

"Splendid," Esther said, heading toward the hole in the wall. "Grab your things and let's go before it gets any darker than it already is."

Miki, Jeff, and Tom all gathered their few belongings in a hurry, with smiles on their cute little faces so big, it could melt an iceberg. They already were half across the courtyard when they heard Milton shout from behind them.

"Wait!" They all turned around to find that Milton hadn't moved an inch.

"What is it?" Esther asked.

Milton twisted his lips as if he wasn't sure how to say it. "We can't go before we fix the problem," he said.

"Yeeees…" Miki, Jeff, and Tom simultaneously agreed, knowing exactly what he was talking about.

"The problem…" Miki echoed Milton's words.

"The problem?" Esther inquired with a blank look on her face. They all nodded their little heads in seriousness.

"You have to be like me," Miki said in an attempt to clear things up only to confuse Esther even more.

"I am afraid I don't understand." She turned toward Milton.

"It's not safe here as a woman," Milton said pulling at his collar.

"Well, that is why we are leaving *here.*" Esther replied in an understanding tone.

"*Here* is New York." Milton clarified.

Was he saying that she was not safe anywhere in New York as a single woman?

"Are you saying that I won't be safe anywhere in New York as a woman?"

Milton nodded. "At least not in these parts."

Esther thought about it for a moment. She was a woman of facts and logic. What Milton said made perfect sense considering it had taken less than an afternoon for her to almost get robbed and God knows what else could have happened. If it wasn't for Milton, who knows where she would have ended up by now. And on top of all of this, she wasn't exactly street smart like these kids. Until today, she didn't even know these parts of New York even existed. How could she take care of these kids if they constantly had to rescue her from another attacker?

"So, what are we supposed to do?" Esther asked, desperate for ideas. But Miki jumped next to her and pulled on her dress.

"You just have to be like me," he said, grinning as the group nodded.

"A child?" Esther asked, wrinkling her forehead. They all busted out in laughter.

"No! Silly!" Jeff tried to catch his breath. "Not a kid. A boy. You have to be a boy." Esther froze. If she wasn't holding the baby, she would probably sit down to digest that better.

"D-dress like a b-boy? I-impossible!" she stuttered. "No one would believe it."

"Yes, they will. They think I'm a boy too," Miki said.

"Wait! You are a girl?"

"Yup." Miki proudly pounded her chest with her tiny fist. "As a boy, bad men don't look at me no more." She grinned.

"People see what they want," Milton declared. "And boys are safer out here than girls."

Esther raised her eyebrows. All of this was starting to get to her. This day had been more eventful than the rest of her life combined. If it wasn't for the kids, God knows, she might as well go back to the pub and have a few drinks to calm her nerves. But then, the more she thought about it, all while staring at Miki who had fooled her all along, the craziness of this whole idea slowly faded to make way for common sense. Looking back, Luigi would not have picked her so easily if she was a man. And then there was Morris, who also wasn't looking for a man. In this time and age, men had doors opened wide for them while women had to fight for everything. And now with five kids—she shook her head in disbelief that she now had five kids—but with five kids she would fare far better posing as their brother or uncle rather than their single, attractive, easy to scam mother or sister.

The group was staring at her in great anticipation.

"Well," she finally said, "after the doctor's we shall stop at a clothing store to get warm men's clothing for *all* of us."

All of the kids, except Milton, now wiggled happily in their places. He smiled as well, but it was obvious that years in the streets had forced him to grow up a bit faster than the rest of them, than any kid ever should.

"And one more thing," Esther said, making her way to the wall. "I want you all to think of a real name for our little love here. The times of calling any of you *Arab* are over, once and for all!"

Miki, Jeff, and Tom jumped ahead to move the box out of the way that covered the hole in it. Milton was right behind them, gathering his things.

They all turned around one more time, looking over to the vent that they once called home for God knows how long, before crawling through the little opening one by one. The evening had turned dark with snow clouds forming. Esther looked to the sky as if her father were there looking down on her. Deep in thought, she kissed little Arab on his hair that was probably brown underneath all that filth. In less than a day she had lost her father and her inheritance, had had to run and find a way to hide until she was twenty-one, become the mother of five street children, and to top everything off, now also had to turn into a man. She couldn't help but grin sarcastically — at herself. If her parents were up there looking down on her, would they be laughing, or crying? Both were possible, considering both of them were as humorous as they were kindhearted.

"Hurry, before it gets too dark," she heard Milton shout from the other side of the wall.

Esther shook her head to return to her new reality, proud of herself for having just as much of her strong mother in her as her father had always told her she did.

"I'm coming."

Those were Esther's last words before she handed the baby to Milton through the wall and crawled from the small, dusty wasteland into a new adventure, forever leaving her old life and self behind.

CHAPTER 4

George put his mug down and nodded at the waitress for a refill. The beer was warm and stale, but he didn't expect much better from a pub in Park Slope, which was one of the poorer Irish Quarters in New York. He wasn't much of a drinker anyway, but tonight was an exception. He scouted the place for his source. The pub was quite typical for an Irish pub: red brick walls, wooden tables, packed with rowdy, drunk Irishmen singing along to some old man fiddling on his violin day and night.

The waitress, a big-breasted woman in her thirties wearing a tiny blouse that meant nothing less than to advertise her little side hustle, filled his mug then sat down on the chair next to him.

"Is dare anythin' else oi can chucker for an 'andsum paddy loike yer?"

With a seductive grin on her face, she leaned over the table making her breasts almost fall out of the shirt that looked like it was about to burst.

George's face reddened in discomfort. "I'm afraid not," he said with friendly smile and handed her a coin nonetheless, which she happily made disappear in her corset.

"Your loss, fella." She pouted, curling her lips like a duck.

He didn't mean to be rude; the woman was just trying to make ends meet. But he was never the sort of man who paid for pleasure. To him, using a woman to please his manly urges had never held its appeal.

He took another deep sip of his beer and ran a hand through his golden hair before his gaze caught another woman, almost too young to be called that, making a try for it by throwing him a kiss from halfway across the stuffy room. She was well kept and dressed in what looked like a rather expensive dress. Probably a lady for the upper classes, he thought. His beautiful blue eyes threw her a wink, followed by a but-no-thank-you headshake.

God had blessed him with his cold-hearted mother's looks—a woman whose beauty had brought her fame and a marriage with his father, the recently deceased and widely respected Duke of Aberdeen. If title was what a woman was hunting for, his mother could have not landed a better match. The dukedom of Aberdeen had been around for hundreds of years, known and respected far and wide not only in England, but in all of Europe. That was, until his harpy of a mother spent his father's legendary fortune into ruin, and if that wasn't bad enough, pushed him into his early deathbed by asking more and more of him when there was nothing left to give. And if things weren't bad enough, she'd now managed to force his beloved sister, who was nothing short of an angel, into a marriage with the most despicable man in all of England. A man who was rumored to be whoring around wearing nappies and fathering more illegitimate children than Genghis Khan. George took another long sip of his beer as if he were trying to wash down the bitter taste his mother had left on his tongue.

A silhouette that soon identified as Murphy, the pub's owner, tore George back out of his deep thoughts. He was standing right in front of his table, holding up a piece of paper in front of him.

"Me lord," the red-haired, short man who seemed rounder than the table he was sitting at yapped. "'Dis jist arrived for yer. Didn't say his name."

George eagerly put his beer down and jerked the paper out of his hand. Murphy curiously waited around, looking at the letter in anticipation of what was in it.

"Thank you," George said without opening the letter, clearly signaling him that it would stay closed until the man had made his way back into the now wildly clapping and dancing crowd again.

Murphy hesitated for a moment, glancing over the letter with greedy eyes, before he threw George an angry look and left. For a moment he just sat there, holding that piece of paper in his hands as if he wasn't sure whether he really wanted to know what was in it. For weeks he had been running around New York trying to find information about his dear friend and business partner Billy. It had been months since he had last heard from him. Months since the earth had swallowed him, leaving nothing but a cold trail to a gold mine. For weeks, George had paid countless lawyers and investigators to find out what had happened—but to no avail.

It wasn't until a drunk man at the pub had told him about a police officer named Wilson who would and could do anything for a few dollars.

And with money running thin, this man was pretty much his last hope.

George took another sip of his beer, marveling at how his entire future was now in front of him in the form of a little piece of paper. It held the power to either continue the legacy of the house of Aberdeen or strike it down like a giant rabbit. Aberdeen Park had survived war and intrigues for centuries, but not the greedy fingers of an exceptional beauty. And according to the creature of rapacity he had to call mother, 'Billy didn't just vanish but in fact ran with the gold, hiding somewhere in riches beyond belief, laughing about the foolish Englishman who was imprudent enough to trust an American with his last funds to mine for gold in the savage lands of the frontier.' Those were the exact words she'd yelled at him instead of saying her goodbyes.

For a moment she had him, for a brief moment he let his mind slip into her dark belief system and doubt his dear friend as well. But Billy was not like that. They had been friends for many years. He was a good man, trying to make a better life for himself—in an honest manner. More in worry than anger, George slammed his fist onto the table. Billy was no con artist. There must have been a reason for Billy's disappearance. Whatever it was, he was here to find out, and if he was lucky for once, this piece of paper would bring him a step closer to finding not only his dear friend, but hopefully a handsome amount of gold along with it.

George took a deep breath, sneaking glances around him, before opening the letter.

I've found him. Meet me at 9 at the East River Bridge. W.

A rush of adrenaline shot through his veins, instantly waking him from the curtain of slight drunkenness. His blue eyes narrowed as he read the note again, just to be sure. The words stayed the same. It felt like his insides were fluttering. For the first time in weeks—no, months—there seemed to be hope. Billy was alive! Wilson, that drunken, corrupt fool, had managed to find out more in a few days than all the investigators and lawyers that he had hired had been able to in months—and that on both continents.

George pulled out his father's golden pocket watch. It was eight now. Although there was still enough time, he thought it better to head out now. Under no circumstances could he risk missing such an important appointment. His very name depended on it.

He slugged the rest of his beer in a single chug and got up. It was instantly noticeable that he was almost a head taller than anybody else who was standing around him. At a lean and muscular six feet, he was considered a bit taller than most men of his time. He straightened his elegant day suit and was just about to head over to the door, when his gaze met with Murphy's. His intense stare directed at the note stood out even at a lively crowded pub like this one. George's eyes darkened as he held the note up to the candle on his table, locking his gaze with Murphy's. The heat of the flame ate away the note, inching closer and closer to George's fingers, but he didn't even flinch. Murphy finally turned away, well aware that his more-than-suspicious curiosity had not only been noticed but also challenged.

George had a bad feeling about this guy, and it was better to let Murphy know that. If the last few weeks in New York had taught him one thing, it was that these parts of town were just as shady as London's West End. George was by no means street-smart, but his time in the army in the Indies had changed him from the naïve spoiled lordling he used to be into a man who knew that life wasn't sparkling wine and endless sunny days for everyone. The three-inch long scar on his left cheek was proof enough. A starving man in Bangladesh had left George with this souvenir to steal the piece of bread out of his hand. Not money, not gold, but bread.

He grabbed his coat and made his way to the door, focusing his attention on Murphy, who here and there threw him a quick glance but looked the other way whenever their eyes met. George stopped right next to him, just enough to give him a silent warning, before stepping out into the dark night.

An icy wave hit him in the face the moment the door closed behind him. The streets were surprisingly busy. Some shops were closing up while others had just opened for the evening. A few drunks were singing on the side, one of them being thrown out from another pub. Women in scantily worn dresses were teasing men, and a few fights broke out here and there, but nothing too much of a concern for the police who stood there laughing. The endless noise and chatter mixed in with the familiar stench of the area that George had somehow gotten used to. It was the same old twilight, nothing new.

A carriage stopped in front of George in the hopes he would ask for a ride.

"No, thank you," he said, shivering as he crossed the street. His fine clothes were like a big target sign on his back, attracting everything from beggars to the mothers of society hunting for European aristocrats for their daughters. He wrapped his coat tightly around himself, a lost battle against the coldest winter he had ever experienced in his life. Locals said that the 1881 winter had taken many souls in December and January and that he was lucky to have arrived right before the spring. But lucky or not, it was still a bloody hell of a lot colder than England — full stop.

Sobered up from the icy attacks of the New York winter winds, he made his way toward the base of the world-famous East River Bridge construction site. A marvel of engineering, the East River Bridge was a declaration of wealth and progress, sent out into the world by the newly emerging world-power — America.

The streets in this area of town seemed to offer much more solace, letting him enjoy the view of the starry cloudless sky, wondering if his sister was also staring at it this very instant. How he longed to be home. But if Wilson had truly found Billy, then not only George, but his poor sister along with his entire estate could be saved—a relief he couldn't even begin to describe with words, making this trip well worth it.

"A newspaper for the fine Mister?" a voice asked from the shadows.

George looked down, squinting at the young fellow who stood behind a gas lamp post. A blonde boy no older than twelve was holding a newspaper up, close enough to George's face that he could almost read it. George waved his hand to get a better look at the boy. He was dressed in warm clothes and looked well fed, a stark contrast to other newspaper boys he'd seen so far. Most of them were caked in dust and muddy clothes, shivering in the cold, nothing but skin and bones. What would drive such young boys to sell papers in the dead of the night, he wondered, feeling an odd jolt in his chest. There was something about this boy's body that made him look like eight, although George was more than certain that he was well over ten. The curse of poverty did this to children. Years of hunger would delay their growth.

George remembered the letter; he couldn't be late.

He wanted to reach for a coin, but the boy must have thought he wanted to leave without buying a newspaper, so this determined little fellow stepped right in front of him, blocking his way.

"An educated man like you should not miss out on the world's news." He smirked, knowing this line would land him something.

George couldn't help but give this little fellow some well-deserved admiration.

"You know your trade well." He smiled at the boy, pulling out a coin for him when all of a sudden, the boy's newspapers slipped from his little twitchy fingers like an invisible hand had just jerked them away. Some fell straight to the ground, while others blew away, scattered by the winds. Muttering under his breath, the boy frantically tried to pick them back up, a desperately futile sight to behold. George bent over to help with both hands, reaching left and right, trying to grab as many he could before the merciless winds made things worse.

Both of his hands full of crunched newspaper pages, George thought to himself that this was exactly why he had left for his meeting with Wilson early. This was America. Anything could happen. No matter what time of the day…everything was possible here…

Esther, now going by the name of Egan, stood outside with Mary and Susan in front of Beth's boarding house. She was wearing male clothes and her once so beautiful long hair was cut short just to the ears. Beth's, the promised sanctuary the kids were so eager to talk about, had turned out to be right next to a brothel. When Esther had first arrived here, standing in front of Beth's footsteps, dressed like a man, with four children and a sick infant in her arms, she had wanted to turn around and leave. But all huddled together in the middle of one of the coldest winters in history, there was no other way than to take a room at Beth's.

"One day," she told the kids back then, firmly shaking her head in disapproval. But just like the children had told her, there was no place in town as clean, safe, and cheap as Beth's. And so, one day turned to several weeks, and weeks to months. Besides, no other place would take her in with five kids, but Beth was as kind as she was smart, so Esther would always have a place there if need be. And as they were all boys now, none of the customers of next door even looked twice at Esther or the kids.

Mary took a sip of her whiskey bottle, then offered some to Esther with a warm lusty smile.

"Herrr lad." Her heavily painted lips twitched in a heavy Irish accent. Esther nodded and took a big sip herself, instantly grimacing as if she'd just bitten into a lemon. Susan, a skinny, young prostitute who despite her age had the look of a woman who had seen it all on her face, laughed.

"There are other ways to warm a handsome fellow like you," she whispered into Esther's ear in a silky, smooth voice.

Esther squirmed to the side, squishing her brows together in annoyance. "Stop that, Sue."

Mary laughed out loud. "That's what yer git for bein' such a hansum lad," she jested, wrapping herself tighter into the blanket she was wearing over her shoulders.

An elegantly dressed couple walked by, staring at them in disgust. From time to time, finer folks got lost in this part of town. Beth's boarding house and the brothel next door did well enough to be right at the border of the parts of town that finer folks frequented.

"How pathetic," the fancy woman cringed in an arrogant voice, holding a handkerchief up to her nose.

Her husband hastily pulled her down the street mumbling: "Don't engage with them, they are not human."

Esther flared. "How pathetic." She imitated the woman in an overly dramatic, high-pitched voice, pretending to sniff a handkerchief. Susan and Mary burst out into loud laughter.

Until the moody lady luck had dethroned her, nobody had ever dared to belittle Esther like this. People used to open doors for her, bowed in front of her. But now, every peacock in town thought he could look down on her and her poverty-stricken friends. The couple had vanished, and her gaze fell onto her reflection in an icy puddle beneath her work boots. Her beautiful, long hair was gone and her once so clean, beautiful face was now as dirty as everyone else's around here. She washed every day, but it was impossible to stay clean in these parts. Besides the occasional lost traveler, everyone she knew was constantly covered in either coal dust, mud, dirt, or all of it.

She was wearing a dark-gray newsboy hat and a gray wool coat that slightly broadened her shoulders. A matching wool vest aided in hiding her female chest just in case the tight wraps around her curves would loosen. At first, wrapping fabrics around her chest to flatten it was quite a challenge. But as money ran out thanks to doctor bills for the children and paying the room before eating herself, Esther had lost weight faster than she could blink, making chest wraps almost unnecessary.

So here she was. Poor, starving, belittled, mother of five kids, and to top things off, constantly under lusty attacks from the prostitutes who thought her pretty face to be the most handsome in town. Of course, some knew right away that she was just a woman wearing pants. Beth was one of the smart ones, but much to Esther's surprise, Milton had been right when he'd told her that most people see what they want. With her hard facial lines from her native mother, one could think her a very pretty-faced man if one had no reason to assume otherwise.

Susan and Mary's loud laughter tore her back out of her thoughts.

"Really lad. Yer make things so much better raun 'ere." Mary's chest chuckled up and down.

Esther did a little courtesy bow.

"It's an honor, my ladies."

All of a sudden, Miki came running down the street. It was already getting dark, so why was she still out and about and why wasn't Helga with her? She threw herself right against Esther's legs, hastily sucking her in for her urgent message.

"It's Milton!" Miki hollered, out of breath. Esther felt a cold shiver ran down her spine, the usual worry of a mother fearing the worst for her child. She grabbed Miki by the arms to try and calm her.

"Is he alright?" Esther's voice trembled. Miki nodded. A slight relief.

"Then what is it?" She kneeled down.

"He is doing the newspaper trick again," Miki bawled pointing toward Murphy's pub.

Esther shot back up; her stomach burned in churning agony.

"After what happened last time?"

Miki just nodded. Esther shot around to Susan.

"Could one of you please take Miki back to Helga and the others?"

Susan was already on her way over and grabbed Miki by her hand.

"Come little one, let's get you a glass of milk before you get tortured again with reading lessons by that dried up nanny of yours," Susan said in a sweet voice.

That dried up nanny she was referring to was in fact a woman Esther had been paying to watch the kids and teach them how to read and write when she was out and about making a few coins in every respectable way possible. Helga, an old German widow whom she'd found begging in the streets, was a sweet old lady, which unfortunately at the time also made her a victim of Esther's street-smart kids. Esther could only imagine how little cunning Miki got away this time.... Milton was the only one allowed to walk the streets freely as he was still selling newspapers to help out with money, but the other kids were 'supposed' to be with Helga at all times. Miki would get her interrogation later on, but for now there was no time.

Esther turned on her heel and ran toward Murphy's. Her heart was pounding against her chest, not from the sprint but from fear. The so-called newspaper trick had almost landed Milton in custody a few weeks ago, which could have placed him in jail, or worse, in an orphanage.

Why would he be so careless to take another risk? Esther's education put her in a position where she was able to do small administrative tasks for shops around here, including Beth's. Although that didn't make them rich, it certainly brought in enough coins to pay for a roof over their heads as well as food—for the kids and Helga at least. So why did he have to gamble away that little bit of happiness he had with that darn newspaper trick he had promised to never ever play on anybody ever again?

Esther picked up speed, her head throbbing in her skull from the whiskey and the sudden jolt of adrenaline. Her heartbeat paced along with her legs faster than she could notice, avoiding the sea of moving bodies, nearly crashing into a carriage yelling slurs back at her.

Just a few more blocks to Murphy's. She wasn't sure if she said the words out loud or in her head, but they repeated themselves over and above again.

"Please God, don't let me be too late!"

For a second, she just stood there, her mouth wide open in disbelief at the scene that enfolded in front of her. The cold wind blew on her face as a storm of white and black papers flew everywhere.

Milton had already dropped all his newspapers, the most important part of his scheme, but instead of the victim leaving and cussing at him for the inconvenience, the tall, lean man had opted to chase them down, fumbling around as if trying to catch pigeons in the dark with nothing but the gloomy light of a single lamp above them. Both his hands were full of crumpled pages, trying desperately to help Milton gather them back into a big pile.

Milton was oddly slow, lazily picking them up one by one before finally noticing her presence. His gaze was just as confused as she was. Never had anybody been kind enough and helped him to get the newspapers back. Esther shot him a glaring look.

The man stopped; a cloud of cold white fog blew from his mouth as he noticed Esther. He straightened himself to face her. His blue eyes cut through her like a razor. She felt a weird tingling in her stomach when their gaze met, and it almost seemed as if the gloomy light brightened to shine on him like a spotlight. Never in her life had she seen a more attractive man before. His short, dark blonde hair was neatly combed in fashion, and his face had extremely clear, straight lines, often only seen in the most handsome of people. As Esther was drawn closer, a long scar on his left cheek revealed itself, giving his incredible smile a touch of exotic manliness. Esther wanted to say something, but she said nothing, for no words would come out. What was going on, where was her voice?

"The fine Mister is inconveniencing himself helping me," Milton said in a tone that clearly tried to signal her something, but what she couldn't make out.

The man swiftly flung around to catch another piece of paper that had flown too close to him to let it go.

"Are you two acquainted?" he asked in a British accent, leaning over to Milton to hand him the pile of papers he had managed to gather. Esther marveled at this man's elegance. His voice, his looks, even the way he picked up newspapers from the sidewalk was as smooth and confident as the movements of a jaguar.

"Y-yes, that's my l-little brother," Esther stuttered, finally finding her voice when her gaze turned to Milton, who now slowly stepped behind the man to throw her signals with duck face lips and a wildly shaking head. Esther squinted, blinking her eyes in confusion. Milton let out a breath in annoyance over her incompetence to understand his made-up sign language. He attempted again, but this time he moved his lips in a silent but slow clear motion that said 'we gotta go,' when the man jerked around. Milton swallowed his own breath as he narrowed his eyes on him.

"Little brother, is it?"

He studied the little boy from head to toe. "You two certainly don't show much resemblance," he declared, bending over to pick up a piece of newspaper the wind had blown against his fashionable leather shoe.

This was not good. Esther could smell his suspicion even against the strong winter winds. He knew something was not right.

"Different fathers." Her innocent voice replied, reaching over to take the piece of paper he held up to her. The man inched closer, scanning her silently with his gleaming eyes that were as blue as the ocean. He was so close that his delightful aroma of soap crawled through her nose, inviting that tingling sense from her chest anew.

"Well, we'd better go," she uttered, finally able to tear herself free from his spell. "Thank you for the help."

Milton rushed up beside her. "Yeah, thanks for the help."

They turned around and started walking. Milton let out a huge sigh of relief. Esther on the other hand swallowed a knot of anger that stuck in her throat like a piece of food. She knew what Milton had tried to do. Her hands twitched in anticipation of turning around the next corner to make him face the music. But just when they were about to turn onto the alley next to Murphy's, something forcefully snatched Milton away from her.

"YOU!" a deep, angry voice growled. Esther turned to find her worries and fears coming true after all. It was Eric, a notoriously nasty police officer assigned to this district. He was holding

Milton by the neck, shaking him out of his senses. "You little rat!" he cursed.

Esther's stomach turned to rock.

"Let him go!" she shrieked, grabbing Eric by his hairy wrist in an attempt to loosen his strong grip on Milton, who now screamed in pain.

"Take your hands off him."

She pulled and pushed at Eric's enormous arm as hard as she could. But Eric wouldn't have it. He fumed like a boar, sending out a cloud of mist from his nostrils. His eyes bulged as he swung the back of his hand which met her face in an audible smack. The blow was so hard, she didn't only tumble backwards, she flew, crashing onto the icy hard pavement.

"I told you I'd catch your rotten, thieving hands one day!"

Eric shook his finger at Esther, dragging Milton by the neck back to the handsome fellow.

Esther rolled herself to the side as her back and shoulder screamed in torment. Clearly there'd be a bruise by the morning. She struggled to push herself up, tripping face first with her head inches from the ground, when a gentle, warm hand grabbed her by the arm to pull her back up. She panicked and swatted the hand away from her. No one was allowed to touch her, discover her disguise. It was a dead giveaway. No matter how manly she tried to look, there was no way to hide her soft supple skin and feminine bones.

"I'm fine," she moaned, wiping the metallic taste of blood and snow from her mouth.

"What is the meaning of this!" the man yelled at the brutal police officer.

Eric shoved Milton right in front of the handsome stranger, presenting him like a trophy. Grabbing under Milton's coat, he pulled out a small leather purse.

"Is this yours?" Eric held the purse up, accompanied by a hoggish wide grin on his gluttonous face.

Esther limped over to Milton, a feeling of panic rushing through her aching body like a galloping stallion. This was the end of it. The end of Milton. And most likely the end of her as well, as she would not let this little boy she'd come to love so dearly get tossed about and tortured in an orphanage without putting up a fight. It would be a spectacularly humiliating one considering that Eric was a modern-day mammoth back from the dead, but she would give it all she had, nonetheless.

"Let me go, please," she heard Milton cry out in pain. The burning sensation of tears formed in her eyes when they suddenly met with those deep blue eyes of the wealthy foreigner. Would he ever show mercy? Or was he just another Morris without a care in the world?

The man shook his head, tearing his gaze away from Esther's begging tears.

"Yes, it is." He now confirmed in an unreadable tone. Eric's face darkened in fiendish delight and he lifted his huge arm up high into the winter sky, ready to strike Milton, when the handsome man launched forward and grabbed Eric by the wrist, stopping him right in his tracks.

"However," he said, narrowing his eyes as he tightened his grip around Eric's wrist, "I gave that purse to him."

"What?"

"Excuse me?"

"Huh?" Milton, Eric, and Esther blurted simultaneously with their mouths wide open.

"Indeed." He confirmed once more to a crowd in utter shock. "I have tasked this fine young fellow to take care of something for me," the man explained further, still holding onto Eric's wrist, not giving him an inch to move. Eric gave in and slowly lowered his arm to signal the man that he would not strike the boy, which in return finally got him his wrist back.

"And what would that be at this hour?"

Eric expressed his suspicion, narrowing his eyes.

"I'm afraid if you can't figure that out as a police officer, I shall have to leave you in the dark." The man crossed his arms. "Quite literally."

Eric scratched his head for a moment, but then formed his lips into a perverted grin. He instantly released Milton, dry washing his hands in excitement.

"Company, aye?" The Irish accent he tried so hard to hide now came out along with an all-knowing smirk.

"Company?" Esther wondered, pulling Milton into her protective arms. Eric turned toward her.

"Didn't use your little lad for more than pissing yet, aye?" He chuckled.

"What?" Esther was now even more confused. Milton came to her rescue and whispered. "Whores…"

Her cheeks flushed bright red as she nodded strongly, a poor attempt to convince the others that she knew more than she did.

"Oh, yes, of course, I know," she mumbled, trying not to peek over at the handsome stranger who just saved Milton from the hell of an orphanage. For some reason she couldn't bear looking at the man thinking about such things. Living next to prostitutes and being constantly hit on by some of them, she thought she was a little more weathered in this subject by now, but apparently this was not the case.

Eric busted out in whiny laughter and smacked Esther so hard on her back that she tumbled forward a few steps.

"Don't worry lad, it's just like pissing!"

Eric hit his leg in uncontrollable laughter, spit coming out of his mouth now. Esther stepped away in disgust. The handsome stranger wrinkled his forehead.

"If you are primitive and don't know anything about it, yes, then it is just like 'pissing,'" he said to alleviate his very obvious detestation of Eric, whose laugh turned dead silent thanks to this very remark.

The Brit pulled a pocket watch out of his fine coat. His eyes briefly swelled.

"For heaven's sake," he said turning on the heel. Something must have been extremely urgent, as the man didn't even bother to ask for his purse back.

"Your money!" Esther shouted after him.

"The boy can keep it."

Those were his last words before vanishing behind the corner.

Esther's breath fumed from the cold as she stared at the corner that moments ago had swallowed one of the kindest men she had ever come across. Not only had he saved a boy who had every intention of robbing him, but had also protected him from harm, and on top of that had given him all his money. Milton tore the purse out of Eric's hand.

"Would you be so kind?!" he barked at him.

"Street rat," Eric mumbled, tugging his clothes in order before leaving as well, keeping a watchful gaze back toward Milton in a silent 'I'm watching you' before disappearing into the dark.

"Does that mean I won't get in trouble?" Milton's voice sounded like that of an angel.

"In your dreams!"

She turned to face him, putting her hands on her hips. "What were you thinking?" Esther yelled, waving her hands. "I work day and night to put a roof over our heads and food on the table. Is that not enough?"

Milton lowered his head in shame, staring at the ground.

"It is," he muttered.

"Then why would you steal again? You promised you would never do it again!"

This was a serious situation, and he had to understand that once and for all.

"For me..." Milton almost whispered, biting his lower lip.

"What do you mean?" Her voice softened.

"You asked if it's not enough. So, I just told you that it is… for me at least."

Esther tilted her head in confusion.

"But not for you. You barely eat," he whimpered, his eyes filled with grief. "And you never sleep, only work all the time. I-I just wanted to buy food for you."

Esther felt a tight knot in her throat. His words broke her heart. He wasn't stealing for toys, or sweets, or anything else a kid his age would dream of — and deserved to do so. No, he had risked his life for no other reason than to feed *her!*

She swung her arms around him, pulling his little body against hers. "I'm so sorry, Milton." She held him tight to her heart like only a loving mother could. "Please promise me you won't do this ever again."

She looked up to the sky, thinking about the pain she would feel if she were to lose him. "There is not enough food in the world that would be worth losing you, you hear me?"

She could feel Milton's head nod in her arms.

Esther was about to tell him that she didn't need him to steal for her, that she would find a different way to make money, an honorable way, when in the distance, the door to Murphy's shot wide open and Big Murphy himself stood in the bare cold. His rusty hair bounced in the winter winds with a crunched-up face that was clearly in a bad mood. Next to him was one of his crook-looking friends. They chattered for a moment before Murphy's friend pointed around the corner and started walking. They passed by Milton and Esther, ignoring them as if they weren't there. Nothing but a bunch of street rats left to rot in the snow.

"I'm telling yer, de nobleman has a treasurr map." Murphy bubbled in his loud, Irish voice. His companion, a tall man with a gaunt drawn face covered under muddy black hair, blew his warm breath onto his hands.

"Yer man is headin' to de bridge, aye?"

"Aye," Murphy confirmed with a smirk that revealed a rotten front tooth. Suddenly, his companion turned toward Esther and Milton.

"Git out o' here, yer rats or you'll get Mossy's iron blow," he growled, clenching his fist, shaking it widely.

Esther grabbed Milton by the arm and pulled him down the street as fast as she could. As soon as they were around the corner, she pressed herself against the wall, peeking back at Murphy and his vagabond who were clearly hatching something out.

"What are they up to?" Milton whispered.

"Nothing good, I'm afraid."

Esther closed her eyes. This handsome stranger was clearly in danger. In these parts of town there were two kinds of criminals. Folks that committed non-violent crimes to get by, and the ones who would make life harder for everyone else. Murphy was not part of the first group. That slimy worm would sell his mother to a butcher shop if he could get a coin for it in return. She had to do something.

"Milton…" She kneeled and grabbed him by the shoulders. "Go run home. If I'm not back in an hour, tell Beth and Helga what happened. They will know what to do." Milton shook his head.

"But—"

"No buts. I'll be fine, I have my pistol, remember?"

Milton nodded his head.

"Go, now."

Milton gave her a quick hug and sprinted off. Esther peeked around the corner again, only to find Murphy and his friend disappear into a side street.

"Damn it," she cussed, a skill she wasn't proud of but came with the rough life of poverty. For the second time tonight, Esther sprinted as fast as she could to catch up to Murphy. And for the second time this night, she was worried about someone else's safety. Not the feelings of terror she'd gone through for Milton, but nonetheless a feeling of worry. But why? Why did she even bother to care? She barely knew that man. Surely it was the honorable thing to do after he'd saved Milton from that pig, but something deep inside her whispered to her that there was more to this than the need to make right.

Esther's frozen feet flew over the pavement through the dark streets of New York, arriving at the base of the world-famous East River Bridge in no time. Its enormous, neo-Gothic stone tower loomed like a huge giant above the East River, laughing at the mere thought of the river trying to separate Brooklyn and Manhattan. Once completed, it would be the longest suspended cable bridge in the world, one of the many industrial marvels of the nineteenth century that made America so famous.

Most of the gigantic columns of the bridge were hidden in the shadows, barely illuminated by a few gas lanterns that lit up the construction zone around it. Esther squinted her eyes to scan the area, which was not easy in this light, when she spotted two silhouettes meeting from opposite directions under one of the sparingly placed lanterns. One of the shadows was short and skinny, the other tall and noble. Without a doubt, she knew who it was.

Esther was too far away to make out the words of their conversation. She crept closer and stopped when she saw two additional silhouettes rush from behind a small construction building into the darkness of the bridge's column. This was not good. If Big Murphy had a weapon, she would get shot if she made herself known now to warn the handsome stranger.

Her heart beat wildly against her chest, teeth clenched in anticipation. She had to do something but be clever about it. Clever, or extremely quiet and sneak up on them. Esther had often heard about the Cherokees' ability to sneak up on others unnoticed. Nobody was better at going about undetected than the natives who had lived and hunted in these lands for thousands of years. They were like ghosts, shadows of the earth. Esther often wondered if her mother was the same, and whether it was something she had inherited and could do out of instinct.

She was about to sneak up on Murphy, when a sliver of light flashed from where he was hiding. Was it a knife? A pistol? Unfortunately, there was no time for mysteries. It was time to put her warrior blood to the test. 'The better half,' as her father always used to say….'The better half…'

CHAPTER 5

The man of the hour, Wilson, seemed awfully nervous. He was constantly licking his lips and looking over his shoulders as if he were expecting someone to be following him. Even in a dark place like this, his red hair somehow managed to have a fiery shimmer to it.

"If I had known what you were getting me into, I would never have taken your money," Wilson said, peeking over his shoulder once more.

George rubbed his chin in a failed attempt to decipher his words.

"I'm afraid I don't follow."

And he didn't, but he was eager to find out. He'd simply paid this man to find his friend, nothing more, nothing less. But something felt awfully wrong here as his eyes wandered into the background.

"Is Billy in some sort of trouble?"

Wilson laughed sarcastically and pulled out an envelope, handing it to George.

"You could say that. He was last seen about a month ago." Wilson nodded. "In Chama, New Mexico."

This piece of information was not surprising at all considering that Chama, New Mexico, was where George and Billy had bought the gold mine and thousands of acres of land with it. But at least he now knew that Billy hadn't just run off with a fortune, drinking sparkling wine in a romantic coastal town somewhere.

"So, he is alive?" George asked, putting the envelope in his pocket. Wilson shrugged his shoulders.

"Who knows? That's some dangerous business you two are getting yourselves into," he snickered.

"What do you mean?" George frowned.

"That land up there. It's bad blood."

Wilson looked over his shoulder again, but this time his gaze got stuck in darkness. "Who knows what the government will do to cover their tracks?"

"Cover their tracks, for what?" George inquired, somewhat annoyed now. Why was he acting like this?

"It's all in there." Wilson pointed at the envelope in George's pocket, his gaze still drawn toward the darkness. "And that is further than I'm willing to go. Now give me the rest of my money." He stretched out his hand.

George was tugging a small, folded envelope out of his inner coat pocket, when he heard the unmistakable sharp metallic click from a revolver's hammer. On instinct, he slid his hand toward the other coat pocket that hid his own pistol.

Wilson shot around in panic, spitting out a fearful whisper at the silhouette of a skinny person approaching from the shadows. Wilson jerked his lantern toward the intruder, revealing the metal of a small pistol barrel aimed toward them.

"Hands up where I can see them." George's cold voice shot at the intruder, holding out his own gun, a rare silver revolver with a rotating cylinder that could hold six bullets at a time. His aim was fixed on the approaching threat, his eyes sharp as an eagle, before they relaxed.

"You," he sighed at the newspaper boy's brother from earlier as he lowered his weapon, not because he thought this skinny lad didn't know how to shoot, but something inside him told him that this pretty-faced boy wasn't much trouble. From his time in the military, George could smell a cold-blooded killer from a mile away. This boy smelled more like fruits and whiskey. He recalled the way he'd protected his little brother. There was honor and selflessness in his heart. George's arm flopped to his side.

"What is going on here?" Wilson's frightened voice whispered to George, who answered with an honest shrug of his shoulders before turning to the boy.

"I'm afraid your little brother has already taken all I have to give," he said with an underlying tone of sarcasm.

"And we are grateful for that," the boy said, his pistol still raised and held steady. George raised a brow. What was going on here? But before he could inquire about that, the boy suddenly yelled into the dark:

"Do you hear that, you rats? Nothing left to steal, so get the hell out of here!"

George and Wilson exchanged confused looks, and for a moment there was silence. Then two men crept out from the shadows of the bridge's mighty tower footing. In an instant, George drew his pistol once more, pointing it at the two men who soon identified as Murphy and one of his drinking buddies. Murphy, that snake, returned the courtesy by pointing his own gun, a long-barreled flintlock pistol, while his friend held up a butcher knife.

George could feel his body tense in anger.

"Is this service included in the price for your filthy beer?" His tone deepened.

"Take another step an' ye'll find out." Murphy spat on the ground, pulling back the hammer of his gun.

"The police will be here soon," the boy now yelled.

George noticed that his slim arm was shaking, clearly nervous. Murphy and his friend focused their gaze on Wilson, exchanging worried looks, when all of a sudden, Wilson jumped for the envelope that George still held in his hand and made a run for it.

"Splendid," George mumbled sarcastically, rolling his eyes.

Murphy and his friends now smiled, revealing the shimmer of yellow teeth.

"What's so funny?" the boy sincerely wondered.

"That *was* the police," George said, letting out a loud sigh.

"Damn it." The boy bit his lower lip. George had to do something before someone got shot.

"Are you somewhat good with numbers?" George hollered over to Murphy, who wrinkled his forehead.

"Gran enoof to know yer have a treasure map from Chama."

Murphy grinned as if he'd just uncovered George's long-kept secret. His friend followed suit, excitedly shifting weight from one leg to the other with a big smirk on his face.

"Ch-chama?" the boy stuttered as if he had seen a ghost. Murphy noticed it too and didn't waste a second to try to turn him.

"Aye boy. A hidden treasure, in Chama," he pleaded his case. "Why don't yer come over here an' join us? We will split it evenly."

George instantly peeked over to analyze the boy's face. Would he fall for this nonsense? Side with that foolish man-child?

"No treasure is worth getting hanged for," the boy shouted with fire in his eyes. "Or shot."

Now it was George's turn to grin. This boy was truly fascinating.

"So, shall we go over the numbers then?" George sassed over to Murphy. "Last time I counted, it's two guns against one gun and a knife. A large knife, but a knife nevertheless." George stepped closer. "And I shall make sure to shoot you first, Murphy."

"Sounds good to me," the boy chipped in, following George's footsteps.

Murphy busted out a chuckle as his rusty hair bounced on his ball shaped face. "I count only one," his gun aimed at George while pointing a finger at the boy. "That lad can barely shoot."

His words seemed to have only emboldened his knife-wielding friend as he now took a step closer. It was impossible to see his face with all that muddy hair in front of it. For a brief moment George wondered whether he could even see them?

"Well, let's practice some shooting then, what do you think, Boy? Murphy first?" George said in a confident tone.

"I think that's a fine idea." The boy played along, smirking straight at Murphy. George shifted his gaze to his unexpected ally who was starting to look older and bolder by the minute. But if Murphy wouldn't bite and stop this nonsense right now, George had no choice but to shoot him to save the boy. Killing someone, even a pig like Murphy, was the last thing he had set his heart on when he'd opened his eyes this morning. George was an incredibly skilled shot, and of course he would aim for Murphy's hand first, but in this gloomy light, there was a chance he would miss his hand and drop all of Murphy straight to the muddy ground.

But the fool Murphy was, he took another step closer, then another...

Damn it, George cursed at Murphy once more. The time for debates was over. George gathered his calm and held his breath, finger on the trigger, aiming for Murphy's hand — and pulled.

The shot boomed across the gloomy night sky, startling everybody but George. Then there was a dead silence which seemed to last forever, until finally, Murphy's gun glinted across the floor with a clanky sound, accompanied by a sharp howl from Murphy who now held his bleeding wrist, shaking and cursing in curses better left unsaid. His lanky friend analyzed the situation, then cursed at George and Murphy alike before turning on his heel, running away to be swallowed by the darkness. Murphy cleared his throat and spat a slimy liquid on the floor in the absolute most disgusting way George had ever witnessed. Then he fled, too.

"Lovely." George turned his head away, repulsed by Murphy, while the boy shivered in clear disgust.

George put his gun away, turning toward the boy with an impression of admiration.

"Thank you for your help." George locked his gaze on the boy. "You were extremely brave here tonight; I am truly impressed," he complimented him.

"I-it was nothing," the boy mumbled with a shy stare as he looked away. George couldn't help but smile in response to such modesty. He stepped closer and stretched his hand out.

"George Astley," he introduced himself with a nod. It took the boy a moment to realize that George had just introduced himself.

"Oh, yes, of course. Egan," he finally said in his soft voice, and shook his hand.

George took a step back to analyze him for the second time tonight. Odd. Egan was rather pretty for a boy. His brown eyes were big like those of a deer and his smile was warm and honest. George's eyes wandered to the boy's full, rosy lips. They were beautiful. No doubt, those lips were made to ki—George violently shook his head to tear himself out of his thoughts. What the hell was he doing?! When had he ever paid so much attention to a man's looks and even worse, lips! He forced a cough to pull his mind away.

"What could Murphy possibly have been referring to when he addressed some sort of treasure in Chama?" the boy carefully inquired in perfect high-society English. George curled his lips and raised a brow. Egan was extremely well-spoken for a street kid. Egan seemed to be reading George's mind.

"I used to work for fancy folks," he explained, looking inward while blinking rapidly. George analyzed him for a moment longer. That explanation was obviously nonsense, but why would he care about the real reasons a street kid was able to form grammatically correct sentences? He was *ankle deep in horseshit*, as the Americans used to say, and had unsolvable problems ahead of him.

"Utter nonsense," George said crossing his arms. Egan swallowed loudly, opening his mouth as if he wanted to explain his suspicious language skills further when George relieved him of this worry. "The treasure map," he clarified. Egan let out a huge sigh.

George started walking, Egan following closely on his heels.

"So, there is no treasure in Chama?" he asked innocently.

"No, not like that." George shook his head. "I have a gold mine near Chama that seems to be more of a headache than all the gold in the world would be worth."

Egan froze to the spot, hypnotized by those very words that had just been spoken.

George peeked over his shoulder but kept walking. Why was this boy so interested in his affairs? A few moments later, he heard Egan's footsteps echo on the pavement to catch up with him.

"So, are you going to Chama then?" he heard Egan's voice from behind, out of breath from chasing him.

"I'm afraid so."

Egan skipped past George and jumped in front of him, blocking his path with arms wide open.

"Well, you got yourself a guide then."

The boy's enormous smile exposed his immaculate teeth. George laughed out loud and simply walked around him. A guide would have been an absolute necessity thirty years ago when people had to travel on wagons or in stagecoaches. But these were the days of industrialization, and America was the frontrunner of trains.

"I think you've already guided enough coin out of my pocket." George picked up speed again to signal that this conversation was over, but Egan was not so easily deterred.

"The Wild West is a dangerous place." Egan kept at it.

"That's why I won't drag a skinny young lad like you along with me. Besides, the comforts of a train will drop me off right at Chama."

George threw a farewell wink at Egan before making his way around the corner, when he heard Egan burst out into loud laughter. George couldn't help but stop and turn around.

"Drop you off right at Chama?" Egan slapped his leg.

"This ain't the Pacific line from New York to San Fran. You don't just hop on for eighty bucks first class and wake up in Chama eighty-four hours later." Egan kept laughing at him, holding his belly as if this was the funniest remark of the month.

George narrowed his eyes, carefully absorbing Egan's words. That was exactly what George had planned. Hop on the Pacific Railroad from New York to Chama.

"And why is that?"

Egan took a quick break from the good laugh George had given him and curled his lips.

"The Pacific will get you as far as Denver. That's it. From there, your ride will be hell."

George crossed his arms. "Keep going."

Egan stepped closer.

"Your enjoyment of the scenic American countryside will be over from there. The ride from Denver to Antonito is a big headache. Trains are often failing this time of year due to heavy snowfall."

George stayed silent. He had no idea that there was heavy snowfall this time of the year in that area. "Oh, but that's just a headache. The real fun begins from Antonito, on the Denver and Rio Grande Railroad," Egan said, all-knowing. He truly seemed to enjoy rubbing this into George's face.

"I'm assuming you have more to say?" George drew his brows together as an addition to his already narrowed eyes.

"I do." Egan smirked again. "The train line there is brand new, connecting nothing more than small mining towns full of gold and silver." Egan said this as if this very statement answered everything once and for all. But George had no clue why that would be an issue.

"So why is that a problem?" Geroge pressed but couldn't help the feeling that he wouldn't like the answer to this question.

"This is the age of Billy the Kid. Every hick with a gun now thinks he is an outlawed cowboy. All this silver and gold being transported on a train in the middle of nowhere with little to no protection…Those damn tracks get blown up like once a month now. But I'm sure you've thought of all of this, so good luck to you." Egan turned around and started walking. "You'll be just fine. I'm sure there will be plenty of trustworthy locals on the train that won't try to take advantage of the foreign nobleman with pockets full of gold in a land of no laws," he sassed over his shoulder, disappearing around the corner.

George stood there rooted to the ground, his mouth wide open, not a word coming out of it. This cunning boy had just managed to do something nobody had ever accomplished in George's entire life. Never. Not once. He had managed to make him speechless. Unsure if he was to laugh about the boy's bold yet sharp aim, swoon over his cunning wits, or about to cry over the newly obtained information of the treacherous trip ahead of him, he did the only logical thing. He run after him to hire him as a guide.

Esther slowed down her footsteps, carefully listening to hear whether George was following her. The moment she'd heard about George heading out to Chama, she knew she had to tag along, no matter the cost. Things were not going well for her and the children. This was the most brutal winter in the history of this nation, and it had depleted her pockets of every penny she'd once owned. At this rate, she would be starved before turning twenty-one to be free to marry whoever crossed her path to save her fortune — which in itself was a whole separate issue. Then there were the kids and Helga.

For weeks she had been giving them her rations, but for how much longer would that last? She was already behind on Helga's wage and Beth's rent and all it took was one more sick kid and a visit to the doctor and they were done. Over with. Back to living above a vent. Besides, Morris was getting closer in his efforts to finding her. The other day she saw a man handing out her picture at Murphy's. Her heart stopped when Murphy had grabbed her by her arm, but then asked her if she had seen or heard of this Esther Silverton lady, which of course she denied.

This couldn't just be a coincidence that she'd run into a man who out of all the places in the country was heading to the same no-name town where Jones had disappeared months ago. He was the only chance to get her fortune back before she and the kids became another victim to this heartless winter that had already claimed so many lives. She had to find Jones or die trying.

There was still no sign of George. Esther felt a painful heaviness around her heart. This was her last chance. She tilted her head back, gazing up to the sky. Dark-blue clouds were forming, and it looked like it was about to snow heavily again.

"Please…" she begged the stars above her and closing her eyes. "You are so many, please let just one shine down on me and the kids…"

"So how do you know all of this?" She heard his curious voice wonder from behind her.

Her heart skipped a few beats, cheerfully dancing in her chest. She slowly turned around, trying hard to put her poker face back on.

"Born and raised in the West," she proudly announced with a Texan accent. It almost felt like she was herself again.

George nodded his head.

"How much?" he asked.

Esther could have jumped up as high as the sky but of course didn't.

"Two-fifty now, two-fifty after you've arrived safe and sound in Chama."

George threw his head back in laughter.

"For that money, I could hire a cavalry."

"Good luck finding one in New York City," Esther grinned and started walking again, hoping to play with lady luck, and for once, win.

"Three hundred," George shouted after her. Esther turned around.

"Four-fifty, and that includes saving you from robbers twice today," she countered in a firm voice, crossing her arms.

"One of them was your brother." George crossed his arms as well.

"Saved nonetheless." Esther stood her ground.

"Three-fifty and that includes not sending your brother to jail… as well as my earlier donation to his pocket." George offered his hand and grinned at her with absolutely the most incredible smile she had ever seen.

Her cheeks flushed in heat, hidden away by the frosty weather and the dark night sky.

"Three-fifty it is," she said, shaking his hand as firmly as she could. George held her gaze for a moment longer as if it were their eyes and not their hands that had sealed the deal.

"Splendid. We leave tomorrow," he said, handing her a card.

"So soon?" Esther panicked. That was too short notice. With that kind of payment, she would be able to relocate the kids and Helga to the better parts of town and even let them go to a real school, not some improvised lessons that Helga, God bless her heart, scrambled together every day. But she needed more time.

"There is no time to lose. Is that a problem?" He raised a brow.

She couldn't risk this opportunity, had no choice but to make it happen.

"Not at all," she said looking at the card in her hand.

"That's the hotel I am staying at. I expect you around noon. The train leaves at two o'clock."

Esther nodded, still going over all the things she would have to do in between now and then. George scanned her once more, and this time he surveyed her head to toe. Was he measuring her perhaps? Though it made sense if he did, you can never be too careful in this part of town. Then he jerked his head away as if tearing himself out of silly thoughts.

"I shall see you tomorrow," was all he said before finally walking away.

Esther's eyes followed him until he was out of sight, fascinated by this compelling Englishman who was as handsome as he was brave. When Murphy had pulled that gun, Esther could feel her arms and legs shake uncontrollably. Though she had practiced shooting over and over at her father's behest from a young age and had rigidly resumed this activity ever since her little run-in with that despicable Luigi, pointing a gun at another person with the intent to kill was one of the most testing moments of her life. She had barely managed to keep herself from throwing up. George on the other hand was as calm as a sunny, cloudless sky. And there was the moment when he grabbed Eric's wrist to protect Milton as if it were the most normal thing in the world for him. Who was this man, she wondered? The thought of him lingered longer than it should, which was odd considering all the troubles that awaited her.

Esther looked up to the sky, something she did quite often lately, wondering if her parents were up there watching her. She slowly released her breath, sending a cloud fog into the cold heavens.

"Now all I have to do is relocate the kids, survive a train ride through the San Juan mountains, and solve the mystery regarding Jones's disappearance," she said up into the sky to her parents. "Oh, and all of that as a man." she mumbled with a sarcastic smile.

Esther thought back to the time her father had taken on the Denver and Rio Grande Railroad line as an investment. Nothing did he ever regret more. It was a non-stop headache. Not a month went by when that darn train wasn't robbed, or broken down in icy weather, leaving the train engineers stranded for days. Esther had always tried to stay positive for her father, telling him something good would come from building the very tracks he came to hate so much, and would now take her to find Jones.

"We'll find out soon enough if I was right, Papa," she mumbled into her wool coat which she pulled over her face to shield it from the icy winds.

"Very, very soon…"

Morris was standing in the family room of the Silverton mansion, holding a glass of whiskey in one hand, while taking another puff from his cigar with the other, filling the room with thick dark clouds. He was staring at the painting above the crackling granite fireplace. It was a family portrait of his old friend who was standing next to his beautiful Cherokee wife. He was holding baby Esther, smiling with that sparkle of happiness only a proud father and husband would possess.

"Are you certain, Mr. Morris?" asked one of the two servants who was standing next to the painting.

"If you ever answer a demand with a question again, you can look for work elsewhere," Morris threatened in his usual, arrogant voice. The two servants exchanged flustered looks.

"Y-yes sir," one of them ultimately said, grabbing the painting on one side while waiting for his colleague to grab it from the other side. Without any more disturbances, the painting was removed and carried out of the room, leaving a discolored rectangle on the wall at the very spot it had been hanging for years.

"Nothing?" Morris turned to Mr. Gorsh who was sitting on the couch.

"I'm afraid not." He twisted his lips into a frown. "She was last seen with five children on the outskirts of New York. Since then we have turned every damnable rock in this town." Mr. Gorsh held up his whiskey as if he was saluting the impossible. "It's like she just vanished into thin air!" he concluded with a dramatic flair.

Morris stared into the dancing flames, looking for a sign, a message, some sort of prophecy as he leaned one hand against the mantel of the fireplace, listening to the crackle of shrieking wood turn into coal. "And the funds, are they still frozen?"

Mr. Gorsh nodded. "Until she is found we won't see a dime of the Silverton fortune."

A pressing stillness crawled into the room, growing louder into deafening silence.

"God damn that bitch!" Morris raged, smashing his glass of whiskey into the fireplace. Glass shattered into tiny flickering pieces, flames scorched high into the chimney, fueled by his hatred. "What about the government, and the police? Aren't they looking for her?" He jerked around, his face turning into that of a dark demon.

"They are. But I doubt they are putting much effort into it. If she is never to be found, they will declare the will intestate and simply keep the funds," Mr. Gorsh elaborated in his usual monotone lawyer voice.

Morris walked down from the hearth of the fireplace. "Well, there must be something we can do!" he shouted, flailing his hands like he was asking for another glass to throw. "I am not paying you a fortune for sitting on my couch and drinking my fine whiskey!"

He jabbed a finger into Mr. Gorsh's face who kept his cool as if he did not possess a single emotion in his boring soul.

"There most certainly are things we could do, but that all depends on how willing you are to use more controversial methods." Gorsh took a sip of the whiskey in his hand. "If you know what I mean."

Morris paced around the room, searching into the depths of his ever-so-desperately darkening mind, only to stop and face Mr. Gorsh again.

"I am a very, very flexible man," Morris pressed with his shadowy eyes wide and glowing.

"That's what I thought."

Mr. Gorsh pulled out a piece of paper and handed it to Morris, who held it close to his face to analyze it in every detail.

"A wanted poster?" he sneered, followed by a bark of laughter. "I have to say, Mr. Gorsh, this is quite impressive. Nationwide, I suppose?"

Mr. Gorsh smelled his whiskey before taking another sip. "Of course."

Clearly in a better mood, Morris handed the poster back to him.

"Double the reward and add a picture of her," he said, walking over to the coffee table to ring the servant bell.

"Double the reward?" Mr. Gorsh jerked forward, almost spilling his whiskey. "But that would make it $10,000! Even Jesse James was worth only $5,000." Mr. Gorsh shook his head. "And that was alive or dead."

Morris's eyes widened as his face turned into a sinister version of joyful.

"You are a genius, Mr. Gorsh!" He beamed. "We only need to find her, no matter the state she is in, is that correct?"

Mr. Gorsh's mouth twisted. "Yes, but—"

"Splendid. Then add dead as an option to the poster," Morris ordered walking over to the family room door to open it wide, startling Ginny who was just about to open it from the other side.

"Ginny, Mr. Gorsh was about to leave."

Mr. Gorsh on the other hand was frozen in his seat, his gaze fixated on the floor.

"Mr. Gorsh!" Morris shouted to pull him out from wherever his thoughts had taken him for a walk. But Gorsh remained rooted to his seat, his gaze still lost in his mind. Ginny exchanged rapid looks between Morris and Mr. Gorsh.

"S-sir?" she whispered more as an apology than a question.

Morris rolled his eyes.

"MR. GORSH!" he shouted, causing the lawyer's head to jerk toward him. "Is there a problem?" Morris asked narrowing his eyes, fixating them on Gorsh like a gun pointing at its victim.

"N-no," Mr. Gorsh apologized, his lips pressed together tightly into a painful grimace. "N-no problem."

Morris turned all smiles again.

"I'm pleased to hear that. Ginny will walk you out now. I expect the poster up tomorrow."

Like a beaten dog, Mr. Gorsh slowly rose from his seat, putting the poster back into his leather bag before joining Ginny and Morris at the door.

"Yes, Mr. Morris, sir," he mumbled before following Ginny into the entrance hall, his every step resembling that of a man who knew he had just crossed a line he could never uncross again — not in this life nor the next.

CHAPTER 6

The train platform was packed. Newspaper boys and other merchants were pitching their goods to get their share of the travelers' coins. People were pushing each other out of the way to get on and off the countless trains. A steam train pulled into its platform, blowing smoke onto the waiting passengers as if it were eating them.

Esther held little Cliff with tears in her eyes. On Cliff's first birthday, the kids had named the baby after her father as a surprise for Esther who had seldom been more touched than by this loving gesture. Miki, Jeff, and Tom launched themselves onto Esther for one last time, all crying like the little children they were. Helga now grabbed Cliff out of Esther's arms and rubbed her fingers through Miki's hair.

"Come on now. She will be back soon," Helga promised in a reassuring voice targeting their little, sad hearts. Milton on the other hand was standing next to Helga with a big frown, his arms crossed, standoffish.

"I should go with you; this ain't safe," he declared for the hundredth time. Esther and Milton had been fighting all night about this.

"*Isn't* safe. Not *ain't*," Helga corrected him with a warm smile, making him roll his eyes. The kids now giggled. Esther grabbed Milton by his arm and dragged him aside a few steps.

"I need you here, to watch over the children." Esther tried to make him feel important. But he was twelve, not five.

"Oh please," Milton brushed her off, "they now live with Helga right next to the University. That's where the fancy folks live." What Milton was saying in between the lines was that unlike the poor Irish and Italian quarters, the middle-and-upper-class districts were patrolled by police and extremely safe.

With George's down-payment, Esther was able to move everybody out of Beth's and into a respectable boarding home the morning after she was hired. Helga was given the task to enroll them all in a respectable school, starting tomorrow. Her money was enough to provide for a middle-class lifestyle and good education for several months, but then they would all be back on the streets.

"I still need you to watch over them. You know how easy it is for the kids to trick poor, old Helga."

Milton seemed to let that run through his head for a moment. It was the truth. Helga was a Godsend, although it was Esther who'd pulled her out of the gutter and gave her not only employment, but a family. Having lost all of her own children to hunger and disease, the woman was starved more to give her love than she was from an empty stomach. Her loving and calm ways instantly made it into the children's hearts. Another tragic life saved from the harsh, unforgiving streets. However, Helga seemed more innocent than the street-smart kids at times, making her as easy to play as a flute.

A train's shrill whistle loudly hollered over the platform they were standing on, warning people to get on before it would leave without them.

"We have to go." Esther heard George from behind her. Had he been standing there the entire time, watching the drama of saying good-bye? Esther had thought he was already on the train waiting for her in the comforts of his first-class train car. But instead he was standing on the train platform carrying his own bag like some third-class passenger, so unlike a duke with hundreds of years of nobility in his blood.

Esther squeezed Milton, something he let happen but did not enthusiastically embrace, his lifeless arms flopping to his sides. He was obviously still mad, but under no circumstances would Esther even consider taking him with her on this mission. He certainly was no ordinary child. In fact, he was more knowledgeable about crooks and the tricks of outlaws than she would ever be, but this trip was dangerous. Extremely dangerous. After Denver they would have to worry about every little breeze blowing their way. She could never forgive herself should something happen to him. She loved him with all her heart — more than her own life.

"I will telegraph you as soon as I can," Esther said with a heavy heart before releasing Milton and signaling George with a nod that she was ready. They didn't have to walk far as the first-class cars were at the end of the train to avoid the smoke from the steam engine.

George led Esther into their private Pullman car. Despite Esther traveling on nothing else in her life than these famous luxury wagons, her months on the streets had reset her memory of what it was like to travel in one of these. Beautiful, red silk drapes covered golden windows, and chandeliers hung from the ceiling that was painted with elaborate designs. The walls were covered in the finest dark walnut, topped off with brass fixtures that sparkled like little stars. Even George seemed impressed.

"This is incredible. As if we were in an estate drawing room," he marveled, putting his bag down next to a queen-sized bed heavily loaded with red satin pillows and blankets.

"The dining car should be down this way." Esther walked past a wooden dresser and desk and held the door to the train vestibule open for him. George walked by her and straight into the parlor car which also served breakfast, lunch, dinner, and drinks.

"Well, if that isn't the sought-after Duke of Aberdeen," a female voice echoed the moment he had stepped into the dining car. It was one of those naturally seductive voices that usually belonged to incredibly beautiful women, and what Esther found when she followed him into the dining car did absolutely not disappoint. The woman this voice belonged to was sitting at one of the two-person tables bolted to the walls, with a smile on her lips that could melt steel. She must have been in her twenties, dressed in a khaki split riding skirt, white blouse, and black silken canvas vest. Her long, blond hair put together into a loose braid shimmered like gold. But nothing was more stunning than her arctic, blue eyes. Esther wasn't sure if she was wearing lipstick or if her lips were naturally red, but her face was by far one of the most elegant beauties she had ever come across. Then there was her whole ranch outfit, one Esther used to grow up in. It gave her an exotic touch in the middle of the most exquisite Rococo furniture while blending in perfectly into the world of elegance with the few other first-class passengers, who seated themselves at the tables. No doubt this was the type of woman men from poor to rich would drool over. A burning feeling made its way into Esther's stomach as she shifted her gaze to George.

Did he find her attractive? *Of course, he did*, Esther scolded herself. He had perfectly working eyes, so why wouldn't he?

"Ah, Miss Wayne." George walked over to her table with a smile on his face.

"Emily, remember?" She grinned back at him and stood up to shake his hand.

"Yes, of course," he apologized. Esther was looking at the two of them standing next to each other. If two Greek Gods would ever come together to make a perfect match, this would be it. Both of them looked like they'd just stepped down from a cloud, gracing the mortals with their presence. Dirty, skinny, poor mortals like Esther, she angrily thought, wiping her face in frustration to make sure she did not have any coal on it from tending the fire this morning to keep the room warm for the children and Helga.

"I see you made it out of last night's gathering alive?" she joked in that pretty voice of hers. Esther knew exactly what she was referring to. By now she had come to know that George was not only a handsome English nobleman, but a Duke, which in Esther's previous circles was close to the Lord himself. When Esther had met with him in the hotel lobby this morning, what could have been a quick walk in and out had turned into thirty minutes of desperate attempts to escape. This man could not walk one step without another eligible-looking woman clawing into him, practically begging him for a stroll in the park or cake and tea in the afternoon. One older lady had come running after him like a cheetah, grabbing him by the coat to introduce him to her daughter, a cotton factory heiress. Coming from a ranch, Esther couldn't help but feel she was at a cattle auction, everybody trying to get rid of their cows.

"I am indeed looking forward to a change in scenery." George tried to be polite when in reality he must be thanking God for escaping New York unmarried.

The train started moving, shaking wildly for a moment. Emily let out a sigh, falling toward George who caught her by her arms to avoid her landing right on his muscular chest, in between his legs. Esther held on to a table next to her, adopting a sullen look. Emily had clearly just thrown herself into his arms on purpose. The train was shaking a bit, not derailing. George helped her back on her feet.

"Thank you," she whispered, her cheeks glowing like little red flames.

"Of course." George sounded polite and emotionless.

Emily now looked Esther's way, her icy blue eyes scanning her from head to toe, not leaving out one inch. "And who are those two servant boys?" Emily nodded her way with a curious grin.

"Two what?" George jerked around toward Esther, his eyes and mouth shooting wide open at whatever was right behind her, causing her to flip around herself.

"MILTON!" she yelled in utter shock. "What are you doing here?!" Esther wanted to grab him by the arm to pull him aside, but the train steward was now right behind him, getting a hold of him before Esther could. People were now looking at this embarrassing scene.

"You! I told you to get off the train!" he barked at Milton, his red uniform with golden buttons blending in with the red satin upholstery theme of the train in such harmony, it almost made him disappear.

"And I told you I'm with the English man!" Milton bickered back at him in a pouting voice.

Esther threw her head back in a mixture of despair and annoyance. What was she supposed to do now? Would George kick them both off the train at the next stop? She peeked over to him to get a feeling of how he was taking this all in. But much to her surprise, instead of rightful anger, George was tapping his lip with his finger, a light smirk on his face.

"How come whenever we have the pleasure you have someone attached to your neck?" he asked sarcastically.

Milton swung his arm in a forceful circle, freeing himself from the steward who now exchanged confused looks with Emily.

"And how come every time we meet, you get robbed?" Milton countered, pulling out an envelope from under his incredibly dirty looking shirt.

Esther couldn't help but roll her eyes at that too. This was a brand-new shirt, how the hell had he got it so dirty so quickly, making her look like she neglected him, which she didn't!

George walked up to Milton with long, determined steps, grabbing the envelope from out of his little hands. It seemed to be the same envelope he'd received last night at the standoff with Murphy.

"How did you get this?" George glanced inside it to make sure everything was still in there.

"Well…" Milton crossed his arms. "While ya'll were so busy with that mushy good-bye at the station, some guy pulled that out of your bag. I followed him and stole it back for you."

Milton proudly lifted his chin. For a moment it was totally silent, everybody staring at the scene in front of them. Suddenly George broke the silence with a loud laugh and turned toward Emily.

"To get back to your question, those two are my guides," he said in a confident, smiling voice. Was there nothing that could break through the impenetrable wall of this man's composure?

Milton happily did a little bow in front of Emily to second his introduction.

"At your service, milady," he grinned at her. This was enough.

"Will you excuse us?" Esther grabbed him by the arm and dragged him out of the dining car back into their private quarters. "Have you lost your marbles? You can't come with us." She shut the door behind her, trying her utmost not to slam it.

"I already am," Milton said unfazed, knowing darn well that Esther would never lose her temper with him. Esther now rubbed her temples in desperation as if she were trying to massage this stubborn kid back to New York.

"It's dangerous, Milton."

"And that's why you shouldn't go alone. I will protect you."

Esther looked at him. He seemed dead serious. This boy would follow her to the end of the world. For a brief second, she felt a warm, fuzzy feeling in her heart. She loved this boy so dearly, it scared her sometimes. But that was also the reason why he couldn't come with her. At least not past Denver. Wait a minute… Denver… An idea crept its way into her mind, lifting some of the headache Milton had just caused her. She would let him roll along until Denver and then put him back on a train to New York. Maybe by then he would have had enough of an adventure and would agree to return? That would also buy her time to give him a feeling of accomplishment, telling him what a marvelous job he had done protecting her all the way to Colorado. Denver was more than fair enough for both of them to convince him that he had done his duty as her knight.

Milton was analyzing her face.

"You're biting your lip," he said, pointing at her.

Esther instantly stopped. "No, I'm not."

"Yes, you are. What are you planning?" he asked with an eyebrow raised. Milton just knew her too well.

"Nothing!" She tried to throw him off her trail. But Esther did indeed bite her lip whenever she was coming up with a plan, a habit she could not break even if her life depended on it.

"Good to know." She heard George enter. "So, when you bite your lip, you are up to something?" He smiled at Esther with that devilish handsomeness, instantly causing her to blush and look the other way.

"Yes, and he always speaks the truth when you ask him something in his sleep," Milton elaborated further.

"Milton!" Esther chided.

George laughed.

"You are already invaluable to this mission, Milton," he said taking his coat off and starting to unbutton his shirt, revealing a muscular chest. Esther instantly jerked around, almost hitting her head on one of the brass lights. She was facing the walnut wall, her nose leaving marks on it from her warm breath.

"A-are we seated in the third c-class, Sir?" she stuttered nervously.

George took his shirt off and opened his suitcase to grab a more comfortable, casual outfit. Esther looked over her shoulder, only to jerk her head around again. Gosh, his upper body was pure, lean muscle. A tingling rushed through her body, making her lightheaded.

"Why would you prefer to be in the third class cramped on top of each other if you can use the beds over there?" He nodded to the wall behind the dark mahogany desk. Esther knew that there would be foldable beds in there. As she had accompanied her father wherever he went, she herself had placed Ginny or other travel companions in those extra beds. But that was different. George was a man. An incredibly attractive one too. And she was a woman who, besides her father's, had never even held a man's hand before. To go from that to sleeping within only a few feet of one, watching him dress and undress himself, that was more than she could bear. The thought of George's naked body brought tiny pearls of sweat onto her face.

She tilted her head to find Milton who was signaling with waving hands and wide-open eyes to get it together. Milton was right. She was acting extremely strangely. As a man, seeing George naked waist up, or even down, should be nothing unusual. She took in a deep breath and turned around again to face the music, or in this case, blazing orchestra.

George was still naked waist up. He was scanning her, clearly noticing her anxiety. *Esther, you fool.*

"That, that is in-incredibly kind. Thank you." She cleared her throat.

"Before I forget," Milton interrupted the whole scene.

Esther let out a sigh of relief, he was coming to her rescue.

But then he suddenly pulled out a brown, leather cowboy hat from behind his back. "Mary wanted you to have this," he said walking over to Esther. He put it on her head and nodded in approval.

"Mary?" she wondered; eyebrows high. Why the hell would she would gift her a hat? Milton totally misunderstood her confusion and tried to clarify.

"Yes, Mary. From the brothel, remember? The one that fell for you." Milton thought he was helping, but Esther froze to the shaking train floor, pulling at her collar for air. Could this get any worse? Apparently, it could:

"Said she was riding all night to get it for you," Milton explained innocently, not knowing what Mary had meant by that. George, who watched the two of them extremely entertained, now burst out into loud laughter.

"That was very kind of Mary, wasn't it, Egan?" He teased Esther, who was now throwing Milton a look that was shooting knives at him. Milton shouted a silent *What did I do?* back at her, shrugging his shoulders. A knock at the door saved Milton before Esther could do God-knows-what to him.

"Sir, your lunch," a voice announced from outside.

George finished buttoning up his shirt.

"Yes, come in."

A man dressed in the train's personnel red uniform stepped in.

"You can put it over there on the table." George nodded toward the two-person table across from the desk.

"This is for you in case you are hungry."

Milton stormed to the table and grabbed a sandwich, biting a chunk off so big, he couldn't close his mouth all the way to chew it. Esther took in a deep breath, while George smiled at him.

"Will you not join us?" she asked.

"I would love to, but unfortunately I have agreed to dine with Emily Wayne."

Esther felt that annoying burning sensation in her stomach again. This Miss Wayne was certainly throwing her bait in the waters for George to swallow it. Did he not see that?

"Believe me, I would much rather dine with you. I can't remember when I have laughed this much," he said, tilting his head in thought. "I actually can't remember laughing this much— ever." He smiled.

"Go ahead. We don't mind," Milton said with a full mouth. "Right, Egan?" He waved her to sit down next to him at the table.

Esther shook her head. "Of course not."

Her words said one thing but her face clearly another. George now smiled at her as if he wanted to smoothen things.

"Thank you. We shall dine together tomorrow, I promise." Those were his last words before he closed the door behind himself, off to join his Greek goddess.

"She's probably changed into some fancy, pretty dress," Esther said out loud to herself in a condescending tone, under the watchful gaze of Milton who was staring at her with a wrinkled forehead.

"What!" Esther told him off, grabbing a sandwich and taking an elegant bite from it.

"Nothing..." he mumbled innocently, still staring at her. "Nothing..."

Esther didn't sleep well at all that night, which was surprising considering she had not slept on a real mattress in months. The kids always came first, so she slept on some blankets, hay or whatever else could be used as a barrier from the cold, hard floor.

The first few hours that she tossed around in her bed were dedicated to why George was still not back from his late lunch. Not that it was unusual to mingle with other first-class guests after dining for a drink and cigar in the parlor car. But for some reason Esther couldn't get the image out of her head of how Emily and George would walk hand in hand, laughing and giggling at each other's jokes, while being admired by others for their endless good looks and charms.

When George finally did come back at nine o'clock, actually quite an early time for first-class social engagements, Esther couldn't help but listen to his every move as he stumbled around in the dark, most likely because he wanted to be considerate and not wake them by turning on a light. The moment he started undressing for bed, her heart almost exploded. Just thinking of him lying in his bed almost naked, just a few feet away, sent heat flashes up her spine and into her cheeks. And so she tossed and turned, even the slightest noise making her jump up in bed.

So it was not surprising that she was already up the next morning when George and Milton slowly opened their eyes to greet the day. Milton, who was willing to take the bed above Esther's, let his bare feet hang from the edge of his mattress.

"Why are you already up?" He rubbed his eyes.

Esther was washing her face in the small sink next to the small bathroom.

"I always get up early," she replied loud enough for George to hear, drying her face.

"No, you don't," Milton disagreed. "It takes forever to get you out of bed."

George let out a little chuckle. Esther bit her lip. *Gosh darn it, Milton.*

George was now out of bed as well. Much to Esther's relief, or disappointment, he was wearing underpants in bed and did not come out from under the blankets completely naked. She let out a sigh of relief to give her constantly heated cheeks a break.

"I hope I didn't wake you last night?" George asked, putting on a white shirt and comfortable but still elegant black pants.

"No, no. No, not at all." Esther made room for George to use the wash basin.

"Well, why don't we get ready and eat breakfast together?"

Milton jumped down from his bed. Like Esther, he had slept in his clothes, but that was due to him not having anything packed for the trip he hadn't been invited on, not because he was worried about being discovered as a woman.

"I'm starving!" He stretched himself.

George opened the upper drawer to the desk and pulled out the envelope that Milton had stolen back for him yesterday.

"I should like to go over these with the two of you after breakfast, if you wouldn't mind?"

"Not at all." Esther shook her head.

"I appreciate it," he said, walking to the door and opening it. "I shall make reservations for a table for three," he said, leaving Milton and Esther behind to give them some privacy to refresh themselves.

Esther looked after him, wondering how such an incredibly kind, brave, handsome, and respectful man was still a bachelor. Esther had never come across a more charismatic man—no, human being—before. His smile genuinely caused women to melt and men to want to be his friend. So why was he still eligible? Was there something he was hiding? Was he one of these secret womanizers, never ready to settle? A feeling of disappointment formed in her heart over the sheer thought of that. Out of nowhere she got the feeling that somebody was watching her. And somebody was, in the form of Milton's eagle eyes. He was standing at the wash basin, his hands filled with water, frozen in the movement of washing his face, staring at her mercilessly.

"What?" Esther tried to sound carefree.

"Nothing…" Milton squinted his eyes and let out a long, deep, audible breath. "Nothing…"

CHAPTER 7

George made his way into the dining wagon that had now been transformed into a breakfast car with a buffet on a long table pushed against the wall. He was scanning the room for the table with his name on it, when he saw Emily waving at him enthusiastically with dancing eyes. For some reason, the idea that he might now be forced to have breakfast with her bothered him. Why, he didn't quite understand himself. He put on a fake smile and walked over to her. She was wearing khaki riding pants and a white shirt, a bold choice for a lady of her standing. As he had come to know from her yesterday, Emily Wayne was the heiress to one of the biggest silver mines in the nation. She was on her way to Denver to visit her father who managed his mining empire from there, as apparently the vast majority of his silver mines were located in Colorado. Her knowledge about mines was probably one of the only things that made spending time with her for several hours bearable. Not that she was not a delight to

169

look at, and she was one of the most cunning ladies he had ever come across, no doubt, but he was not here for romance, which couldn't be said about Emily Wayne.

"Did you get a good night's rest?" She sparkled, her beautiful white teeth exposed by her charming smile.

"Yes, thank you. I apologize for retiring so early last night, but it has been a rather eventful week."

"As long as you don't make a habit of it." She grinned. "But you can make up for it now. Come have breakfast with me."

George looked at the table which was only a table for two.

"I would be delighted, but I am afraid I have to go over some business with my assistants." He tried to sound as friendly as possible, feeling a little bad for brushing her off again.

"I don't mind." She got up, waving the waiter over. George opened his mouth, but Emily was faster. "We need a table for four," she ordered the waiter, "and pick that up," she demanded, pointing at a napkin she had dropped earlier. The waiter did a courtesy bow and instantly rushed off to set up one of the larger tables, her napkin from the floor in his hand. "You two don't mind, do you?" she said, looking over George's shoulder who turned around to find Egan and Milton standing right behind him. Milton shook his head, but Egan seemed to look at Emily for a moment as if he were seriously thinking about how to answer her rhetorical question.

"Wonderful," Emily blurted and took a seat at the new table. Milton followed her, a plate in his hand that was piled up with ham and eggs. When the hell had he got that? He was just standing behind him, George wondered, smiling to himself.

At first, he was concerned that his newly hired guides might become tiresome to be around all the time, but it turned out to be quite the opposite. They were the most entertaining sort of fellows he had ever come across. He was constantly smiling, laughing, or grinning at one of them.

Growing up in a house with a mother who must have been brought into this world by a creature of the underworld, laughter or smiles were scarce during his childhood, considered inappropriate for a future duke. Having those two around was an absolute delight. Especially the older of the two, Egan. There was something about this boy that drew George in like a fly to a flame. He had barely known him longer than a few days, but it felt like he'd already got to know Egan better than ninety-nine percent of the people he had spent years of his life with. He couldn't believe his eyes when he'd seen him step out of the dark, a pistol in his hand, to save him. Selfless and brave, he'd stood by George's side without even knowing him. And to learn that Egan was using all his money for a troop of street children he cared for as if they were his own, that literally sucked George's breath right out of his lungs, leaving him speechless. But meeting Egan had also stirred up sad emotions for a man like George, who had grown up without the tender touch of his mother or the loving hug of his father. Watching Egan hug each and every one of these children at the train station, he couldn't help but feel a strange loneliness and longing, as if he wanted to belong to someone like those children and Egan belonged to each other.

"George, you shall sit next to me," Emily blurted at him, waving him over. George took a deep breath and took his seat right next to her. Although she was one of the prettiest women he had ever laid eyes upon and most men would probably kill to be in his shoes right now, he couldn't shake off the feeling that Emily was luring him in for marriage—a daunting thought to be quite frank. Of course he had considered marrying an American heiress to save his poor sister from a marriage to the most despicable man in England; these loveless matches were made all the time, a title for a coin, but for now there was still a chance to mine his fortune back—at least according to the documents in his pocket. So why start another doomed, loveless marriage quite yet?

"So, what kind of business are you conducting here? Please tell me a-a-a-ll about it," Emily inquired, taking a sip from the cup of coffee the waiter had elegantly placed in front of her. She certainly was a straight shooter, something George could actually respect if it didn't seem like her end-goal from all of this was a ring on her finger.

Milton and Egan were both eating, one of them more like a wild animal. But oddly enough, the other was carefully using a knife and fork as if he were born and raised among the highest circles of society. George's brows slowly furrowed as he watched Egan take a careful bite of a tiny piece of egg on his fork. Milton seemed to have noticed too and let out a fake cough to get his attention. Egan now looked around, realizing that everybody was staring at him. All of a sudden, he shoved an enormous scoop of eggs on his fork, wolfing them down, barely able to close his mouth. Milton nodded, even smacking Egan on his back in approval. George, like so often when he was around them, had to bite his lip in an attempt not to laugh, but a little chuckle came out, nonetheless. He looked back up at Emily who was still waiting for an answer.

"Oh, yes, the business." George straightened his back to face her. "As I mentioned last night, I am on my way to an investment in a mine that unfortunately did not turn out to be as lucrative as I had initially anticipated." George poured milk in his coffee and stirred it.

"What's the issue with it, if you don't mind me asking?" Emily leaned over, her hair shimmering golden next to her beautiful blue eyes that were sparkling like icicles. The morning sunshine that made its way in from the window illuminated her like a holy altar at a church. She was a true beauty, he had to give her that. The money-hungry harpy he had to call mother would be more than pleased if he came home with a match such as this.

"Not at all." George shrugged his shoulders. "Apparently, the mine my friend and I had purchased is located on tribal land. So you can understand the sensitive and problematic nature of this matter."

Emily furrowed, then gently released her eyebrows in a widening curiosity. "I thought they had settled that with the Brunot Agreement a few years ago?" she asked in a casual tone.

"That was further north with the Ute tribe. This time the government encroached on Apache land." George flexed his finger repeatedly, a clear sign that the whole matter bothered him and concerned him deeply.

"What is a Brunot?" Milton asked with an empty plate in front of him that was shimmering so clean, if George had not seen him eat a few moments ago, one might think he had only just got the plate.

"A few years back," Emily started to explain to Milton's eager ears, "the Ute tribe was killing the poor miners in the San Juan mountains. It went on for years before Felix Brunot was finally able to talk sense into those worthless savages, finally removing them from the miner's lands."

Those words were like listening to nails scratching a chalkboard. George narrowed his eyes, carefully analyzing the beauty in front of him once more. He never expected her to be compassionate or selfless, but the way she had just spoken disturbed him deeply. Of the many versions he had heard about the Brunot Agreement, hers was by far the most ignorant his ears had ever had to endure. He was about to say something ungentlemanly, when Egan suddenly threw his head back in loud, disrespectful laughter. The whole train car was staring at him for a moment. Emily laughed a bit herself, most likely thinking Egan found it humorous how she was calling the natives savages. But if George knew this boy even half as well as he thought he did, this was certainly not the case, and Miss Emily Wayne was in for an unpleasant surprise.

"Absurd," Egan laughed wholeheartedly, slapping his leg before putting a hand on his chest to try to calm himself. "I apologize, but that was by far the most uneducated remark about the Brunot Agreement I have ever heard, and I live on the streets."

Emily's smile vanished in a fraction of a second, her blue eyes darkening with hatred. She wanted to say something, but Egan wouldn't let her.

"For years, white men have illegally mined on the reservation that they imprisoned the natives on. In 1873, Brunot pretty much forced the Ute tribes into signing their land away for an annual hand full of dirt in return, or they could insist on keeping their land and get removed by force by the military with no annual hand full of dirt. And that is the Brunot Agreement. Everybody who tells you otherwise has his..." Egan paused, turning toward Emily. "Or *her* hand full of dirt themselves."

Then there was dead silence. Milton exchanged looks with George who carefully peeked over to Emily. Her elegant, soft hands were clenched into tight fists, trembling as they squeezed the table's cloth, probably picturing it was Egan's head. He couldn't help but feel a sense of pride for Egan standing up for the truth like that. But before George could use his calming charms to agree with Egan as well as try to stop Emily from shooting him on the spot, Egan got up and adjusted his clothes.

"Now, if you'll excuse me, I think we are about to stop for a water-refill, and I would like to stretch my legs."

Egan rose and walked out the dining car, his pretty chin held up high.

"It's the train... It makes him edgy." Milton jumped up, apologizing nervously with a little courtesy bow to Emily before running after him.

The train stopped in a shaking motion, spilling some of George's coffee onto the glowing, white tablecloth. Leaving was the best thing Egan could have done, as Emily most likely would have escalated the argument to never before climbed heights—at least that is what her raging eyes and shaking fists suggested.

His eyes followed Egan through the window as he stepped onto the train platform.

"How did you meet those two again?" he heard Emily inquire in a cold, trembling voice.

"One of them tried to rob me," George responded with his usual calm, still watching Egan through the window. "The other one saved me from a robbery...twice."

Emily let out a high-pitched, ugly laugh, her eyes widening in disbelief. "Surely you cannot be serious?"

"I'm afraid I am. Now that I'm thinking about it, it would be more accurate to say they both saved me from robberies. If you count the envelope incident at the train station that is," he said in a serious tone, still glued to Egan's every move. Milton had joined him by now and although he couldn't hear what they were saying, it was obvious that they were arguing about something. George tilted his head, focusing in on Egan's face. How fine and clean his facial lines were. Women of high society would pay a pretty chunk of coin to have that boy's clear skin, thick eyelashes, and full, rosy lips. He was incredibly handsome for a boy. But that wasn't what naturally drew George to him. There was something else, something he just couldn't put a finger on quite yet. The way he stood up for the natives confirmed once more that this boy was pure and honest. A little prideful maybe, but fair.

Egan slowly shifted his gaze, looking his way as if he felt him staring at him. For a brief moment, George wanted to look away, like a schoolboy caught gazing at the pretty schoolteacher. What the bloody hell was going on? Maybe the train was making him 'edgy' too. George nodded over to Egan in a manly manner before pulling his eyeballs back toward Emily who just sat there, following George's gaze with her icy blue eyes like an eagle its prey. She was studying him, her brows tightly squeezed together, disapproving of whatever conclusion she must have come to.

"And you think you can trust them?" Emily mocked him, playing with one of the pretty strands that had fallen out of her braid.

The waiter came over and started clearing empty dishes off the table. George pulled out a coin and pushed it toward him.

"I do," he finally answered with a grin on his pretty face, composed and calm as always. "Now will you excuse me; I have to tend to some business."

Emily jerked up, her mouth wide open, as if she wanted to apologize to make him stay. But George was already halfway to the door.

As he closed the door to his private car behind himself, standing somewhere in the middle of Ohio, George couldn't help but feel discouraged and awful at the same time. He almost fell off his chair when he first read the documents Wilson had sold him at gunpoint in New York. Had he known that Billy was investing in a gold mine that was on native land, he would have never agreed to this. It was not even ten years ago when it made news all the way to England how the natives were cheated out of their land in Colorado. Of course, there were plenty of ignorant people, like Emily Wayne, who twisted and turned the truth to their own advantage. But George was no man of the old ways and therefore did not dare to call the Brunot Agreement anything less than theft.

And now here he was, years later, deeply entangled in another version of the same old story of white men taking what they wanted—no matter the cost. Was he a thief now too? Stealing land from people who had been deprived of everything they have ever held dear? And what about Billy... Did he know about any of this? Was the poor fellow even still alive?

In the midst of all of this, somehow George's mind was wandering off to Egan again. What would he think of him when he presented him with these documents: the entire truth. None of this was George's fault. He'd had no idea about any of this. To him, this gold mine sounded like a gift sent from the heavens to save him from ruin, but more importantly, his beloved sister from a marriage to some perverted old man. But would Egan see it this way?

George threw the envelope carelessly onto the desk, shaking his head in frustration. Why did he even care what Egan thought of him? He'd hired him as a guide—nothing more, nothing less. Yet for some reason, deep down inside, he feared that those beautiful brown eyes that were always so full of life and passion would judge him differently. The thought of it was like a whispering tune inside his head, growing louder and louder.

One way or the other, he couldn't conceal this information from him. Soon the train would start moving again, and George would have to face the beat of the pounding drums.

Esther took a deep breath, trying to shake off the frustration and hurt that had swallowed her heart again, just like it did every time someone indirectly called her mother, and half of herself, a savage. This Emily Wayne was nothing but a shiny apple that was all rotten on the inside, filled with worms. She had heard of the Wayne family before. Miners who had their greedy little fingers in every piece of land they could steal from whites and natives alike. That was one of the reasons why her father had never invested in mines. It was a dirty business—literally. Rarely had she come across more hard-working folks than miners, sailing here from as far as China, to risk their lives to be treated like dirt in return, earning no more than a few coins a week. That was probably why it felt so darn amazing putting Emily Wayne in her place.

"Are you out of your mind?" she heard Milton reprimand her from behind. She turned to face him.

"Why? Because I taught the beautiful Miss Wayne something about the real world?" Esther defended herself, crossing her arms. Milton's little eyes stared at her, almost as if he was looking deep into her soul—or heart.

"Is it about him? George?" He narrowed his eyes.

Esther's mouth fell open. She couldn't believe he'd just said something so absurd.

"Don't be ridiculous." She waved her hand in front of her as if she were swatting a fly.

Milton shook his head.

"I didn't live next to a brothel for months and not learn a thing or two about the bees and flowers," he insisted, "and you are a bee trying to land on a flower." He pointed his finger right at her. If this situation wasn't closer to the truth than she would like to admit, Esther would have laughed at his notion of love.

"First of all, we will have to have a talk about the bees and the flowers," she said, pushing his finger out of her face in annoyance. "And second, I do not want to land on his flower."

A woman walked by, stopping for a second with a confused gaze at Esther's words before moving along.

Milton wrinkled his forehead, nodding his head into the leaving woman's direction, as if her glance at Esther was proof that he was right. Esther rolled her eyes. Milton shifted sails, trying a softer approach.

"It's okay." He leaned closer to whisper, "Esther, I get it. If I was a girl, I would fall for George as well." He leaned back again. "I mean, he looks so handsome, and then his smile with that manly scar…he is also a duke, and, and kind-hearted. I get it, really. He is stunning!" Milton blurted and threw his arms up into the air.

A man passing by threw him a disturbing glance. This silly conversation had to stop. It was nothing short of ridiculous. Absurd. She wasn't falling for George Astley. Granted they had already been through a lot more together than ninety-nine percent of couples who usually got married with nothing more but a stroll through the park together; however, love was out of the question.

Esther put a hand on her little knight's shoulder.

"Milton, I promise you, I am not falling—" She froze, her gaze finding George's blue eyes looking at her from the train window. The sunlight was at such a perfect angle, highlighting every inch of the irresistible features on his face. A warm tingle rushed through her stomach, all the way into her fingers. "Not...I'm not...," she stuttered, her own eyes locked in on him as if she were hypnotized. She saw him nod at her and nodded back before ripping her eyes back to Milton.

"...What was I saying?"

Milton sighed in a mixture of frustration and empathy, his face in his hands, slowly shaking his head. But then he focused on Esther again.

"We need this job," he finally said, something that struck with her instantly. She might not agree with him about her being a bee and George her flower, but he was right about this trip. They needed this job. The kids depended on it. She depended on it. The Silverton fortune along with her father's legacy depended on it. Most likely even her life. She needed to find Jones, and time was of the essence. Milton made a good point here. She was out of line with Emily Wayne. Rightfully so or not. If George took a fancy to Emily, he would not allow her to speak this way to her, no matter how insulting and ignorant she was.

"You're right, I'm sorry. I will apologize to her," Esther promised with a hint of shame in her voice. Milton nodded empathetically.

"She is unbearable, but that would be better."

A steward shouted to get back on the train and set people on the platform back in motion. Esther grabbed Milton's hand as they slowly walked back to the train.

"Besides, I think you're prettier than her," he assured her. His words warmed her heart like the first sunrays hitting the grass after a long rain shower.

"Really?" she asked enthusiastically, her eyes sparkling.

Milton tilted his head. "Well, on the inside for sure."

Her sparkle immediately turned dull.

"Thank you, Milton." She smiled sarcastically.

"You're welcome," he rambled, jumping onto the train with not a care in the world, clueless that his 'compliment' was not one any woman would like to hear.

The train had been delayed for several hours, pushing their arrival time back to tomorrow morning. It was not uncommon for trains to break down. It was just ironic seeing a later train from New York to Denver halt at the platform right across from them. They had left New York almost four days ago, and the ride was as peaceful and scenic as Esther had promised. It filled her with pride and joy to watch George admire the American countryside, often in awe of its diverse landscape, from sky-high mountains to miles of flat fields. This would have been the most exciting trip of her life if it weren't for the beautiful Miss Emily Wayne, who, whenever George was not around, didn't let any opportunity slip through her fingers to bully Esther. On one occasion she even had the audacity to demand that Esther clean her bathroom, 'like a good servant would do,' but luckily George came to her rescue and asked for her assistance in going over maps of Colorado and New Mexico. So, it was no surprise that Esther hadn't had a chance to apologize to her as of yet. It didn't help that Emily was constantly adding more and more problematic incidents to their already sour relationship. By now, Esther had to apologize for countless interactions that always seemed to end in Esther upsetting Emily even more. She could not stand this woman, but Milton was right. Nothing was worth endangering their mission over, especially not a ten-cent woman such as Emily Wayne. Esther would have to swallow this rock and just get the apology over with.

George was looking out the window, his tired eyes staring at the same, boring train station for hours.

"At this pace we would be faster walking to Denver," he sighed, getting up from his seat. They had just finished dinner. Esther got up as well and walked over to the door. "Where are you going?" George asked, getting papers out of the desk.

"I wanted to see if Miss Wayne is in the dining car."

"And why is that, if I may ask?"

"Well, to apologize to her for my behavior—s earlier." Milton was still sitting at the table gulping down his meal, nodding in approval. But rather than tell Esther what a great idea that was, George grinned at her.

"Oh, please don't."

"No?" Esther and Milton asked simultaneously with big deer eyes.

"I shall treasure your words and remember them every time an ignorant person opens his or her mouth again."

Esther's chin fell to the floor. Did he just really say that? Wouldn't that also mean that there was no romance between the two of them?

"Besides, I have to talk to you two about something important." He walked over and handed Esther the documents he had just pulled out of his desk.

"You can read?" he inquired kindly. Esther nodded and sat down on a chair next to the desk. "Are those the documents from the envelope?"

George nodded. She started reading them. Each page had a big warning stamp on top stating: 'For Government Eyes Only.'

It wasn't until the third page, after all the bureaucratic nonsense that the government loved so much, that Esther clearly read keywords that caught her attention—in a very, very bad way. If she understood this right, these documents would push the Jicarilla Apache off their lands to round them up and march them to Utah. And for what? So the whites that were illegally mining their land could claim it in the eyes of the law. The veins in her body tensed as she jerked the papers down on the desk, her palm tightly pressed against them.

"Is this an actual agreement they are trying to enforce?" Her voice sounded emotional, and rightfully so.

"I am afraid so," George said, pouring himself a drink from a little tray next to his bed. Esther shot up in her seat.

"But that would rob them of the tiny land they have left! Not even offering them that despicable hand of dirt the Ube tribes got for theirs!" Esther almost shouted. Milton was watching the whole scene quietly.

"Yes, it would," George said, his eyes looking down, clearly embarrassed by the situation.

Esther flopped back into her seat, her mind working like a steam engine. Things started to make more sense to her now, in so many ways. Jones must have known about this agreement and thought it wrong. Otherwise he would never have just left overnight to be involved in this despicable transaction. Esther remembered how back then when word had finally made it out about the Brunot Agreement, the vast majority of the nation had found it despicable and thought it unfair. The government had tried to keep the whole affair as secretive as possible, but to no avail. They certainly had all the more reason to try the same now, especially as this 'agreement,' if you could even call it that, was far worse than the Brunot contract.

"That is probably why he hasn't replied to us yet," Esther mumbled, thinking out loud.

"Who?" George pursed his lips.

She gasped, almost choking on her own breath. *Darn it. Did she just say that out loud?*

"Y—Your friend. Billy, was it?" she said, scratching her cheek with unease.

George narrowed his eyes on her for a moment, but then shook his head as to tell himself *don't be ridiculous.*

"Yes, Billy," he confirmed without suspicion, finally relieving her anxiety.

Phew. George had no clue as to her true intentions for being here—to find Jones. The thought of it almost made her dizzy. What would he say if he were to find out about her deceit? That she was a woman? It was very unlikely that he would still let her tag along into the lawless frontier, no matter the amount of pleading and begging.

"So, you think that the government is somehow involved in Billy's disappearance?" George nodded toward the documents pinned underneath her hands.

"I don't think they would do anything to him, but they might simply have cut Chama off the map until the whole situation with the natives is settled." Esther stared at the documents once more in growing annoyance.

"To avoid alarming the press?" George wanted to clarify.

"Amongst other things."

Esther bit her lip. How much was he involved in this? She was afraid to find out but had to.

"Did you know about this when you bought your mine?" Her tone sounded more provocative than she had intended. Her heart was pounding louder and louder. She locked her gaze on George, who now returned the favor. Even now, she couldn't help but adore the way he looked at her, his eyes shimmering in the dim light of the gas lantern, passionate and unraveled. His white shirt was unbuttoned around his neck, exposing bits of his chest.

"No," he said holding her gaze. "No, I did not."

Esther stared a few seconds longer, before tearing her eyes from his, dropping her gaze down onto the floor.

"I believe you," she said in a tender tone, a flush slightly visible on her cheeks.

George let out a sigh. His shoulders dropped down, his body hung loose, almost vulnerable. Was he relieved? Did he care what a poor street boy made of him? He leaned on the desk, throwing his head back to face the ceiling.

"Any ideas what I am supposed to do about all of this?" he asked, letting his guard down. "I can't just mine on stolen land," he said, closing his eyes in vain. "I would detest myself until my last breath."

Esther was not surprised that he would do the honorable thing after all. For some reason it felt as though she knew George, and he was nothing like the usual rich, entitled people who thought they were better than everybody else.

"Why do you need this mine? Is it important to your family?" Esther wondered. George let his head fall forward.

"Very much so. I'm afraid without it I am ruined." He waved his glass up and toward her with a nod, before taking a deep sip.

"That is terrible." She truly felt for him.

"It's even worse." He shook his head, his mind seemingly wandering off into parts he would rather not visit.

"My sweet sister would be forced to marry a monster in human skin. I haven't heard from her in months, but that is most likely the doing of my angry mother cutting me off from her and burning my letter. Who knows, she might already be married to him, if my mother has finally got her way. Knowing my sister, she would sacrifice herself against my wish if she knew that this mine will not save us."

A heavy silence filled the room. Esther had no idea that George had found himself in such dire circumstances, almost reminding her of herself. Unknowingly, they had more in common than he knew. This trip to Chama was not just about money to him; his very livelihood, and that of others, seemed to depend on it.

"I don't see how the Jicarilla Apache would be able to win this no matter what," Esther said, shaking her head in empathy for those poor natives while at the same time trying to encourage George that he might get his mine even if he didn't want it this way.

"You aren't really at fault here. You could simply wait until the agreement is signed and the land becomes legally yours. Then sell it."

It was a terrible suggestion, but maybe a little better than constantly having to deal with a mine that only filled his mind with guilt.

"I'm afraid I still could not look into the mirror again."

"Is it a lot of land that you bought?" Milton now entered the conversation; they'd almost forgotten he was there.

"Enormous. Half of the bloody mountain." He let out a hard sigh.

"Why don't you go and talk to the Apache?" Milton wondered, scratching his neck. George let out a laugh.

"Just go there and talk to them? They would kill me." He chuckled some more.

"But would they?" Esther muttered, rubbing her chin. Despite what the white man thought, not all tribes were the same. Most of them were very peaceful, only resorting to violence when threatened. Before the white men started to steal their lands, they had been peacefully trading with one another for many years.

"Maybe," she announced, becoming the focus of attention, "if you were to offer them a deal. Trade. Maybe they would hear you out. They aren't savages." George reached over to the whiskey bottle and poured himself another drink.

"And trade what?" He had a big smile on his face, finding all of this comical. "The profits from the gold mine?"

196

Out of the blue, his smile turned numb, eyes drawn out, lips parted. He jumped up from his seat and started pacing back and forth with a finger waving in the air like a stick.

"That's it! I could offer them half of the profits. Or better, I could offer them to keep the land and let me mine it for half the profits in return!"

Esther now got up as well, her eyes sparkling.

"Yes! That could interfere with the government forcing them off their land too. If a white man, especially a duke, does legitimate business on their land, then they could face a whole lot of legal issues if they would just cease it without your permission. Your business, that is."

"Will the government not try to stop you from going to the natives in the first place so you can't make this deal with them?" Milton didn't seem so enthusiastic about all of this, despite it being his idea in the first place.

Esther shrugged her shoulders, still sparkling. "They would try. But only if they knew our intentions."

George thought about it. "We could make something up, so they'd let us pass."

Then, as if someone was turning on a lantern in the dark, Esther had the most marvelous idea. Why not use this whole situation to her advantage as well? It's not like it would hurt anybody. She could bring Jones into all of this. Esther had no doubt in her heart that he would assist her. He was an honorable man and most likely already arguing with the government over this horrid piece of paper they called an agreement. Jones would be able to draft a legal contract for George and the Jicarilla Apache to settle their mining deal. And more importantly, she would find Jones and get her own mess sorted out. But she had to make finding Jones the priority.

"If I am not mistaken, I read in the papers that one of the negotiators is a man by the name of Doug Jones." She tested the waters.

Milton jerked from his seat to face her, his eyes squinted in silent accusations. He knew all about her situation and was smart enough to put one and one together.

"What about him?" George raised an eyebrow.

"He is famous in all of New York for his progressive mind," Esther said, telling herself that she wasn't lying. "He is most likely one of the reasons why the negotiations came to a halt."

"Are you saying he is advocating for the natives?"

Esther was guessing here but did so with confidence. She had known Jones her whole life and had never come across a kinder and more respectable man, besides her father of course—and George.

"That's what I'm assuming."

George tapped his lip with his fist, slowly walking up and down again.

"We could tell the government that we are here to talk sense into Mr. Jones. That we need this agreement signed." George was contributing to the plan that was forging in front of them.

"We could tell them that we are very well acquainted with him—even friends." Esther perfected it.

"It's risky. If Jones doesn't play along with us, they could throw us in prison, or jail as you Americans would say," George remarked in such a calm and composed manner, his bravery nothing short of admirable. He had no idea that Jones would recognize Esther in men's clothes, short hair or not.

"They won't throw me in jail, I am just a guide," Milton chipped in, which made George laugh in warm response.

"Of course, I shall take full responsibility. I promise you two will never see a Wild Western jail from the inside. Though, I hope you will try to break me free at least?" he joked.

Milton scratched his head, seriously thinking about the proposal.

George threw Esther a wink with a smile that warmed her heart. For a moment, Esther wondered what George would do if she just told him the truth about her. But that noble notion was shortly taken over by the reality that he would put her on the next train to New York, telling her it was for her own safety. But he needed her more than ever. Just thinking about taking the train from Antonito to Chama gave her goosebumps. Not a month went by when her father wasn't informed about trouble on those lines, from robberies to train failures. Every white hick in the region was trying to pull a Jesse James these days. Despite the line generating a respectable profit for the Silvertons, her father was talking to Jones about selling his stake as no money in the world was worth this headache.

George looked like a huge weight had been lifted off his shoulders, or at least part of it. He walked over to Esther and stopped right in front of her. She froze when she realized that he had gently placed both hands on her shoulders. His grip was so tender, it made her feel breathless, dizzy.

"This is the first time in months that I feel like I have a chance again," he said in a soft, grateful tone.

Esther could feel his breath on her; it smelled of whiskey and fruit. A tingling overtook her whole body. She couldn't help but direct her gaze at those beautiful lips of his and wonder if they were as soft as his touch. She opened her mouth to say something, but nothing came out. A strand of her short hair fell into her face, and before she could even move her hand, George went ahead and gently tugged it back behind her ear for her. Gosh, she wanted to kiss this man although she didn't even know what kissing really was. Her knees weakened thinking about it, and just when she thought they were about to give out, a loud knock tore both of them out of the moment.

"George?"

A familiar voice penetrated the air through the door, followed by a second loud knock. Esther jerked away from him, while George stepped back, brows closely squished together in confusion, still staring at her as if he were lost over his own actions. What had just happened? The way he had tugged her hair back... Did he know who she was?

Another knock, almost aggressive, clearly demanded to be answered.

"George... I hope I'm not interrupting?" Emily's voice echoed from the other side.

George slowly released Esther from his gaze and turned to make his way toward the door. Esther's eyes now met Milton's, who was biting his lip and slowly shaking his head, almost like an adult who'd just caught two kids stealing forbidden cookies.

The door opened to reveal Emily dressed in a beautiful evening gown of the finest blue silk and of the latest fashion. Her golden hair was put up tightly into a bun and she was wearing a diamond jewelry set that sparkled just as bright as her beautiful eyes and white teeth. Her face curved into the most charming smile the moment her eyes saw George. Esther tasted bitterness in her mouth.

Emily looked nothing short of stunning. No man, George included, could withstand a beauty like that. It was simply not possible. Her heart sank from the highest point she was at moments ago, to the deepest depths of the underworld.

"Emily, what a delight," George welcomed her.

"Would you mind if we had a word in private," she inquired in the most elegant, angel-like tone.

George turned to Esther and Milton, almost as if he were asking them if her request was an issue. Esther took the initiative and nodded Milton out the door. "Not at all." She tried with all the strength she possessed to sound as casual as possible.

Milton followed her, but not without stopping for a moment to get a good, long glimpse of Emily, whose beauty clearly robbed him of his breath.

"Milton!" Esther barked at him, dragging him out of the room. *Let her draw her shiny harpy claws into George, but she would not get the boy, too,* Esther thought to herself, ignoring the fact that for the first time in her life, she was getting feasted on by nothing else but pure jealousy.

CHAPTER 8

W hat a blessing that the train had pulled right into a small train station somewhere near the Colorado border. Esther craved nothing more in this very moment than to get a deep breath in from the cool Kansas night breeze! It was dark out and the station was lit by small gas lanterns attached to wooden poles. Passengers on the platform were now an equal mixture of cowboys, Western locals, and East-coast travelers.

At the other end of the train, third-class passengers were lining up for the wooden lavatories that could only be considered inhumane even for animals. Weeks of human waste was piling up in a hole dugout in the dirt, covered by wood walls. If the wind blew the right way, or the wrong way as far as Esther was concerned, the stench would swallow the train as a whole, suffocating its passengers in an unbearable, nausea-provoking cloud of reek all the way to the first-class cars.

For months Esther had had to use the New York lavatory version of this train station shithole, so she couldn't help but whisper a relieved *thank you* to George for letting her stay with him in his train car with private bathroom amenities.

Esther was about to ask Milton if he would like some sweets from the vendor next to the ticket office, when he walked straight past her, his mouth and eyes wide open in utter shock.

"Milton, what's wrong?" Esther worried, but he continued dragging his feet over the pavement without stopping.

"What is it?"

She followed him, grabbing him by the arm to make him talk to her. But Milton pulled loose and kept walking until he stopped right in front of a train steward who was dressed all in green and most likely worked for the train that had arrived at the platform across from theirs. He was hammering something to one of the numerous wooden poles that held up the station's more than modest roof and lanterns. Esther was just about to ask Milton once more why he was acting so strangely, when the steward walked to the next pole, giving them full sight of the poster he had just hung up there.

A breathtaking fear tightened Esther's throat, driving all the color away from her face. Anxiety swirled around her head, making everything feel light but weighty as more and more people stopped to read the piece of paper that now had become the biggest threat not only to her mission, but her very life.

Esther stumbled backwards in a loss of footing when she bumped right into a huge cowboy in dirty ranch clothes pushing her back closer toward the pole.

"Wanted. Esther Silverton. Dead or Alive," he read out loud with a huge grin on his face.

"Te-Te-Teyn thousand?!" another cowboy stuttered as a crowd of people gathered around them, smothering Esther in the middle, making it impossible to breathe. She tried to push her way out, panicking, almost ready to scream, when she felt a hand grabbing her trembling arm. It was her little knight, Milton, who'd used his crowd reading skills from years of fleeing from the police once more to pull her out, bumping shoulder to shoulder before completely sliding by the last few bystanders like a slippery fish from its captor's wet hands.

"This woman better not squat with her spurs awn or sher's maahn," another cowboy whooped to the crowd, exposing his yellow teeth in hysteric excitement. An older woman dressed in a simple ranch dress and dusty boots stepped next to Milton and Esther several feet away from the crowd. She held her hand up to her mouth in shock. "Te-yn thousand… That's double thuh ballast thay offer for Jesse James." She shook her head. "What she done?"

"She was born a woman," Esther heard herself say without even realizing that she said those words out loud. The words must have slipped out in sheer distress. The old woman now looked at her with sad eyes, almost as if all the hardships a woman in the nineteenth century had to endure just flashed in front of her. "Ahm guilty of that crime too."

Esther instantly turned away and pulled down her leather hat to shade her face. More and more people rushed by her toward the poster. Their faces all looked alike, a bunch of wolves in sheep's clothing, hungry for fresh meat.

"This sage hen will keep my scamper juice flowin' for life," another cowboy joked in a wet, spitting voice that was fading in the distance as

Milton and Esther hurried back. Everybody was now laughing, cheerful and elated, but to Esther it all sounded like a blur of moving bodies squirming upon each other like maggots on a dead carcass.

She somehow managed to drag herself back to first-class wagons before her legs gave out and threw her against the cold metal of the train car. She leaned her back against it, trying to hold herself steady. Her heart raced like a frightened stallion in a burning forest, with no way out.

"Egan!" Milton's voice brought her back, holding both of her hands, rubbing his thumbs into her cold palms to force the frozen blood to circulate. "Look at me," he begged. "It will be okay. They are looking for a woman, and I will protect you," he promised her with big, teary eyes.

Esther glanced at her rescuer. It was not his job to do so—it was hers. She had to be strong, for everything that mattered to her. Esther took a deep breath in, slowly blowing it out again. Milton was right; they were looking for a woman, so all she had to was keep a low profile. For God's sakes, they were so close.

"Morris," she mumbled. This man had crept back into her life like an incurable fever. And what was fear that had paralyzed her moments ago now turned to anger, making her blood simmer.

"I'm fine." She lifted her hand up to Milton's cheek whose look of worry was imprinted in his eyes like a tattoo.

"Really," she said once more, forcing her voice to sound steady and true. A train whistle reverberated through the station, halting the chattering of the people.

"We have to go." Esther took in another deep breath before pushing herself off the train, her first steps weak and shaky, but quickly changing into her usual, determined walk.

Milton was right at her side, his little mind also deep in troubling thoughts.

"Don't worry," Esther comforted him, grabbing his hand. "I swear awn maah cousin Bobby's guh-rave, none awf thayse chuckleheads will be drinkin' from maah bounny," she joked into Milton's ear in the strongest Texan cowgirl accent she could come up with.

Milton threw his head back in laughter, hitting his little leg with his hand to cope.

Esther smiled at him, on the outside, but on the inside, she was boiling with rage. The thought of

Morris invaded her once more like an eerie light pulsing in pitch darkness. He wasn't slow-witted, she had to give him that. All he had to do was prove that he didn't have anything to do with her disappearance in New York. Having her corpse shipped from the West by some bounty hunter would shift the blame and open his path toward the Silverton inheritance like a pleasant walk on a field of roses, trampling on every fragile flower in his way. But Esther was not even close to giving up. Roses have thorns as well, in case Morris had forgotten, and her blood grew hotter than the scorching sun. Something seemed to have awoken in her. Something raging and wild, determined to take the war straight back to Morris and win it like a true Silverton. And there was no better way of doing that than making it to Chama—alive!

Emily was standing by the window, leaning against it with her back. George was looking straight at her, but his mind wandered off yet again to the boy he was so fond of. What the bloody hell was he doing tugging the hair back behind his ear like that? Since he had met Egan that dreadful, cold night in New York, things had progressively turned more awkward between them. Or to be more precise, not between the two but with George, as poor Egan had most likely no idea what was going on here. But George didn't either. Was he attracted to his own sex all of a sudden? Had stress pushed him over the edge of the truth of who he really was? Was that the reason why he had never fallen in love and gotten married? No. That couldn't be. His past was full of occasions, especially when he was young and more foolish than wise, in which he had felt sexually attracted to women, and not once to a man. But whatever he felt when he was looking into those loyal, adventurous brown eyes was definitely more than just some simple friendship. He was old and experienced enough to know the difference. Deep in thought, George was walking over to the whiskey tray. Suddenly he remembered that Emily was with him. He turned toward her, but she seemed lost in her own thoughts.

"May I offer you a drink?" he asked, picking up one of the bottles, snapping her right out of wherever her own mind had just wandered off to.

"No, it won't take long," she said pulling something out of her little purse. She held it inside her palm without handing it to George just yet. "I will get straight to the point." She smiled

211

Denise Daye

nervously, her beautiful red lips revealing her perfect, white teeth.

George had laid eyes on her many times, but he was always surprised at her beauty every time he saw her again. Was that not a good sign, proof he was still the same George who was looking for love with a woman? "How can I be of service?" he asked to jumpstart the conversation.

Emily looked down onto the piece of paper in her hand, which seemed to help her relax her tense shoulders.

"I... I know I seem very confident and entitled at times," she said, still staring down onto her hand, "but there is more to me than looks."

She now had his full attention as he knew exactly where this conversation was heading. Too many times he had been asked by a woman, or her mother, to have a word in private.

"Emily—"

"Please let me speak my mind," she interrupted him, now focusing her arctic blue eyes on his. George nodded.

"I overheard the gossip in New York that you are from one of the most respectable and oldest noble houses in Europe." There was nothing

212

George would have liked better in this moment than to stop her right there, but he was too much of a gentleman to do so. "And by God, I have never met a more bewitching charmer than you, Lord George Astley," she teased before lowering her gaze again. "I know that marriage is not on your mind right now, not with me, not with any other heiresses."

George was leaning against the desk, preparing himself for the 'but' that would soon follow, just as it always did with the more aggressive women proposing to him.

"But," Emily said, focusing her gaze on him again, "I also know that you are at the brink of financial ruin and your sister is engaged to an animal with means."

And there it was! George didn't say it out loud, but in thought he congratulated himself for having won the imaginary bet he just placed against himself once more.

"So, all I'm asking..." Emily now hesitantly walked over, stopping right in front of him. "All I'm asking is that you think about it for a night or two. Don't just say no right away."

She held the card up in front of him, which most likely had her information on it. He would not marry her, but the way Emily had opened up in front of him, made herself vulnerable, she didn't deserve to be treated unkindly. George would take the card and respectfully decline her offer, just like he had done many times before with all the women he knew he could never love and therefore never make happy. But right when he was about to grab it, to show her respect, the real Emily Wayne broke free again, swallowing that skittish, innocent girl in front of him to reveal the cunning, manipulative, entitled woman she truly was.

"It would be very selfish to sacrifice your poor mother and sister's comforts by turning down my offer of marriage. To be thrown into poverty from such noble birth... Could you live with yourself knowing you had done this to them?"

Emily tried to sound caring, as if she only had his and his family's best interest in mind—almost like a savior from his own foolish actions. But George was not a man who liked the taste of emotional blackmail on his tongue—even when it came from a goddess like her. He lowered his arm again, refusing the card he had been just seconds away from grabbing. If Emily Wayne thought she could walk in here and trap him in a marriage of hell with a few cunning threats, then she was as far from reality as the sun from the moon. He remembered it as if it were yesterday. Isabella, his sister, and he were standing in front of their father's grave, swearing to one another that they would only marry for love. His beloved sister was the only reason he was in the lawless Wild West in the first place. He would manage, with or without money and an estate, but his poor sister was not to be married to that disgusting pig Lord Warrington, not as long as George was still breathing.

George didn't say a word. His narrowed eyes stared right back at Emily, who ultimately was the first to turn her gaze away. With a grin of victory on her face, she stepped right in front of him, only inches away, to reach around him and place the card onto the desk. This was clearly an attempt to seduce him, leaning into him so closely, her breasts rubbed against his steel-hard chest like a soft summer breeze. But George still didn't move an inch, staring at her with cold, narrowed eyes, his body as dead inside as a graveyard, no arousal—nothing. Emily waited just a moment longer before she finally stepped back again, disappointment clearly written all over her face.

"Just think about it," she said in a cold voice, acting as if nothing had ever happened.

And just like that, she walked out, leaving behind the scent of her perfume that certainly drove countless men into insanity of lust, but not George. Nothing turned him off more than a cold-hearted, controlling woman. For God's sakes, he had grown up with one. No one knew better what it was like surviving one, whether they looked like Aphrodite herself or not. Besides, his mind was already occupied with nobody else but Egan, who was just to enter the room before getting pushed out of the way by Emily like he was an annoying fly.

"What was that all about?" Milton asked, walking behind Egan.

George frowned and waved his hand at the two of them. "Nothing of importance," he said, putting the card away into a drawer on the desk.

The raucous, metallic sound of iron wheels penetrated their ears as the train slowly started to move again. "Finally." George rolled his eyes.

"We should be in Denver by tomorrow morning," Egan said, sitting down on his bunk bed. He took off his hat and used his fingers as an improvised comb to get his hair in order, hair that was brown and naturally wavy, just falling over his ears.

George noticed that Egan still wore the same clothes he was wearing when they'd got on the train. He never saw him unbutton it, not even a button or two to make himself more comfortable. Was he perhaps shy around George? Men often loosened their shirts and pushed up their sleeves in the cigar room after dinner to make themselves more comfortable, and from what George knew about living in poverty like Egan did, men were sharing bath houses and changing rooms. But Egan acted more like a maid in waiting, not even revealing the slightest bit of skin on his arms or legs. As if he knew his thoughts, Egan met George's gaze, but unlike last time, George was the one to look away.

"Well, we should all get some rest. Tomorrow we have to make our way down to Antonito," George mumbled, hiding his face behind a map.

"We will need the rest for sure," Egan worried. "If we make good time, we might be able to continue straight from Antonito to Chama—on the Rio Grande Railroad."

George peeked over the map to find Egan shake his head in disbelief. Whatever was lying ahead of them clearly troubled him.

"Might there be anything we could do to prepare us for the dangers on that ride ahead of us?" George wondered.

"Keep our guns ready and loaded," was all Egan countered before stretching out in his bed.

George looked over to Milton who was sitting at the table playing cards with himself. Egan had promised George that he would convince him to return to New York as soon as they reached Denver. This was no place for a child, not even a smart and loyal one like Milton. George was growing less convinced that he should even bring Egan along. The thought of him getting hurt became unbearable to him and drove a sharp sting into his heart every time he revisited that idea. George walked over to turn off the light, except for the one Milton had next to his table.

"Five more minutes, Milton," he said to him.

Milton drew another card and placed it right in front of himself.

"But I'm winning!" he protested.

George threw him the 'raised-eyebrow-no-negotiations' look that a father would use on his child.

"Fine." Milton rolled his eyes, drawing another card. He didn't notice that George was still staring at him with a satisfied, faint smile on his lips. What a weird, warming feeling it triggered in him talking to Milton like that. Similar to the love he felt for his sister, but still different. Was he developing the love of a parent for this child? Perhaps a fatherly figure that was lost to the boy in the past? George looked over to Egan who seemed to have fallen asleep. How bizarre his journey in America had become. He had come here to find gold, but so far had found nothing but trouble and more mouths to feed. And worse, he seemed to be falling in love with two boys. One of them in an innocent, parental sort of way. The other one, God, he didn't even know what to call that. Attrac—*no, don't even think of it!* he yelled at himself inside his head.

The room turned darker as Milton turned the light off, but George was still wide awake, staring at the train's wooden ceiling into darkness. Something odd was definitely happening here. And if he wasn't more careful, his financial desperation would turn into the least of his worries.

Emily was sitting in the parlor car, waving the waiter for another glass of champagne. Rage bottled up inside her. Never, not once in her life, had a man rejected her. All she had to do was blink, and they'd fall onto their knees and beg to be of service. The line of broken hearts she had left behind was as long as the train tracks from New York to Denver. This rejection was the absolute worst feeling she had ever experienced—period. To her, even losing her own mother was not as painful as the feeling of not getting what she wanted. Who did George Astley think he was to reject her? He needed money; everybody knew that. The whispers of an attractive duke at the brink of ruin had made its way to American heiresses long before he had even set foot onto this continent. When she ran into him at the hotel in New York, she knew at first sight that this was the man she would marry. Not only was he the duke of one of the oldest houses in England, but his looks and charms were something no sane women could ever resist. She didn't care if he was an honorable or kind man, faithful or not. All she cared about was his title and his looks and she swore to herself the night she met him that she would possess him, no matter the cost. Admittedly, never had she felt anything for another person but herself. But whenever George smiled at her, a soft sultry tingling spread through her stomach, the closest she would probably ever get to feeling love.

Unfortunately, she didn't get that smile even a tenth as often as this insufferable guide of his. If Emily didn't know better, one could almost think him in love with him. She hated this young, big-mouthed boy. Both of them. If it wasn't for keeping face in front of George, she would have had this guide boy thrown off the train the moment he voiced his opinion over that silly business with the savages. How dare he reprimand her in public! No one was allowed to talk to Emily Wayne like this.

Emily felt the trembles of hatred rushing through her body again when she noticed a small crowd gathering around a pole outside the window of the parlor car. People were shouting in excitement, laughing out loud.

"What is all this noise about?" she barked angrily into the train car demanding an answer.

"The commoners are delighting over a warrant," a gentleman dressed in a fine black tailcoat explained, making his way over to her. He was in his thirties and quite handsome. Emily scanned him head to toe, instantly dismissing him as a candidate for marriage. He was no George Astley.

"The train that caught up with us from New York. It carried warrants for the Silverton heiress. They are spreading them everywhere," he said in the usual snobbish tone of society holding up a piece of paper.

"Of the Silverton Empire?" Emily inquired curiously.

"As incredible as it sounds." The man raised an eyebrow, handing the poster to her.

Emily shifted her gaze toward it when in seconds, her whole body shot up from her seat. "Impossible!" she shouted, her eyes and mouth wide open. Her legs almost gave out, shaking, breathless, letting herself fall backwards into her chair again. "This c-can't be!" she stuttered, her face full of manic joy.

The gentleman narrowed his eyes in curiosity.

"Are you acquainted?" But Emily had no eyes nor ears for him as her spirits lifted from the dark place she was in moments ago up high into the sky.

"I have never met her, few were lucky enough to have moved in her circles, but this will certainly cause gossip for centuries to come."

She heard the man bubbling in the far distance, but her mind and gaze were glued to the piece of paper in her hands.

"I doubt she will be alive that long," Emily rejoiced, clearly confusing her new friend.

"May I?" the man asked politely putting his hand onto the chair across from her.

"No," she declared in an arrogant voice, "you may not." Her usual, fake smile had made its way back to her lips, making her blue eyes sparkle like little stars before she added: "Now will you excuse me; I have some business to attend to."

When Esther opened her eyes that morning, George and Milton were already up looking out the window. George was wearing a khaki colored sable brushed cotton vest and matching trousers over a white dress shirt and lace up leather boots. His new look was topped off by a black cowboy hat and a gun holster with two guns. He looked like a real cowboy. As long as he didn't speak with that sexy, elegant accent of his, people could mistake him for a local who had just gotten on the train from the frontier. A far cry from what you'd expect of a duke from England.

"To remove the target sign off my back." He threw Esther a wink.

"What time is it?" she asked rubbing her eyes. This was the first time in weeks that she had slept through the night. Maybe that was due to the fact that she was actually lying on a real mattress instead of the floor, George in the room or not. Back home, the kids would always get the bed while Esther rested next to them on the floor. Funnily enough, one by one, they would come down to sleep cuddled up next to her and when she woke up in the morning, she would be walled in by five kids—well, four, as Milton would sleep on the floor as well but in one of the corners a few feet away from them. A heavy knot formed in her throat. She missed the children horribly, but she was doing this for them as much as for herself.

"It's almost nine." George checked his pocket watch.

"Look Egan, look out the window! The mountains, the mountains are as high as the sky!" Milton pointed out at the Rocky Mountains that were sitting in the distance like a herd of giants.

Esther remembered how excited she was when she first saw them as a little girl. Her father had taken her on a business trip to Denver, and it was nothing short of breathtaking. Since then she had seen them several times, impressed by each and every one of them nonetheless. Suddenly the train started slowing down drastically.

"We are in Denver. You should get a bite in." George nodded toward a plate with breakfast on it. "I doubt we will have time to get food at the station. The steward said that the train to Antonito leaves at nine-thirty."

Esther stretched and walked over to the table and grabbed a sandwich. Deep down she felt a bit of a sadness that their train journey with George would come to an end so soon. If, and the emphasis was on 'if,' they wouldn't run in to any trouble from here on George would go his way as early as tomorrow, never to be seen again.

She watched him stand next to Milton, talking about the history of the Rocky Mountains, almost like a father would teach his son. For a moment she let her mind wander to the insane thought of what it would be like if they all would be a family. She had no doubt that George would be the most incredible father to her children. And in regard to herself…Esther's imagination went wild… picturing his strong hands holding her tightly pressed against his tall body, kissing her gently with those beautiful lips of his. Her cheeks flooded with heat as she shook her head to escape this romantic daydream. She was hopeless. Maybe Milton was right. Maybe she was falling, or most likely had already, for George Astley, the stunning Duke of Aberdeen.

The train wheels made that horrible shrieking noise again, changing countryside views into pictures of streets and tall stone buildings. Denver was on its way to becoming a real city, growing from five thousand working souls to over a hundred thousand residents in the short span of a few years. Grand buildings, including the monumental Union Train Station they were pulling into, were popping up everywhere. But underneath all this new bling was still that old miners' town. Streets were still made of mud instead of pavement, a reminder that the city was barely able to cope with never-ending construction zones and the constant flock of people settling down here.

The mighty high ceilings and white showy pillars of Union Station were already in sight when the train tracks took them right along the brothel and gambling district. Prostitutes were lining up at the side of the tracks, welcoming the passengers with seductive laughs. One of them threw George a wink, pulling down her shirt.

Milton let out a sigh. "Just like New York."

"I didn't expect it to be so...lively," George commented politely with a grin on his lips.

"It certainly is a great place to lose your hard-earned money," Esther replied, turning her gaze away from a prostitute who ran after the train and lifted her skirt for her.

The train stopped abruptly, giving everyone a good shake. Stewards were shouting in the distance, tearing open the train doors to let out the waiting passengers who now flooded the station like an untamed ocean wave. Their marching steps could be felt rippling across the train.

"Is everyone ready?" George asked, picking up his bag from the floor realizing too late that nobody but him really had any belongings that could have been packed for this trip. He opened his mouth to apologize when Milton shouted in a muffled, shrieking voice.

"The police are here!"

He instantly ducked down from the window, pressing his little body against the wall. Esther rushed over to join him; her chest stuttered, biting back a loud gasp. George curiously leaned sideways to peek out the window and investigate the situation.

"There are certainly several policemen pointing toward this train car," he announced with a face turned into puzzlement. Eyes squinted as he stepped closer toward the window. "With Emily Wayne spearheading them. I wonder what she's up to now."

A sense of dread washed over Esther. She felt stuck, her mind slowly being pulled into hot quicksand. Had Emily Wayne found out about her?

"Unless it is illegal in America to turn down an entitled heiress, this honor must be indeed for you, Egan," George concluded calmly, crossing his arms in silent demand for an explanation.

"We didn't do anything, really!" Milton pleaded with big eyes. Esther threw her head back against the wall. This was bad. George had no reason to cover for them. If he had common sense, he would block the only escape at the back of the train car and keep them in here until the police arrived—which was any moment now. She looked up at George who was mercilessly staring straight back at her.

"I can explain it later," Esther blurted out in a desperate tone, breaking the anxiety-filled silence in the air. "Please..." her voice pleaded, begged.

George's intense gaze kept her hostage for a few more seconds before letting out a loud breath.

"Get out the back," he instructed them, hurrying over to the window to analyze the situation once more, "and meet me on the train to Antonito in thirty minutes."

Milton threw himself into George's arms, giving him a quick, big hug with an even bigger smile. Esther would have loved nothing more than to do the same, but of course she didn't. If she had ever wondered who this man truly was, she would never, not in this life nor the next, do so again. Despite all logic and the odds stacked against her, George trusted her, believed in her, had her back no matter what. That was all she needed to know about this man, that and nothing more...

"Go now!"

George rushed them out the back door. Esther and Milton climbed down the train coupling and onto the tracks. "I shall deduct this off your pay," he joked with the most handsome smile on his face before shutting the door behind them, locking it from the inside.

Esther had to run, but for a moment just stood there in awe about this man. There was not the slightest doubt in her mind any longer…she loved him with all her heart!

"Hurry," Milton said, pulling her arm and leading the way around the train cars and into the safety of the bustling crowd of the train station. Esther dared to look over her shoulder to witness a horde of police getting on the train when she felt a brick hit her on the chest and staggered backward a few feet, almost tumbling to the ground.

"Hey, watch out!" an old man pushing a cart of coal yelled at her. "Useless kids," he murmured as he continued onwards.

"Let me help you there darling," a prostitute flirted in a tempting voice. "What a pretty young lad you are, looking for company," she purred, squishing her breasts together with matching pouty lips.

230

"Come on!" Milton yanked her forward. Gathering herself together, they ran across the winding crowd, met by a burst of sweltering sunlight as they made their way to the train platform to Antonito. If they made it onto the train and George would be able to throw the police off, they had a fair chance of staying hidden.

Esther had to find Jones as soon as possible or be back on a train to New York most likely dead as a trophy of some bounty hunter. She could see Morris with a hidden smile on his face when he identified her corpse, pretending to be outraged over the warrant, swearing to find out who did this to her, leaving no trace behind that he was the killer.

As she and Milton snuck onto the train to Antonito, she prayed that from here on nothing would interfere with her mission to find Jones any further. But something deep inside told her that this adventure was far from calming down and was most likely just starting to warm up.

George was sitting at the table reading the newspaper when the police, dressed in blue uniforms with shiny copper buttons, swung open the door to his train car without knocking. There must have been four of them entering with more waiting outside. All of them looked so alike, it was hard to distinguish between them. Except for one of them whose enormous mustache instantly made him stand out.

"Oh, thank God." George put his newspaper down on the table and shot up from his seat. "Did you find them?"

He sounded hopeful. All four officers exchanged confused looks. Emily Wayne, looking her best in a yellow dress with a long, heavily decorated train in the back, pushed the police officers out of the way.

"Where are they!" she fumed.

"What do you mean?"

"Your so-called guides. Where are they?"

George tilted his head to the side, pursing his lips.

"Are you saying they are still out there? Still on the run?" he asked perplexed.

"We thought they were here," one of the officers remarked hesitantly.

"Here?!" George acted outraged. "Why would they be here? I reported at the last train station that they had fled. Like thieves, in the middle of the night. Gone."

The policemen looked truly puzzled, not sure what to say next. "Did you know that one of them is worth double the bounty of Jesse James?" the officer with the ridiculous mustache said, snooping around the car.

George had no idea. This was the first time he'd heard about this bounty. "Of course, I did! And it is still my lord to you!" he belittled them in the almighty tone a powerful nobleman would unleash on his peasants.

Emily and the officers exchanged looks again, but this time they turned more and more from confusion to worry and embarrassment.

"I—I am very, very sorry, my lord, we thought they'd made it all the way to Denver," one of the officers said, carefully avoiding eye contact.

"Well, clearly they have not, or do you see them here?" The room was drenched in silence, grown men staring onto the floor like little children being scolded by their papa.

"Now do not bother me again until you have found them, and I highly recommend you hurry as they might be halfway back to New York by now."

George crossed his arms, his brows squished together in annoyance. Emily surveyed his facial expression, somehow searching for the truth buried in there. Too bad for her, as George had grown up with a monster of a mother who would torment her children for matters as trivial as running down the hallway, so he'd had no other choice but to learn to hone his emotions to perfection. Time out at his estate's former torture cellar depended on his ability to hide the truth, and as a small child, nothing was more traumatic than that dark place filled with rats and lost souls. Nobody, not even a cunning snake like Emily Wayne, possessed the skill to get information out of him that he was not willing to give.

Emily must have decided to believe him as she angrily stomped her foot on the ground, both hands clenched into rageful fists. For a brief second, she looked as if she was about to shatter into millions of hateful pieces, but she was able to get a hold of herself again as soon as she noticed how George was judging her with his noble, captivating eyes.

"Let's telegraph the train stations located on their path back to New York," she said, trying to seem as composed as George was.

"That would be wise." George complimented her idea to further clear all suspicion, thinking to himself how despicable she was.

"Yes, my lord, at once," the officers shouted in a subordinate cheer, rushing out the door. Emily didn't follow them but remained standing in the middle of the room, her mouth twitching, as if she was trying to apologize but didn't possess the skill to.

"It might be to our advantage if someone with the intelligence above an average pigeon accompanies those incompetent policemen to send out the telegraphs, or else they will fail at that too and will never find those criminals."

George pretended that he was simply thinking out loud. In reality, he was baiting her like a fisherman his dinner, and luckily for him, Emily took the bait. Flattered that she could be essential to this task but also clearly anxious that the police would mess up and let her enemy, Egan, slip away, she turned toward the door.

"I better join them to oversee those telegraphs. Shall I keep you informed?" She sounded hopeful as if her success in this mission would bring her the reward of marriage after all. Was this woman that delusional, not living on planet Earth?

"I shall be indebted to you forever."

George forced himself to smile at her. It worked and her face lit up like a shooting star, her mind most likely filled with delusional pictures of becoming the next Duchess of Aberdeen.

"I shall telegraph you as soon as I have news. Call on me when you get back to Denver."

She smiled back at him. And just like that, Emily Wayne rushed after the police officers, thinking she was on a mission for George, who in return was leading her further from the truth than she could ever imagine. At least they would be looking in the wrong direction, which should buy George, Milton, and Egan enough time not only to make it to Chama but also to come up with a plan to get him out of this mess.

George grabbed his bag and jumped off the train. His feet were gliding over the busy train platform like an eagle ready to descend for its prey. He could not miss that train to Antonito for anything in the world, as now two additional people depended on him — and one of them meant more to him than he could possibly ever have dreamt of.

CHAPTER 9

Esther nervously turned around again, staring at the train door with worried eyes. Milton was anxiously scooting back and forth in his seat next to her. Outside was another one of those damnable posters haunting her wherever she went. It attracted a few glances once in a while, but nothing like the rowdy crowd when the posters had first gone up. She pulled her hat onto her face, trying her best to blend in with the small crowd around them. The Denver and Rio Grande Railroad was a small-town train line with no first-class wagons. Only a few train cars were designated for passengers, leaving the majority of the train for supply wagons to stock the military forts and mining camps that were scattered in the untamed West. The interior of the wagons was far from what could be classified as lavish, with wooden seats lined up in rows like church banks and the walls made of wooden planks, some of them with gaps in between. Except for two families with children and several cowboys, their passenger car was almost empty.

Esther stood up to get a better view of the door, but still no sign of George. If he were to miss this train, her chances of making it to Jones would go down to zero. She didn't know for certain but highly expected that the government had not only cut off all communication to Chama, but passenger rides as well. Without a duke who argued to push the agreement along by talking sense into his lawyer, Jones, there was no chance of getting on that train from Antonito to Chama. She would have to get a horse and ride the treacherous mountain terrain by herself, a guaranteed death sentence. Besides, she had anticipated spending that one more day with him before parting ways. Taking that from her was almost worse than not making it to Jones.

Milton let out a heavy sigh.

"Where is he?"

The train whistled at the passengers and the workers on the tracks to warn them that the train was being set into motion. Esther rushed over to the train door, stopping right behind the steward who had just closed the door as the train slowly started to roll off.

"Wait," she shouted into his neck, causing him to jerk around in surprise.

"What for?" he asked, shoving her off his back, his face grimaced in annoyance when a voice boomed across the distance.

"Hold it!" George's voice yelled, out of breath, sprinting along the train in an attempt to jump onto it.

"What the blazes?" the steward cussed, stumbling backwards as George maneuvered himself next to the train door, gripping the metal bar that was put in place to help people get on and off the train.

Esther forcefully pushed the steward aside to throw herself against the heavy door, swinging it wide open, almost falling out herself. The speed and winds around the train had picked up quite a bit by now, pushing and pulling George around as if he was an unwanted flea on a dog. He finally managed to use a heavy blow of wind coming in from his back to throw himself right through the opened doorframe and into the train. But instead of an elegant landing worthy of a duke, he fell straight past Esther and the steward and flat onto his stomach. Under flabbergasted mumbling from the other passengers, he instantly pushed himself back onto his feet and used his cowboy hat to dust off.

"A bit of a downgrade from our previous accommodations, don't you agree?" he leaned over and whispered to her before doing an elegant courtesy bow for the disturbed passengers. "My apologies. Delighted to make your acquaintances."

He smiled in the most handsome of his smiles, causing the women and children alike to giggle. The men on the other hand mumbled in annoyance, putting an end to the show by going about their business—reading newspapers or looking out the window.

Esther was left speechless by this stunning entrance but not motionless. Without thinking, she threw herself around his neck.

"You made it!"

Feeling his iron chest pressed against her body, the smell of his sweet scent of fresh soap instantly brought her back to reality, reminding her who and where she was and more so what the hell she was doing. She jerked away, staring onto the floor with cheeks as red as a campfire.

"You did not think I would let you have all the fun by yourself?" he joked.

"Meh. I was just worried that I would have to pay for our train tickets." She brushed him off with a smirk.

George scouted the train car to find Milton wave at him, the smile on his little lips as warming as the rays of the sun. Still staring at Milton, he leaned in, but she knew all too well what he had on his mind so she talked before he could.

"I couldn't put him back on the train to New York. It would have been too dangerous."

George pursed his lips but nodded in sympathy.

"But I've already talked to him; he will stay at a hotel in Antonito until we're done in Chama."

"Considering the circumstances, that would be best," he agreed.

Esther now noticed for the first time that George was without his bag.

"Where is your bag?"

"Somewhere on the train tracks." He straightened his shirt and vest. "Now will you excuse me? I shall sit for a bit to admire the Colorado scenery and recover from this chase and then you will explain to me in detail why I have had to lie to the police and jump on a train like Jesse James." He put his cowboy hat on and walked straight to Milton, who instantly pointed out the window at the Rocky Mountains.

"Can you explain to me now how mountains grow?" He begged George to continue the conversation where they had left off before they'd pulled into Denver.

"If you don't interrupt me incessantly with new questions before I have even answered the previous one," George countered, sitting down across from him.

"I won't."

"Well then…" George took a deep breath. "Mountains are formed when the earth's tectonic—"

"Why are they called mountains?" Milton interrupted.

George wrinkled his forehead. "Well, the word mountain originated from the word montem, which is Latin for—"

"Do the Latins still live?" Milton blurted out again, cutting George off once more. George opened his mouth, but Milton was faster. "Don't the Latins fight with swords? And what do they look like?"

George started rubbing his temples with his hands.

"Bloody hell," he mumbled to himself. Esther couldn't help but burst into loud laughter, rejoicing over his agony of the everyday pains of having a child.

It must have been several hours since they had left Denver. The train ride to Antonito would take about half a day, so they must have been closer than they thought.

George and Milton were pretty occupied marveling at the breathtaking Colorado countryside. Even the locomotive smoke creeping in through the gaps of the planks could not diminish the beauty of the golden plains that unfolded in front of them as wide as an ocean, the majestic Rocky Mountains constantly in the backdrop as if they would watch over the state's beauty. Where George had found the seemingly endless patience to endure Milton's thirst for knowledge, Esther didn't know, but it had taken him further than any other human being has ever managed to withstand Milton's interrogations.

George stared out the window again, his eyes as peaceful as she had ever seen before, then shook his head in disbelief, something he had done several times so far.

"I have never seen anything like it."

Words he had also mumbled in awe repeatedly on this ride. Suddenly he turned toward her. "Well. I think I am ready now for the explanation you owe me," he declared, standing up.

Milton and Esther exchanged nervous looks.

"Where are we going?" she inquired.

"Somewhere quieter and more soothing for this sort of topic."

George headed toward the door that connected the passenger wagon with the supply cars. Milton and Esther followed him. The coupling that connected the train cars was out in the wide open. The loud sounds of the train wheels and winds of the racing train danced wildly around them. George took a big step over the coupling, reaching his hand over to Esther and Milton to help both of them over the fast-moving tracks underneath them. The supply car they broke into was filled with wooden chests. There was no window in it, but its wall planks had gaps so big, it let the cold April sunshine penetrate the inside of the car like bright lanterns, lighting the whole room up in shadowy daylight.

George sat down on a pile of three stacked boxes, crossing his arms as a sign that he was ready. Milton scratched his neck, avoiding looking at him. Esther also avoided him, staring at the floor to gather her courage.

"Well?" he broke the silence, his foot jittering against the floor. A fluttery, empty feeling filled Esther's stomach. What if he was angry at her for using him to get to Jones?

"Well," she cleared her throat, "t-there are people who are searching for me."

George stayed quiet as she stated the obvious, barely scratching the surface he expected from her confession, and she knew that.

"First of all, I haven't done anything wrong," she promised him to silence the sudden worry that he might be thinking that whoever was chasing her, at this point all of America, was doing so with good cause. George crossed and un-

246

crossed his legs, not a single word or smile escaping his handsome lips.

Milton was pretending to inspect the wooden boxes to avoid being dragged into this conversation. The only thing that could make his performance more suspicious and fake would be for him to start whistling.

Esther walked over to George, sitting down next to him. For a moment she was fumbling with her sleeve, preparing herself to continue. Now came the hard part.

"My father just passed away." She kept staring down at the sleeve between her fingers, trying to swallow down the tears of his memory. "And now his business partner is hunting me to claim my father's business for himself."

"He is a very bad man," Milton chipped in, still pretending to inspect the boxes.

Esther peeked over to see how George was taking this in, only to find his face grimacing in deep empathy and sorrow.

"I'm very sorry to hear that. I lost my own father not too long ago."

"Are you an orphan too, then?" Milton asked, leaving the boxes to themselves for the time being to join the conversation.

"No," said George, taken aback by the question, almost refusing to elaborate. "I am afraid my mother is not of this world and would survive the apocalypse, riding on the back of a flying daemon."

"That bad?" Esther gasped, surprised by this newfound information, which somehow now made sense of why he'd been a bachelor all these years.

"If you consider spending and emotionally torturing my father into the ground and then engaging my poor sister to a monster to continue her lavish lifestyle bad, then yes, that bad," George said, closing his eyes. "But this is not about me."

His gaze found Esther's sky-blue eyes. "This man, your father's former partner, how can he claim your father's business for himself?"

"By forging my father's will and killing me," Esther responded in an unemotional tone, almost as if it were nothing unusual, just another day in the life of Esther Silverton. By now, excruciating poverty, Morris's constant threats, disguising herself as a man...all of it had become the new normal to her.

George abruptly stood up, both of his hands clenching into tight fists. "Are you saying this man is trying to kill you?" His voice sounded low, almost like a threat that was scary enough that it would make it all the way to New York right to Morris to send a shiver down his spine.

Esther nodded. George's joyful eyes darkened. Never before had she seen this light-hearted, calm man this angry before. He walked right up to her, placing one of his hands onto her shoulder.

"I swear to you, this man will not harm you." He narrowed his eyes. "Even if I have to put him into the ground myself," George vowed with a face so serious, it could crack a mirror.

Esther couldn't help but feel safe for the first time since that dreadful day of her father's passing. Not even for a brief moment did she doubt this man's promise to take care of her and sort things out. But luckily it wouldn't have to come to this if they made it to Chama and Jones without further problems. Since Denver, Lady Luck had been looking their way. The weather was milder than most Aprils in the Colorado mountains, so a snowstorm was unlikely. And if

Esther was right about the government shutting down Chama, then there should be military all over the place from Antonito, which made it very unwise for any wannabe Jesse James to rob the train from Antonito to Chama. In short, the stage was set for Esther to come out with the rest of her story…She took a deep breath, half to get the courage to continue and half because George's close proximity and soft grip of her shoulder sent butterflies through her body.

"There is something else," she finally mumbled, tearing her gaze away from him and down onto her hands.

"No, don't." Milton leaped toward her, his voice shaking in distress. Esther looked up to him with a faint smile on her lips.

"It's alright, Milton," she said, trying to reassure him. She trusted George with her life, so why not with this secret? This man had saved her from the police twice, both times all odds and evidence stacked against her. Not only did he have a right to know, but her heart craved to tell him her secret so he could look at her with those eyes for who she really was—not a pretty-faced boy with a high-pitched voice but a woman! *A poor woman, skin and bones with short hair like a man,*

250

not even the shadow of a beauty like Emily Wayne, a voice in her head nagged at her confidence. *And with five kids,* that festering voice mercilessly added to her self-doubts. No. No, no, no! She tried to shake it all away. She had to tell him the truth before her secrets came out and he lost his trust in her. Or worse, before they would part ways and he would never have known who she really was, and how she felt about him. Her heart fluttered wildly in her chest, making it harder to breathe. She unfastened the top of her collar with her finger, a desperate attempt to help her get more air. Now or never. She slowly opened her mouth, her eyes holding on to his gaze. Do it!

"I... I... I am —" the words stuck in her throat, clogging the air trying to reach her lungs. "I... am —" *just say it, it's not like it will kill you...*

She forced her every breath in her body to finally, once and for all, lift the curse, ready to tell the truth.

"I am a wo —"

The aggressive loud shrieks of gunfire shots startled all three of them in utter surprise. George jumped up, instantly pulling his guns out while jerking around to the source of the noise. Esther rushed Milton over to the stacked boxes to seek cover.

Senses sharpened with adrenaline as George stomped over to the connection door, tearing it wide open, stepping out onto the coupling platform to see what was going on. The wide-open door intensified the sounds of the never-ending gunshots, now accompanied by men hollering frantically to the beat of galloping hooves.

"I thought you said we wouldn't get robbed until later?" he shouted back to Esther as loud as he could to out-yell the hollering and shooting. Esther felt her hair lifting on her arms and neck. She had tried to prepare herself for this very moment over and over again, yet it still left her with the cold feeling of nausea, frantic prayers racing through her mind that Milton would come out of this alive.

"I doubt we can just tell those wannabe Jesses that they are too early, but you are welcome to try!" she shouted back, rushing over to Milton who was cowering behind a pile of boxes, ears held tight with his hands. Esther pulled her pistol out of a little holster she had made for her ankle.

"Milton, you will stay here, you hear me?" she said in a firm voice, checking the bullet count in her pistol — only two.

He just nodded, his wide eyes screaming in fear.

Esther forced herself to smile. "Have I ever missed a target?" she asked in a confident, almost sassy tone.

Milton took the bait and shook his head, seemingly a little less frightened.

"I won't start with it now. Now hide. I'll be back as soon as I take care of those Luigis."

Esther threw him a wink before running over to George who quickly scanned her pistol in her hand.

"Do you know how to use that?" he shouted as loud as he could against the nerve-wracking soundtrack of a speeding train's yowling winds, human howls, gunshots, and galloping hooves hitting the shaking ground.

Esther jumped over the coupling. "You'll find out!" she yelled back, tearing the door to the passenger car open while holding her hat to keep it from flying off. George was right behind her. The car was empty. The passengers of this wagon must have grouped up with the other travelers in the car, so they kept moving. But instead of being welcomed by their allies, they were greeted with guns pointed right at them. Women were hovering over their frightened children on the floor while the rest of the passengers, the unarmed ones, were seeking shelter behind the metal linings of the wooden benches. There were five armed cowboys as she counted, from Esther's age all the way up to an old rancher with a long white beard, most of whom had Colt revolvers, except for the old, bearded man who was brandishing a rifle. And as things stood right now, their outnumbered and out gunned barrels were pointed at the wrong folks.

"Easy…" George lifted both hands to calm their nerves. The old rancher narrowed his eyes.

"It's thuh flannelmouth," he announced, repositioning his rifle back out the opened window and at the real threat. The others mumbled something and followed suit.

George and Esther exchanged looks. "As long as he can shoot, I don't care what that means," he declared loudly before running over to one of the unguarded windows and pressing himself against the wall underneath it.

Esther did the same, covering her head with her hand as if that would protect her from incoming bullets.

George quickly peeked out the window. "There are six of them on this side," he shouted over to a young cowboy in a red shirt, barely able to get his message across over the endlessly, insufferable hollers and howls coming in from the open windows. The cowboy nodded and scouted out the situation on his side of the train.

"Five lunkheads hair," he yelled back at George who drew his brows together in confusion.

Esther translated. "Five."

George now confirmed this information with a nod. All of a sudden, the outlaws' bullets changed directions, unpredictably hitting different parts of the train which only fueled the fearful screams of the women and children to new highs.

"They aren't thuh friendly kahnd," the old cowboy with the white beard shouted, holding his rifle against his chest.

Without saying another word, George and the other cowboys started to shoot back in a constant pattern of seeking cover to reload, waiting a few seconds before standing up and firing out the windows. Esther couldn't tell how successful the cowboys were on their side of the train, but George managed to land a hit, causing one of the masked robbers to force his horse to an abrupt halt, launching himself into the dust. And in a moment of brief silence from the sounds of flying bullets, with a racing heartbeat pounding against her chest so hard it hurt, Esther jerked up and stretched her arm. Her fiery eyes scanned the remaining five robbers on their horses, her gun glinting in her hand before her gaze froze on a robber with a red mask who was pointing his own gun straight at her—so she fired. Instantly, the man was propelled off his horse, plummeting onto the ground, withdrawing from the race against his will. Esther dodged under the windowsill, smiling over to George who was staring at her, eyes and mouth wide open.

"If that's how you use this thing then I guess I know how to," she answered his earlier question with a cheeky grin. Despite all the adrenaline rushing through her shaking body, she couldn't help but feel proud to gain his approval and admiration. But then there was also that sudden feeling of overwhelming guilt. Never in her life had she killed a man before. And if it was only her on the train, she might have not done it. But she was a mother now and shooting a man who was endangering her child was only the beginning of what a mother was willing to do to protect her child.

The fire exchange continued, and with a loud cry, one of the bullets had found its way into an old cowboy's chest. The women and children screamed as they watched him sag to the ground like a lifeless sack of potatoes, using his last bit of strength to cover his wound. The young cowboy in the red shirt crawled up to the old man, checking his injury, only to shake his head to let the others know how bad it was.

"If thay get awn board thay will beef us all," he announced in a failed attempt to boost morale.

"Fort Garland idn far from hair," the middle-aged cowboy with a goat beard yelled over his shoulder. "If we kayun keep the train goin' we kayun mayk it!"

Everybody nodded silently in agreement with this plan which they all knew was their only hope.

Esther shot back out the window again, hitting one of the attackers in the hand, but rather than going down, he fired right back at her before he simply switched his pistol into his other hand

and continued firing. She managed to dodge just in time, when the metallic, loud shrieking of the train's wheels sent shockwaves up everybody's spines.

"Thuh train is stopping!" the young cowboy shouted over to George and Esther, who'd just dodged another bullet storm.

"We're all dead!" the injured rancher cried out in pain, releasing frightened screams and cries from the women and children.

Esther had to do something. This train could not stop, no matter the price!

"We have to get to the locomotive," she announced before she threw herself onto her stomach and crawled to the door that connected the passenger car with the train locomotive.

George followed her, then pushed by her to take the lead of the dangerous task to open the door to the unknown. He tore on its handle, but it was locked. Without hesitation, Esther stepped back and fired with her freshly reloaded Derringer at its keylock, letting in sunrays through her bullet holes.

George then threw his body against the door and managed to push it wide open, only to find

Esther getting hit by the force of black, smoke-filled winds so strong, if she hadn't grabbed the metal door frame in reflex, it would have blown her off her feet.

The steam locomotive was now in front of them, only separated from the passenger car by the uncovered coal supply wagon attached to its back. The smoke was unbearable, penetrating Esther's lungs with sheer aggression. She and George coughed uncontrollably until both of them were smart enough to cover their mouths and noses with their sleeves. It was hard to see, but even with constantly blinking eyes it became clear that the locomotive's engineers were nowhere to be found. Had they been shot? In fact, it seemed like the train had been left to drive itself.

"Cover me!" George shouted, lifting himself up to climb into the coal wagon, when Esther saw one of the robbers lurk up out of nowhere from the locomotive on the other side of the coal wagon.

"Watch out!" she heard herself scream, and without realizing it, as if her body had a puppeteer maneuvering her moves, she launched herself against George to knock him into the coal wagon, out of harm's way.

A sharp, cold pain, similar to a snake bite, gnawed at her shoulder as a loud thundering sound echoed into the sky, leaving Esther in a state of deafening silence. Her body stumbled backwards against the doorframe, her motions frozen by a pain more agonizing that she had ever, in her whole life, experienced before. It took her a moment before she realized that she had been shot. Things happened so fast from here on, all she heard was another shot right before she saw the silhouette of the robber on the locomotive fall off the train and disappear in the dust of the desert. George must have gotten him. She threw her head back in pain. George was now kneeling right next to her.

"Are you hit?" he shouted against the loud noise of the winds and gunshots in the distance. Esther nodded her head. Her shoulder burned like hell, and her skin felt oddly cold, but she decided she did not feel like her life was fading — not yet. George tried to pull her coat down to reveal the wound, but she wouldn't let him. There was no time!

"I'm fine," she growled under tightly clenched teeth, putting on a brave face and pushing George off of her. "Go!" she yelled at him as loud as she could and nodded toward the locomotive. The train was losing speed by the second, soon making it impossible for their outnumbered and outgunned group of makeshift heroes to defend it and prevent the robbers from boarding the train and killing everyone on it. But George ignored her order, for some reason insisting that she was his priority; he tried to hold her arm down to get a better look at her gunshot wound. She forcefully jerked it out of his hands. "If the train stops, they will shoot us all!" she cried out in pain, tears in her eyes thinking about what would happen to Milton and George.

"I — said — go!"

She gathered all her strength to push him toward the coal train with her foot, triggering a burning sensation in her shoulder that felt as if someone had just stabbed a fork into her wound. George stood there for another second, fist clenched, clearly in despair over the reality that leaving her was the right thing to do — their only chance. With a face full of anger, pain, and desperation, George turned to jump back onto the coal car, disappearing inside it for a few moments only to reappear at the other end of it.

Esther pushed her torso against the doorframe to help herself back up on her feet. She only saw parts of George in the locomotive, but it looked like he was helping up one of the train's frightened engineers who then pointed at something on the floor before pulling back a handle next to the locomotive's fire that kept the train running. George and the engineer were now both frantically shoveling coal into the hungry heart of the train, its flames flickering angrily to the left and right, demanding more. Shovel after shovel, without rest, shoveling coal like their lives depended on it, the two of them gave it all there was to give, with success.

The train started to pick up speed, the sound of turning wheels becoming louder and louder, faster and faster. But Esther didn't dare let George out of her sight yet. Instead of pressing her hand down on her bleeding wound, she held her pistol tightly clenched in her fist, ready to shoot whoever dared to come close to him again. For how long she stood there protecting George feeding the feasting engine of the train, she didn't know, but what she did know was that the cheerful shouts and gunshots coming from behind her meant that they were getting close to Fort Garland, and that the robbers must have given up the chase. And not a moment earlier than that did she let her legs give in to slowly slide onto the floor, partially in relief, and partially because her legs would carry her no more.

CHAPTER 10

George kicked the door open to the doctor's home in Alamosa, a small town that had quickly become the Denver and Rio Grande Railroad's construction and shipping hub and was heavily guarded by Fort Garland soldiers. He was dragging Egan in by placing his arm around his neck, holding him up with his own arm wrapped around his waist.

"We need help!" George shouted, stepping into a simple Western that had not much more in it than a stove, a cupboard, and a wooden cross hanging on the wall. Two plainly dressed women were sitting at a wooden table and were feeding a baby. One of them was older, the other younger. Identical facial features gave them away as mother and daughter. They must be used to injured people as neither of them seemed too disturbed by George's cries for help.

A man in his late forties with silver streaks in his hair now came running from the back of the house. He was wearing a black vest and pants and the typical, round doctor glasses. The doctor didn't even stop to analyze the situation but pointed into the back of the house from where he had just come, turning on the spot.

"Follow me," he said in a composed but firm voice. The younger of the two women got up and followed them as well, handing the feeding spoon over to her mother. The group was led into a small room with a metal table right in its center. Medical jars, books, and strange looking metal instruments filled up shelves and tables pressed against the walls.

"Place him on the table," the doctor instructed George as he walked over to one of the shelves to grab a bottle of liquid and a pair of scissors.

From his time in the military, George knew what the scissors were for and was silently praying that Egan would let the doctor use them to cut his shirt open. He had tried to take a look at the wound on the train, but Egan was fighting him tooth and nail, insisting to wait until they reached Alamosa, a small town right before Antonito. Never before had George felt so helpless and angry than when Egan wouldn't let him clean the wound right away with whiskey transported on the train. Judging by the blood flow, he didn't think that an artery had been hit, but seeing Egan grimacing in pain, and even worse, enduring all of this because he'd sacrificed himself to save George, had brought the burning sensation of tears to his eyes.

"What happened?" the doctor asked calmly without making the situation seem unimportant. He must have been used to seeing much worse, working so close to a military fort, George thought to himself. Nothing was more horrid than seeing the terrors of war first-hand. Egan also seemed to have somewhat adjusted to the pain in his shoulder as he barely made any sounds unless he moved his shoulder a certain way or somebody touched the wound.

"We were attacked by a group of bandits," George explained, frantically turning his head left and right to search for Milton. He found him standing in the corner of the room, tears running down from his eyes.

"I'm alright, just need a bit of rest," Egan protested again. He tried to sit up on the table, but the doctor placed an elbow onto his chest.

"Hold still," he demanded, placing the scissors wide open at the upper end of Egan's shirt to start cutting it open.

266

"No!" Egan snapped trying to jerk up, but the doctor who had probably held down hundreds of soldiers fighting all they could to keep their limbs, just put more pressure on his elbow, pinning Egan in place again.

"Stop!" Egan clenched his jaw, trying to roll off the table this time and with some success managed to squirm his arm free.

"Hold him down," the doctor yelled over to George and the younger woman who most likely was his wife and nurse. Both of them came running, and each grabbed one of Egan's arms, placing their weight on them.

"Please stop!"

Tears were now running down Egan's red cheeks, as he kicked with his thin legs like a wild mustang battling his captors to remain free and untamed. But the doctor kept cutting the shirt open, his face totally emotionless.

George on the other hand was not as immune to Egan's heartbreaking cries, clenching his jaw in response to deal with the wave of guilt overcoming him for pinning Egan down against his will.

The doctor was now all the way through Egan's shirt and pulled it open, when Egan cried out for one last time, this time begging:

"Please don't!"

George tried to calm him.

"We are just trying to he—" George froze, abruptly releasing Egan's arm without even realizing.

The doctor and his wife both halted in motion as well, staring down onto Egan's bare chest with their eyes and mouths wide open. In front of them wasn't the flat, bony torso of a young street boy as they had all expected, but the curvy breasts of a woman!

George tumbled backwards a few steps, pressing his fist to his mouth, his lips pinched between his thumb and index finger. How was this possible?! How was this even possible?! Egan... no...

The short-haired woman in front of him shot up, covering herself by closing the shredded shirt around her like a cape protecting her from a snowstorm. She was staring down at the wooden floor, biting on her lip so hard it started to bleed.

The doctor's wife was the first to regain her senses.

"Out!" she commanded. "Everybody out!" she yelled again before placing a motherly hand onto the back of the woman they had called Egan up until now.

It took another aimed stare from the doctor before George was able to shake himself out of the endless train of thought and clear the room, dragging Milton out with him. He walked straight out of the house into the little vegetable garden in front, passing the older woman who was feeding the baby in the doctor's kitchen. The warm rays of the spring sun hit his face, pulling him back into reality, away from the idea that maybe all of this was just a dream. For a moment Milton and George just stood motionless, in total silence, gazing off at the white Rocky Mountains, listening to the wind blow the smell of fresh prairie grass right in front of their feet.

"Fool!" George shouted suddenly, throwing his hands high just to have them land on his hips again. How the bloody hell did he not notice that Egan was a woman? It was obvious at every step they took. The way (s)he smiled, laughed, the fine voice. Her eyes that sparkled like a thousand stars up in the night sky. And then there was that whole attraction thing.

George started pacing up and down, something he did quite often now, shaking his head back into that same endless train of thought. How could he have doubted his own character before coming to the most logical conclusion?! Not that he minded men who were attracted to their own sex, love was love and it was not his business what others should or should not do, but to think he was falling for a man himself…

"I'm such a fool!" he barked out loud again, angrily kicking a rock in front of him. No, he wasn't falling for Egan, his brave, loyal, selfless guide. He was falling for… for… for God's sakes, he didn't even know her name! What if she had died on the train? George would have stood by her side while she was leaving this world, not even able to call her by her real name. It was tearing him apart, piece by piece, that he knew close to nothing about this woman who had risked her life for him not once, but twice. TWICE! And almost losing it, too.

Milton now stepped closer, avoiding eye contact by staring at a rock he was pushing around with his dusty, little boot.

"Please don't be mad at her. It was all my idea," he apologized.

George turned around, searching the boy's face in front of him. Another person devoted to his cause whom he knew nothing about. Here he was, George Astley, the honorable Duke of Aberdeen, dragging women and children along on his dangerous quest to save his despicable investment and title. George felt another wave of gut-churning guilt flush through his body. He clenched his fists in anger, only to notice Milton's body shrinking in on itself with a darting gaze at the floor. George instantly calmed himself, letting out a sharp, whizzing breath instead.

"Milton. I'm not angry with either of you. The only person I am angry with is myself." He stepped closer, putting a gentle hand onto his shoulder. George suddenly frowned. "Your name *is* Milton, isn't it?"

Milton nodded.

"So you are a…"

"A boy," Milton answered with a faint smile on his face.

"Unlike Miki—she's a girl, too."

"I see. And who is Miki?"

Milton seemed to become more of his usual self again, rolling his eyes in annoyance as if that was a silly question.

"Well, one of us six, of course," he explained. "Me, Miki, Jeff, Tom, little Cliff, and of course Esther."

"So that's her name? Esther?"

"It's not Cliff, Tom, or Jeff," Milton joked, managing to put a faint smile onto George's face.

"Fair enough."

Even now, this boy had the power to make him smile, feel like everything was going to be alright. George loved both of them, he truly did.

The door opened and the doctor approached George, wiping blood off his hands onto a white cloth.

"She is as strong as she is lucky," he said, turning his hand to see if there was any blood left on it. "Went straight through, no artery was hit."

"Does that mean she will be okay?" Milton asked with big, teary eyes.

"She will have to keep the wound clean," the doctor said, bending forward to level with Milton and give him a warm smile, "but if she follows my orders, I don't see why not."

Milton threw himself into the doctor's arms.

"Thank you, thank you, thank you!" his buried face mumbled into the doctor's vest. George was a grown man, but almost threw himself into the doctor's arms as well, so relieved and grateful was he. It was like an elephant sitting on his chest had just walked off, letting him finally breathe again.

"You didn't know?" The doctor now turned to face George, Milton slowly letting go of him.

"No," he almost whispered, his voice soaked in shame. The doctor didn't say anything but simply nodded his head as if it wasn't his business to ask any more questions. George was about to ask whether she had said anything, when the train's loud whistle screamed through the town from the distance, warning passengers that the train to Antonito would leave in a few minutes. George looked over in the direction of the train. Time to go. Alone. Esther had to rest, but more importantly, he would not allow her to continue to Chama with him. It was simply too dangerous, and the bullet in her shoulder was proof enough of that. He would have to manage on his own from here on. And of course, safely get back to Alamosa to check in on her as soon as possible.

"Will she be safe here for a few days?" George asked, fishing some money out from his coat's inner pocket. The question seemed to have left a bitter taste in the doctor's mouth as he frowned for the first time since they'd arrived.

"I swore an oath to save lives, not to destroy them," he informed George, chin held up high.

"Of course," he apologized, handing him some money to pay for his services and a little extra in gratitude.

"No-one can know of this," George said in the kindest threat ever spoken, but a threat, nonetheless. The doctor nodded.

"I understand." He put the money in his vest pocket and turned around to walk back inside. George now stepped in front of Milton, whose lips twisted downward, knowing exactly what was to come. "Tell her I will be back soon."

Milton kept staring at the ground. "Can I come with you?"

George placed a hand on Milton's head, gently rubbing it. "I need you here. To watch over her."

Milton nodded in silent agreement.

"Good," George said, standing up and handing Milton several notes. "Give this to her."

Milton held the money up as if it were evil, didn't want it. "You're not coming back?" his wet, big eyes accused him.

"Of course, I am." But what he couldn't tell Milton was the uncertainty of it. He might not even make it to his destination for all he knew. From here onwards, there were far too many folks who would have a problem with him, with his mission—the government and the natives for instance. Add outlaws to it and his plan was nothing short of insanity. But there was no time for doubts or whining as the stakes were higher than ever. Two more souls he cared about had been added to the list of people he couldn't let down. He had to find a way to get his fortune back so he could help Esther and Milton, get rid of this ridiculous warrant, and... and... *and what, George? Take care of them? Offer them a home? Return to England with five children and a wife?*

The train whistle howled again, breaking him off from his thoughts. It was time to go. He leaned over to Milton.

"Tell her she can trust me; I will make things right."

Those were his last words before he turned and headed back to the train station through a small cowboy town in the middle of nowhere, far away from his home, lost in the deepest American Frontier the continent had to offer. At least the rumors of those God-forsaken, lawless Western towns that high society loved to babble about at dinner parties seemed to be nothing but bed-time stories. So far, those little Wild West towns seemed rather peaceful and well taken care of by their sheriffs and community.

"For once, fortune seems to smile my way again," George mumbled to himself, pulling down his hat to greet a group of women and children passing by on a wagon. Antonito was less than an hour away by train. He was so close and yet had the battle of his life ahead of him.

"Bloody fortune..." George cussed as he stood rooted to the dusty ground in the middle of downtown Antonito, a town that was as Wild Western as the sun was bright. Unlike serene, little Alamosa, or any other Western town he had passed by so far, this tiny town was bustling with more life than a carnival. It was sheer madness! Soldiers dressed in blue were tumbling by, blackout drunk, with giggling prostitutes hanging around their necks. One of them was about to fall onto George, who managed just in time to jump aside, watching the soldier fall flat onto his stomach—passed out cold. George wrinkled his nose at the stench of booze oozing from his body. The two women who were with him moments ago now leaned over, their hands hastily going through his pockets, stealing everything they could carry.

George now directed his shocked gaze toward a group of young cowboys storming out of one of the countless saloons. They jumped hollering onto their horses, riding off, shooting their guns. Shortly after, the bartender of the very same saloon and two of his helpers came flying out the batwing doors, shooting after the fleeing cowboys, without success.

Loud laughter and piano music accompanied his every step down the dusty, crowded main road. Most buildings were wooden, two-story structures with flat facades and horses tied up in front of them, patiently waiting for their owners to return. But there were also a few hastily thrown together tents that were packed with railroad workers, prospectors, soldiers, and even lawmen. George stopped, perusing the situation before letting out a long, frustrated, hot breath of air. He had parted from Esther less than two hours ago and was already in need of her help.

The next train to Chama was not due to leave until tomorrow, but even that was an issue. 'Military ownlee,' a sign read at the Antonito train station office, and George was bemused by the poor spelling of 'only.' So, in order to be on that train, George still had to somehow convince the military commander that he was on their side — which he wasn't.

He would deal with it later. For now, he would need a room for the night. On their way to Denver, Esther had told him that there were many different types of saloons, some more respectable than others. According to her, his best chance of finding a clean room was at the restaurant saloons. But how the bloody hell would he find one in between all those billiard saloons, gambling saloons, drinking saloons, dance hall saloons, and opium dens? He looked down the street in front of him that was nothing short of a war zone. How could there be so bloody many of them? Discouraged, he started reading some of the saloon names: "Tanglefoot," he mumbled to himself, "Forty-Red, Tarantula Juice, Red Eye, Coffin... Coffin?" He stopped and rubbed his face with his hand in impatient annoyance. This was a nightmare.

"Kayun ah help thuh faahn Mister?" a young man in a dirty suit and missing a front tooth asked.

He was wearing a melon hat above his black frizzed hair and was trying to look like a trustworthy gentleman—which he clearly failed at miserably. Like everyone else, the stench of booze was on him, as if he had bathed in liquor. George did not trust this man as far as he could spit, but it couldn't hurt to ask which one of all these places was a restaurant saloon.

"I need a room," George tried to lose his British accent. The man's face lit up, exposing his missing tooth in a huge grin.

"Alone, no women," George clarified much to the disappointment of the man whose grin didn't vanish but diminished.

"Well, ya came to thuh right man they-n." He slapped himself on the chest.

"You came to me," George reminded him, narrowing his eyes. The man tapped his hat with his index finger in some sort of howdy gesture.

"No need t' be so suspicious. Wer all friends hair," he said in a far from trustworthy tone.

"Hair."

He pulled some sort of ticket out of his jacket and held it up to George, who didn't move an inch. The man kept holding it up right in front of him anyway. "It's a ticket for a free heyrcut at Bob's. Awn thuh howse."

George was truly puzzled. Had this man just offered him a free haircut?

"Did you say haircut?" he asked, eyebrows raised high.

"Yes, Sir. At Bob's," the man confirmed with a smirk.

George shook his head. This was absurd. He almost wanted to accept the ticket simply because he was curious to see if indeed it really was the ticket he claimed it to be, so bizarre was the whole situation. But just as he was about to accept the offer, he heard an all too familiar voice coming in from behind him.

"Get out of here, you saddle bum!"

George turned to find the brave, incredible woman he had left less than two hours ago. She was still dressed like a man, one hand holding the reins to a brown horse, the other in a white makeshift sling. The sun was shining right behind her, almost like a knight coming to his rescue—from a haircut.

The swindler, who obviously did not appreciate her interference, changed his oh-so-helpful and friendly demeanor in a matter of seconds, his face now grimacing like an angry wild cat.

"Git out awf hair, ya purty puss!" he spat on the dusty ground, reaching into his pocket while taking an abrupt step toward Esther to threaten her. George had had enough of this theater play and lifted his coat just enough to expose a glimmer of his gun in its holster.

"I wouldn't do that if I were you," he cautioned. The man instantly shot both of his hands up, stumbling backwards.

"Easy now." He nervously smiled. "Was jus' about to cut a path anyways."

And just like that he turned on his heel and was gone with the wind, the ticket slowly tumbling onto the dusty ground. A heavy silence took the stage where a moment ago this jester had been performing.

"The good ol' heyrcut trick," Esther nervously joked at George to break the silence. But George still didn't say a single word. He didn't have to. His whole being had a glum of displeasure around him, quite likely visible from space.

"They do that one in New York as well. Lure you into the barber shop with a free haircut. Then the barber feels out your wallet and cuts a mark into the back of your head to let the thieves know if you are worth the trouble," she babbled nervously, stepping closer, acting as if there was nothing unusual about her riding here on a horse, with a gunshot wound, to continue this treacherous journey to Chama.

"Rather daring, wouldn't you agree?" he finally said, crossing his arms.

"Well, the barber and the thieves all are—"

"I am referring to you," he interrupted her, winning that round as Esther slowly let her gaze sink to the ground to avoid his judging eyes. She bit her lower lip, something George had noticed she did often when she was nervous. He knew why she was here, but it would rain pigs before he would let her tag along and put herself in danger — again.

"You are not coming with me... *Esther.*" Hearing him say her name seemed to have struck something in her as she instantly jerked her head up to meet his gaze.

"I know I wasn't quite honest with you..."

"I saw that," George countered in his usual calm and composed voice before realizing that this statement didn't sound right. A brief image of her perfect curves flashed into his memory, flooding his thoughts in a short burst of elation.

"I-I mean I know... I know that," he clarified, rubbing his neck and blinking his eyes away from the image in his head. How could he even think about her like that? Here... Now? Rather unlike him, but Esther thankfully didn't pay it much attention.

"Please, George. I really need to get to Chama," she begged with her big deer eyes that were more beautiful than ever. Had any man ever managed to turn those begging eyes down, he wondered?

"Well, not with me you won't. You need to rest and it's too dangerous. Please go back to Alamosa and wait for me there."

George stepped back into the carnival-like mingle of the street when he heard Esther shout:

"Jones is my friend!"

He froze, then turned to face her.

"What do you mean?"

"He has been my father's lawyer and friend of the family since I can remember." She urged the horse to slowly move closer. "He vanished in Chama, just like your friend Billy. A few weeks before my father passed away." Esther looked away as if she were trying to shake off the very notion of a sad memory, a memory she had no time for right now. "He is the only one who can save me. Please, George."

She sounded desperate, which instantly drove a dagger into his heart. He stepped closer, gently putting his hand on her arm that was holding the horse.

"I promise you I shall find him. But you have to wait for me in Alamosa. It's too dangerous for you to come with me."

"It's not safe there for me any longer. Who knows, people might already be looking for me as we speak." She argued a good point. Alamosa might not be safe any longer. Emily Wayne, in her endless hatred for Esther, had most likely already telegraphed to New York that she had seen her on the train to Denver. If that Morris guy was smarter than a three-year-old, he would add one and one together and know that she was on her way to Chama to find Jones.

Suddenly Esther turned around and started to walk off. George followed her, kicking dirt and sand as he trudged behind her.

"Where are you going?"

"To Chama." She lifted her chin.

He let out a frustrated, sharp breath. "Please stop."

She didn't.

"You mustn't blame yourself when they find my dead body in the desert," she calmly remarked, getting all the dirty tricks out of her toolbox.

"That's not fair, Esther," he yelled after her, trying to keep up.

"*If…they find my body,*" she shouted back over her shoulder without slowing down. "The desert has swallowed many souls before. Just tell the kids I love them for me, will ya?"

She had played the winning card in this poker match. George stopped in his tracks, bitterly speechless. He had to give it to her. As mad and frustrated as he was, never, not in his wildest dreams, could he have ever imagined meeting a woman like Esther. She was incredible, amazing, and stunning without a doubt. Something told him that she would do just as she had threatened and ride off to Chama all by herself on an old horse…with a gunshot wound. Of course, he could not let that happen.

"Wait!" He took his hat off, dragging a hand through his now sweaty hair. But Esther kept going without even bothering to look his way. Gosh darn it this woman was as stubborn as she was smart. She had set him up yet again, and he'd fallen for it like a mouse following a trail of cheese.

But not everything she said was without merit. As things stood, nowhere was safe for her right now. It made sense to be on the constant move. It was her only chance. Finding Jones had to happen now, not later. And George was determined to do whatever it would take to help her. At least she'd somehow managed to keep Milton somewhere safe this time. Unless—

"What about Milton? How do we know he hasn't already followed you? Is he here somewhere? Gambling or handing out tickets for free haircuts?"

Esther laughed, but it was more of a giggle. Her brief smile glinted in the sun that highlighted every soft curve on her face, from her flushed brows to her reddened lips—gosh she was beautiful.

"I told him that it was important for him to stay behind at Alamosa with the doctor's family so he could telegraph us as soon as the sheriffs started looking for me."

George was not convinced.

"It's the truth so he believed it. Milton wants to protect me, and he can do so best from Alamosa."

George put his hat back on, relieved to hear at least some good news. He would only have to protect a wounded, outlawed woman, not a child on top of that.

Esther nodded down the road. "This way."

"Where to?"

"We need a room." She led the horse around drunken soldiers and cowboys who paid her no attention with her boyish outfit. George followed closely just in case. "Did you forget what I told you about saloons?" she asked, eyebrows raised high as they walked.

"No, but I was rather taken with all of them... I mean, Coffin, Red Eye, Tarantula juice... Who could resist?"

Esther grinned at him. "The answer lies in the façade." She stopped in front of a brick building called 'Desert John's' and tied her horse up to a hitching post.

"Brick..." She smiled. "To be able to afford brick walls you must have good business and have been around for a while."

With a faint smile on his lips, George watched her enter the saloon, wondering if there was anything he wouldn't do for this hell of a woman. He wasn't surprised to find that he couldn't think of anything...

CHAPTER 11

Esther felt a bit of relief when they walked into Desert John's and it was indeed a restaurant saloon with rooms for rent, just like she had told George it would be. She was raised in the West; however, there was still a big difference between growing up as a privileged heiress on a secure ranch and actually surviving the harsh life in a frontier town. Her father had moved both of them to New York when he thought it was time for her to become a lady, so her exposure to the lawless frontier was limited to accompanying her father on the occasional, heavily guarded, business trips out West or the colorful tales from the cowboys working on her ranch.

Desert John's was a typical saloon with a long mahogany bar that was polished to a sparkly shine. Steer horns, saddles, and a few taxidermied mountain animals decorated the walls, staring at the arriving guests with glazed eyes. There were several tables with somewhat decent-looking folks eating and drinking, giving the saloon an overall tamer atmosphere, which didn't seem like the norm in this town.

"Kay-yun I help ya?" the short, overweight bartender asked while cleaning a glass with a white rag. He had an enormous curled mustache that swallowed parts of his voice and was wearing a white shirt with black stripes. Esther and George stepped up to the bar which seemed to also operate as the reception, as indicated by the room keys located on a wooden shelf in between all the liquor bottles.

"We need a room," George said.

The owner placed the glass aside and studied Esther and George from underneath his mustache.

"Eend two firewaters to wet the throats," Esther added in a cowboy accent.

The bartender placed two dirty glasses in front of them and was about to pour whiskey out of an unlabeled bottle, when Esther grabbed him by the wrist, stopping him right in his tracks.

"Not the rotgut, the good stuff." Her eyes narrowed. The bartender growled something from under his mustache and replaced the unlabeled bottle with a bottle whose label read 'Old Grandad' and finished his pour. Esther swung down the whole contents at once. She almost gagged, burning up from the inside, but put all her strength into her poker face before signaling George, who was about to sip on it, that this is how it's done here.

George looked around the room and noticed a few pairs of eyes on him, so he pounded the whole thing as well, his iron face not giving away for a second that he too was on fire from this hundred-proof attacker.

The bartender now nodded in approval, turning around to grab one of his room keys.

"That's all ah gawt." He slammed the keys onto the counter in front of them. Esther stared at them for a brief moment, her heartbeat racing. George sneaked a glance at her from the corner of his eye. They would sleep in the same room again. But this time without Milton and as man and woman. *So, what? Is this seriously all you concern yourself with right now?*

"That's faahn." Esther grabbed the keys, trying to play it cool in front of George. The bartender's direction to the room was nothing more than a dry, short nod up some wooden stairs at the end of the saloon. Esther responded with a hat nod and was about to head to the wooden stairs, when George grabbed her by the arm to stop her.

"The military…" He directed his attention at the bartender who was now pouring whiskey for one of the saloon girls.

"What's with thuh blueskins?" he growled from under his beard.

"Would you happen to know if their commanding officer is here?" George inquired, asking for another glass of that hellish whiskey by tapping his finger next to his empty glass. Esther was somewhat surprised how fast George had learnt the talk of the West.

The bartender mumbled something that was hard to understand, filling George's glass just to watch him swig it down again, like a real cowboy. George was looking over to Esther for a translation, but she simply shrugged her shoulders.

"You get better at reading his mustache after a few weeks of being trapped here," an elegant, strong male voice addressed George from a table in a corner of the saloon.

George and Esther walked around the bar to discover an older gentleman dressed in a spotless, blue military uniform. His balbo beard was combed to perfection, a sign that he was one of the finer folks. And unlike all the other soldiers they had come across so far, this man was covered in medals and had two golden stars on each shoulder, revealing him to be higher up there on the military ladder. He was not looking up but continued to use his knife to finely cut the meat in front of him.

"I was rather hoping to stay a day at the most." George instantly changed back from a whiskey-pounding cowboy into his duke persona, noble accent included. There was no doubt in neither his nor Esther's mind that this commanding officer would respect a man of society by more than what the rest of the town judged folks by — how they ordered and drank their whiskey. The officer now leaned back in his chair and gazed at George in curiosity.

"And who if I may ask do I have the pleasure with?" the major general now inquired, tapping his mouth with a napkin.

"George Astley, Duke of Aberdeen. Delighted to make your acquaintance." He lifted his hat a little in a formal greeting despite it being a cowboy hat. The major got up from his chair and pointed toward the seat across from him to invite George to sit down.

"Major General Patterson."

He sat back down at the same time George did. Esther wondered if she had heard that right. What in the hell was a major general doing here? None of the forts within hundreds of miles could produce such military nobility. She could only hope that George knew that. Unfortunately, she had no place at this table or even in this conversation to help him. The commander would not bother with a poorly dressed guide, so she had to let George win this battle for them. She stepped a few feet back, just enough not to be a bother but still close enough to hear their conversation.

"You're far away from home," Patterson remarked, waving the waitress over to refill his glass of water. He wasn't a drinker…a family man then? Perhaps forced to be here?

"So are you, it seems," George countered.

For a brief moment, Major General Patterson's gaze darkened and drifted off wherever his mind took him, perhaps to his family and home he missed dearly? Esther almost smiled… She had to give it to George, he was as clever as he was handsome and kind.

General Patterson shook himself back from his tender memories to the dusty, devilish town he was in.

"All the way from Maryland. They were hoping to avoid a massacre of the Indians, so they have sent something more civilized."

"I can see that," George joked sarcastically nodding toward downtown Antonito. The major general laughed.

"You can only tolerate the whining for permission to go to the saloons for so long. At a certain point, the begging becomes more insufferable than actually witnessing your men giving in to flesh and sin."

George nodded with an understanding faint smile on his lips.

"I was in the military myself. I understand perfectly well."

The general studied George's face, looking for the former soldier in him. Ultimately, he seemed to have found him, slowly nodding with pursed lips.

"So how can I be of service to you?" he asked in a curious tone. George leaned forward to make strong eye contact.

"I need to be on that train to Chama tomorrow."

General Patterson thought about it for a second but then shook his head.

"I'm afraid I can't do that. We have strict orders. Military personnel and cargo only. No one else is allowed in or out of Chama." His voice was strong and clear, leaving no doubt he would not bend. George looked down at his hands, as if debating his next move. Esther started to wonder why he wouldn't follow their plan and make something up about Jones, telling the general that he was here to push the agreement onto Jones for the sake of his mine. But George did none of that. Instead he decided to go a totally different route.

He locked his serious gaze on Patterson.

"I shall not waste your time by telling you fairytales."

The major general now stopped eating, raising his brows.

"You don't deserve that horseshit, as they say around here." George leaned back in his chair, crossing his legs. "But the fact is, you do not strike me as a man who enjoys soaking the desert ground with blood."

For a moment there was silence between the two of them. Esther almost expected the general to laugh, or at least ask who the hell George thought he was to just walk in here and demand for the rules to be bent, but for some strange reason, he didn't. Instead, he leaned back in his chair, wiped his mouth with his napkin and stared George down into tiny little pieces. From toes to head and head to toes. He then locked in on George's gaze with dark, meaningful eyes—the kind of eyes of a man who could find a needle in a haystack on any given day without much effort.

"I could have you home by the end of the week without a single drop of blood spilled," George declared, breaking the silence.

The major general crossed his arms, giving George now his undivided attention.

"Tell me about your time in the military," General Patterson asked, catching George and Esther both off guard.

"My time in the military?" George repeated in surprise. General Patterson nodded.

"Yes. That is what I asked."

George looked down at the table as if an invisible hand had pulled him back into his army years right there and then. Whatever memory had just haunted him, it filled his eyes with emptiness, despair. He shook it off again, put it back into the box he must have locked it all away in.

"My time in the military…" George mused, straightening in his seat. "I'm afraid, sir, you might not like my answer."

"Try me."

There was another heavy moment of silence between the two of them before George gave in.

"Very well. My time in the military… I've been to war. I've seen men shot and blown to pieces, seen mothers hold the lifeless bodies of their children, and heard grown men cry in their sleep like little babies." George locked his gaze back on General Patterson. "And with all due respect, at some point, blood is just red, no matter what side it's from."

The air between the two fogged up like a cloudy spring morning before a storm. Esther tried not to stare over to them, but she just couldn't help it. Was all lost now? And just when she thought that the major general would get up and walk off, he picked up the knife and fork from his plate again, nodding the whole way through.

"You shall be on that train tomorrow, George Astley, Duke of Aberdeen."

A tingle of excitement made its way through Esther's stomach. He did it! He really did it! Not even a major general could resist this man's charms.

George kept his calm and composed demeanor, but Esther had a feeling that he was cheering on the inside just as much as she was. But just when things finally seemed like they were going according to their plan, insane or not, just when Lady Luck finally seemed to have joined them for a little while again, the major general added:

"But I am afraid you might not have much time. I am expecting marching orders any day now."

"Marching orders?" Esther blurted out without thinking, her face frozen and pale. She was instantly greeted by the major general's clear disapproval of making herself noticeable. But he answered her, nonetheless.

"The Jicarilla Apache. To put an end to all of this."

Just as expected, the room was simple. The walls were made of wood panels. The whole furniture and décor pretty much consisted of no more than a bed barely big enough for one, a wash basin on a small table with two chairs, a dusty, round rug on the floor, and a window covered by dusty, red curtains that looked more orange than crimson.

Esther closed the door behind her, hanging her head down like a beaten dog. Her initial worry about being in a room with George had been replaced by a deep, sulking sadness. General Patterson could receive a telegraph at any moment now, which would not influence her own, dire circumstances as she would still find Jones, but it almost felt unimportant to her now that an entire tribe's future was at risk. Her legs were starting to betray her. The poor natives would not stand a chance. They would be forced off the little land they still had left, or even worse, the whole tribe could be wiped off the map for good. The times where the military would take hostages and send them to white farmers to work, like they had with her mother, was over. The natives had fought back, more than once, to reject the white man's demands and defend the bodies, souls, and land which rightfully belonged to them. Every thought pulled Esther deeper into murky darkness, trapped in the midst of an unrelenting quicksand.

George walked over to her and stopped right in front of her. He gently lifted up her chin to make her look into his tender, sky-blue eyes.

"We still have time. Tomorrow morning, we will take the train to Chama and I promise you, I shall not waste any time. The moment you are safe with Jones I will get the fastest horse money can buy and make it out to the natives to settle this."

Esther stared back at him, unconvinced with her brown eyes that seemed to have now turned black. But he did not give up so easily.

"The cards are still in our hands. If I can arrange to return the land, to mine the gold for them, the government won't have much grounds to insist further on claiming this land for a handful of small prospectors. I am certain nobody else was foolish enough to purchase as much land as I did."

Esther nodded hesitantly.

"And if need be, I could offer the government a share in the profits as well. What do they care about winning back land for a few miners if they can fill their own pockets with gold without the bad publicity of a massacre?"

This new attempt at cheering her up sat rather well with her.

"You think they would agree to that?" Her big eyes flickered with hope.

"Are you jesting? Governments love getting their pockets filled with free gold." He smiled warmly at her.

Suddenly, a sharp pain in her shoulder made her jerk up her arm.

"Your wound." He lifted her vest and shirt at the side of her neck to discover a blood-soaked bandage. Riding a horse like the devil was after her was most likely not the best idea she had ever had, especially not with an open wound, but then, she also hadn't had much of a choice.

"It's nothing." She brushed him off. But George locked his hand around her wrist and pulled her to the bed with the wash basin and fresh towels next to it.

"Don't even start with that again." He took his hat off and nodded at her to sit down on the bed. The strict tone in his voice did not leave much room for defiance. He poured water into the basin and soaked one of the clean towels in it.

"I will get some of the hundred-proof; please take off your vest and shirt," he said before leaving the room in big, hurried steps.

While he was gone, Esther debated whether to listen and take her shirt off or not. Her skin tingled thinking about George seeing her chest almost naked with nothing more than a bandage wrap around her breasts. But then, it wasn't as if she currently was in any shape or form desirable—at all.

She took her hat off and examined the reflection staring back at her in the round mirror that leaned against the wall across the room. She looked awful. Her beautiful, thick hair was cut at ear length and she had shadows under her eyes that made it seem as if she hadn't slept in months, which in all fairness she hadn't. There was not even the slightest possibility that George would see anything else in her than a guide boy, even now that he knew the truth. With the heavy feeling of disappointment sitting on her chest, Esther carefully undressed herself.

The door opened and George stepped in with a bottle of John's rotgut, almost dropping it when he first saw her sitting half naked on the bed with nothing more than a wrap around her breasts. He hastily closed the door behind him again.

"Th-this one has mushrooms in it for some unexplainable reason," he stuttered, staring at the bottle he was holding. "It might help to prevent an infection."

He walked over, kneeling in front of her. She couldn't tell if he was avoiding eye contact while using the wet towel to clean the wound, because she herself was avoiding him for sure. Her whole body was on fire before the darn rotgut had even touched her. It was the most amazing feeling that she had only ever felt around the man who was now closer to her than ever.

"This might burn...a lot," he said before pressing a towel soaked in liquor onto her shoulder. And by God it did. Without thinking, Esther snatched both her arms up, pulling him closer. Her jaw clenched in pain as her grasp forcefully closed in until the sensation of raging flames in her wound slowly wore off.

She opened her eyes, only to realize she had pulled George so close; his face, his eyes, his lips, they were only inches away from her own. He wasn't moving, only breathing slow and heavily, as if he wanted to freeze this moment in time forever. Heat curled down her spine, arousing a desire that had fought to come to light the first time he had smiled at her. His breathing had become incredibly fast, as fast as hers. She dared to tilt her head back enough just to gaze into those beguiling eyes that shimmered with a fire she had never seen in him before. Was that longing she saw in them? And before he could even dare to pull away from her, to apologize, to compose himself, she gave in to the dreams that had filled her head every night when she lay awake in that train car, smelling his scent of fresh soap, listening to the very breath that she could now feel on her skin. Her whole body on fire, she leaned forward and softly brushed her lips with his. An electric shock wave sent a painful longing to the area in between her legs, as if she would never feel complete again if she did not satisfy it.

"Esther," he whispered, gently running his arm up her naked waist, pulling her closer. His lips descended onto hers, gently pushing them apart to enter her mouth with his warm, delicious tongue. His kisses deepened, passionately pushing and stroking her tongue.

Aching with pleasure and as if she were bewitched, she got off the bed and slowly lowered herself onto his lap, wrapping her legs around him. She gasped the moment her longing heat found his big erection. It was hard and long and pushed a bit into her opening through her clothes. She started rubbing herself against it to ease the painful longing his steel formed at her wet center. George buried his head in her neck, growling as if he too was in joyful pain.

"Esther, we have to stop," he moaned, releasing his tight grip around her waist.

But Esther was far beyond reasoning. She was a grown woman who knew what she wanted, craved.

"I can't," she whispered against his lips, intensifying the pressure of her rhythmic motions on his erection. George's eyes darkened with lust as he carefully pushed her onto her back, spreading her legs with his knee.

"I can't control myself much longer," he begged while softly running his lips down her neck. But Esther didn't stop. She threw her head back in pleasure, wrapping her legs tightly around his hips.

"Then don't," she demanded, looking at him with half-shut eyes as she continued to rub herself against him. All of a sudden, George let out a sharp breath, as if he'd just let go of all reasoning himself, pulling down her trousers and underpants in one motion. His hand was running up her inner thigh to the very place she craved him the most.

"You are so wet," he moaned against her lips as he slowly slipped his finger inside her waiting lady part. Esther threw back her head to let out a loud moan. She reached for his pants, anxiously fumbling at the buttons to open them. George's trembling hand rushed to help her, pulling down his pants without parting his lips from hers. And before she could beg for making this painful, hot feeling between her legs go away, she felt his hard member at her wet core, gently entering her with a loud and lustful growl. At first, she felt a sharp sting, the initial pain of giving her maidenhood, but that faded quickly to give way to this incredible, tingling longing that demanded to be relieved no matter the cost.

And as she lay there, her whole body moving in the rhythm of her lover's gentle thrusts, tears of happiness formed in her eyes. She loved this man with all her heart, soul, and now, her body, too.

George couldn't breathe. Feeling Esther's wet center wrapping around his shaft was more than he could handle. For a moment he had to stop, or he was afraid his heart would stop beating, so amazing did she feel. His flesh tingled like never before, his heart scattered as if it was a racing stallion. He slowly started moving again, looking down at the beautiful woman who was aching for him, calling his name under heavy breaths every time he gently thrust into her again. George's movements became faster, feeling that tingling buildup that demanded to be pushed over the edge.

Her body understood perfectly well, and she dug her fingers into his buttocks, holding him tight in between against her core, moaning and panting in pure pleasure. The exciting sensation of her heat tightening around his shaft pushed him closer and closer to climax. And just when he threw his head to the side in a desperate attempt to hold his own relief back to wait for hers,

Esther's whole body trembled and twitched as she threw her head back to let out a loud cry. Right at that moment, he too climaxed, pulsating his seed into her twitching warmth with a loud moan, collapsing onto her lips to finish their most intimate moments with a loving, passionate kiss. And when he slowly opened his eyes again to gaze at the beauty underneath him, there was no doubt in his mind that he loved this woman, with all his heart and soul, and if she asked it of him, he would cross the wildest oceans and fight lions with his bare hands.

He gently rolled himself off her warm body, looking deep into her bewitching, brown eyes that sparkled like a thousand ice crystals.

But as the sun slowly made way to the colorful plays of twilight, reality started to kick in again. What had he done? Panic briefly flashed across his face. Like a youthful fool guided by lustful urges, he had just claimed a woman to whom he could offer absolutely nothing if the natives rejected him. To make things even worse, she had five children to feed as well and couldn't afford to be the wife of an impoverished duke looking for employment in a country that had just come out of a civil war, leaving hundreds of thousands of men without work. And as things stood financially right now, he couldn't even afford a ticket back to England for one person, so how the hell would he care for all of them? What was he thinking, losing control like that? The very thing he always prided himself on, his composed nature, had just gone out through a dusty saloon window in a matter of seconds. This woman had indeed bewitched him.

Esther seemed to have noticed the change in his mood as she now locked in on his gaze, studying his eyes with a faint smile.

"Isn't the woman the one who should have regrets?" She tried to joke, sitting up to reach for her shirt and pull her pants back up. George pulled his pants up as well and got up to grab the white bedsheet off the bed. He inspected it before he started tearing it into long shreds.

"I would only have regrets with Egan," he grinned kneeling next to her, "but not with an outlawed gunslinger woman of the wild frontier."

Truth was, as foolish as it sounded, he could not think of any other woman he would want to spend the rest of his life with but her, five children or not. And by now, he'd learned to love Milton as if he were his own. Certainly, he would love the other children just as much... But how would he provide for all of them? And what about his poor sister? He would never allow her to marry that foul-smelling pig, no matter the outcome with the natives.

He kept a strong façade for Esther, but the truth was, his life and everybody else's now depended on this gold mine, or more precisely, striking a deal with the natives and preventing the government from slaughtering them.

George was smiling, but something was the matter. His mind kept wandering off to far-away places. Was he worried he would have to offer her his hand in marriage? That he was now trapped, dragging along five street children? Esther looked at her handsome lover wrapping the torn bedsheet around her chest and over her shoulder to make a pretty decent makeshift bandage, considering what he was working with.

"George," she said, gently placing her hand on his, stopping him in his tracks. "I do not expect anything from you. Not marriage, not money, not to take care of me and five children."

Her voice sounded tender and sincere. She knew this man before her would do the honorable thing and marry her, even if that meant his own unhappiness and ruin. But what had happened between the two of them was her doing, not his. "Besides," she shrugged, ignoring the pain in her shoulder and heart, "I have absolutely no intention of getting married soon."

"No?" One of his eyebrows shot up.

"Not in the least. I value my freedom and once I find Jones, I shall take over my father's business from that thief and provide for myself."

She tried to sound jolly, hiding her true feelings. Of course, it had crept into the farthest corner of her mind that George could be the one to marry her after she turned twenty-one—if Jones didn't find a way out of Morris's fraud of a will that is—a distant dream she pictured at night to fall asleep with a warm and fuzzy feeling in her stomach. Mr. and Mrs. Astley, a happy family, together until the end. But that was before she seduced him, forcing him to marry her without love.

"Esther, I was hoping—"

"You are reading too much into this," she interrupted, putting her shirt back on. He tried to help her, but she rejected him by jerking away from him.

312

She loved this man with all her heart, which meant, no matter how painful it would be, she would have to let him go so he could marry who his heart, not his honor, desired.

George didn't seem to be quite finished with this topic as he stepped right in front of her, inches away from her face. Her heart instantly picked up speed, sending this beautiful tingle all the way into her fingertips all over again. He gently lifted her chin, a move that would always freeze her in place, begging to be kissed. He opened his mouth to say something, when they were both distracted by loud screams from the street.

"What's going on?" Esther frowned. Suddenly a loud knock banged against her door.

"Lord Astley!" a man shouted, urgency vibrating in his voice. George and Esther exchanged confused looks before he walked over to the door to open it. The voice was now paired with a young soldier, who nervously saluted George and handed him a letter.

"From the major general. The train leaves in thirty minutes."

...What?

"But I thought there was no train until tomorrow?" George asked, his brows squished together in worry.

"That was before we received marching orders."

Esther stumbled backward, an icy shiver expanding deep into her core. "Marching orders? Tonight?"

"The train in thirty minutes is for supplies only, but the major general said you should be on it."

"So, no troops are moving out tonight?" George clarified.

"No. All supplies will be sent to the troops in Chama first."

Esther managed to regain control over her body again.

"How long will that take?" she almost shouted.

"Don't mean nothing to me." The soldier shrugged his shoulder, disengaged.

George grabbed him by his collar. "How long?!"

"O-one or t-two days," the soldier stuttered in fear before pulling himself free and fleeing the scene, almost falling down the stairs.

For a moment both of them just stood there, unable to speak. Why did Lady Luck have to beat them down over and over again?

George slammed the door shut and ran to grab his hat and coat. Esther did the same.

"What's in the letter?" she asked, scanning the room anxiously to make sure they didn't forget anything.

"I don't know, it's not addressed to me but to a certain Major Wicks."

"Help for Chama I hope?"

George pursed his lips.

"We will find out." He put the letter in his pocket. "We will find out." He repeated his words as if it was a plea to the moody Lady Luck herself that this indeed be the case.

Without wasting another second, they paid for their room and fought their way through an endless crowd of nervously moving and shouting soldiers, filling the streets like busy ants preparing for battle.

CHAPTER 12

L ady Luck seemed to have a questionable sense of humor, Esther thought when a strong, sharp pain in her shoulder woke her once more, so close to the finish line. She was lying in George's arms on the floor of a freight wagon, surrounded by military supplies, heading for Chama. It must have been the middle of the night. The moon's bright, silver light was shining in through the big door they had opened to air out the smoke that was creeping in through the big cracks of the wall planks. For a short moment, Esther forgot her pain and stared out onto the ancient mountains and rivers that sparkled silver underneath the mystical moonlight. Her lover's warm body was shielding her from the cold as the rhythmic sound of train wheels on the tracks felt hypnotizing. Despite her pain and dire circumstances, she felt happy, more than words or thoughts could tell.

"Are you alright?"

She heard George gently whisper, softly running his hand down her cheek. Esther nodded and closed her eyes, as she let his beating heart swoon her to sleep. They were so close to Chama, what good would it do to make him worry? Besides, the train from Antonito to Chama had no major stops, only small mining towns and refill stations for water and coal. In the morning she would finally make it to Jones, and from there on she would have plenty of time to rest.

She felt George lean closer, his cheeks softly touching her hair and without a second to waste, felt his supple lips, and a long, tender kiss onto her head. She focused on the calming waves of his breathing chest to push the intensifying pain of her shoulder into the distant background, slowly drifting off into a slumber again.

"The hell?"

An angry voice demanded an explanation, waking both of them from a night of constant waking. George was the first to slowly get on his feet, stretching his head from left to right to drive out the stiffness from sleeping on a train floor. Esther would have done the same if a stiff neck and back would be the only annoyance her body was complaining about. But what was a painful wound yesterday had now turned into an almost unbearable ache spreading through her whole body, almost paralyzing her.

"Who are you?" the young soldier asked, pointing his rifle at them. He must have been barely eighteen and had red freckles all over his face. Young men, also called battle maidens amongst their own, were easily startled and fast to pull that trigger.

"Easy, my friend."

George slowly lifted his hands taking a step closer to the soldier.

"We are here to see Major Wicks."

This was nothing but a hopeful guess as they weren't even sure if Major Wicks was in fact stationed here. The soldier narrowed his eyes but then swung his rifle over his shoulder with a big grin.

"Well, follow me then."

George and Esther exchanged confused looks. This was too easy, but the soldier who had already walked a few steps turned around again. "Come now, we ain't got all day. War is coming to town."

Esther tried to get up, but barely made it onto her knees before that unbearable ache almost made her cry her lungs out. Luckily George, who was climbing out of the train, didn't notice her face that must have every muscle frowning in agony. She bit down onto her lip. She had to get it together. So close, she told herself before forcing herself onto her wobbly legs. She was so damn close...

George turned around when she finally stood tall, hiding her misery with all she had left.

"Are you alright?"

"Yes, just a bit stiff," she lied. This was not the time to make this all about her. George had to get to the natives to work out a deal and save them from destruction, not sit by her bedside holding her hand while the military rolled over the Jicarilla Apaches like a train on full steam. George nodded over to her, his watchful eyes on her every move. He was smarter than that, clearly unconvinced.

Unlike Antonito, Chama had barely enough buildings to be considered a town. The vast majority of accommodations were white military tents swallowing the little village like a blue whale its krill. The few wooden makeshift saloons were packed with soldiers; however, the lack of prospectors, prostitutes, and cowboys made everything rather settled and calm. Orderly, military boozing...

The soldier walked them downtown, past a saloon built out of wooden planks that read 'Billy's' on it.

"If you got money and need a drink and rest, it doesn't get better than this one." The soldier pointed at Billy's without stopping.

Esther felt too weak to turn her head around to give Billy's one more look. Her aching body started to feel more like a ravaging fever, made only worse by the sweltering heat that made her head feel weighty and her eyes begging to shut down. Just a little longer, she told herself, biting her lip to keep herself from passing out. Her mind locked on every wavy step ahead of her, one mistake away from tumbling forward.

"Esther?"

A sharp pain radiated through her body, stemming from her festering wound. Little pearls of sweat were running down her face.

"Just a few more steps," she whimpered to herself, concentrating so hard on dragging her feet, she didn't even notice that the soldier and George weren't next to her any longer.

"Esther!"

She heard George call for her before she realized they had stopped. Why the hell was he calling her by her real name in front of the soldier?

"Esther!"

Her name rang like thunder across the dusty plains. She eyed George from a distance, but his lips weren't moving.

"…ESTHER!" the voice cried once more. And right there, just in front of Billy's, stood Jones. She would recognize this short and round man from miles away. For a brief moment she couldn't believe it, rubbing her droopy eyes. Was she hallucinating? But when she opened her eyes again, Jones was now right in front of her, his eyes and mouth ripped wide open in utter shock. Despite all her pain, an overwhelming feeling of relief took a hold of her, tears welling up behind burning eyelids.

"JONES!" she wailed, throwing herself into his arms, her body revived with a hidden reserve of energy that she must have saved for this very moment. Jones instantly wrapped his arms around her, holding her up to make sure she didn't fall, squeezing her tightly like a father his long-lost child.

"I don't understand," he murmured, his voice a mixture of worry, confusion, and joy. "What are you doing here?" he stood to face her, holding both of her shoulders.

Esther felt the numbing pain return, not only from the gunshot wound but also the wound deep in her heart. Her father, Morris, starving for weeks, the children, pretending to be someone else…

Tears started gushing down her dusty face like rain down a desert mountain.

"Oh Jones…it's father…"

Jones's eyes filled with panic.

"What is with your father? Is Cliff in trouble?"

"Ya know each other?" the soldier interrupted, scratching his head.

George also stepped in.

"Mr. Jones, might there be a place for a more private conversation?" he asked with a tone that implied that the conversation was rather 'explicitly' private. Jones gave a firm nod.

"Yes, of course. Come, child."

Placing his arm around Esther, gently steering her toward the saloon.

"I can't let ya do that," the soldier announced, reaching for Jones's arm to stop him in his tracks. "Ya'll have to see the major first. No-one in or out, those are the orders," he added like a teacher's pet reading the classroom rules.

"Well, why don't you take *Egan* here," George said, nodding toward Esther, "to your room and I shall talk to the major?" George turned to the soldier. "That shouldn't be a problem?"

The soldier took his hat off and scratched his dirty head, flinging dust off from his hair. "I guess," he finally said.

"Splendid," George said, joining the soldier who started walking again. "I shall join you shortly," he reassured Esther and Jones.

She nodded back before they parted ways, disappearing into the saloon with Jones who had nothing but worry written all over his face now.

"My poor child…," he whispered to her, shaking his head in disbelief. "My poor, poor child."

★

Jones gently placed Esther on a chair in his room, a struggle which took a while, before closing the door behind him. The room was simple, with nothing more than a table, two chairs, a bed and a wash basin. No rugs, curtains, or any form of décor. Yet, it was obvious that someone had been living in it for quite some time.

Clothes were hanging off the bed's railing and documents were scattered all over the table and floor. Jones kneeled in front of her, grabbing her hand. He had lost weight, she thought to herself as she studied the deep wrinkles under his eyes that his glasses unsuccessfully tried to hide. His silver hair was combed neatly as always, and he wore a black day suit with a tie. Even trapped out here he looked like a lawyer ready to go to court — or battle in this case.

"Your father…," he whispered, suspecting the worst. "Is he…?"

Esther now met his gaze and silently nodded, her tears bearing witness to her pain.

Jones's gaze sacked onto the floor, his hand trembling with eyes now tearing up as well. "I am so sorry…"

He turned to wipe his tears in private. Jones was a proud man and Esther gave him a moment before continuing with her story from hell. As her father's one and only true friend, he deserved nothing less.

Jones cleared his throat to compose himself, turning back to face her once more.

"But that isn't why you are here?" His voice was shaking, almost afraid to hear her answer.

"It's Morris, he is trying to take everything from me. He showed up with this lawyer, Gorsh. And then they presented a copy of a will in which father named Morris my guardian."

And for the first time since she had come to know Jones as a child, she witnessed him, a man who had never even raised his voice before, lose his temper. He barreled toward the table, slamming his fist onto it, his knuckles flushing as red as the evening sun.

"That son of a bitch!"

He slammed his fist again, causing the papers on it to flock wildly into the air, before tumbling toward the floor as if they too were outraged and in deep despair. Jones locked in on her gaze, his brown eyes darkening into hate. "I swear I shall not rest until he gets what he deserves."

"That will…" Esther took a deep breath, trying to ignore the pain that had crept further into her arm. "It was signed by father. It stated that Morris shall be my guardian until I marry or turn twenty-five."

Jones sneered, followed by a bark of laughter dedicated to the far-away Morris.

"What a fool! Does he really believe I would not challenge him in court the moment I return from this mess here? I shall have him for breakfast."

Jones put his hands on his belly that used to be bigger before he'd come out here but was still well-fed enough to demonstrate his love for good food.

"He must have thought of that when he made further plans to have me killed before you could make it back." Esther shook her head once more in disbelief about the whole mess. Talking to Jones was reminding her again of who she used to be, before Morris, that rat, had tried to claim the Silverton dynasty with all the monstrous tricks the devil's cards could hold.

Jones stopped laughing and analyzed her head to toe, his brows and forehead wrinkled with a look of worry and pity. She must look truly awful. Dressed like a man, covered with dirt and grime from riding a horse through the desert, and not only surviving the streets of New York but also a wild train ride that ended in her getting shot. She tried to suck in a deep breath but felt like she didn't have enough energy to do even that any longer.

"Is that why you are dressed like a man? To hide?"

Esther nodded, giving in to the urge to slump her body, letting it slowly slide out of the chair and onto the floor. Jones rushed over just in time to prevent her head from hitting the ground. He jerked off her hat, which was soaked in sweat from the little pearls that were forming on her forehead.

"My dear child, are you ill?"

She tried to shake her head, but it kind of just flopped instead. Jones pulled her into a sitting position and leaned closer to reach a hand to her forehead.

"You are burning up!"

Esther wanted to say something but could find neither the spirit nor the energy to do so. Her whole body was aching, flaming, crying in protest that drained every bit of strength she had left. She finally gave in to the heavy eyelids that were begging to shut down just for a moment or two.

"I should have never come here. They wanted me to deceive the natives, make them sign their lands away for free. I told them that Doug Jones does not steal from anybody."

She felt the warmth of Jones's hands under her knees and arms but was too tired to even dare a look. Only his voice was left to her comfort.

"All these terrible things that have happened to you during my absence. And now Cliff is dead. Silvia must be sick with worry… and what for?"

She felt the soft mattress of Jones's bed underneath her back and legs.

"Esther?"

She heard his voice fading, followed by a soft tap on her cheek.

"Esther!"

Then his voice silenced as Esther fell into the deep trance of her fever. Her last thought played an image of a once happy memory—George Astley smiling at her the first time they met. An outstretched hand reaching across the dim light, aching to hold onto it for one last time as she mumbled his name:

"George…" Was her last word, a faint smile on her face as her body went limp.

Unlike Major General Patterson, Major Wicks was a true frontier soldier. Born and bred locally, he had years under his soldier belt, fighting for different presidents of varying agendas, some of them fair, others not to speak of these days. But his work was always out here, in the Wild West, where he belonged.

George was standing in front of his desk, watching Major Wicks read the letter from Major General Patterson. His office was horribly dull, nothing but a desk with chairs and a little table with a bottle of whiskey on it—an appropriate décor for such a plain-looking place besides the nails on the walls holding his military hat and jacket.

His muddy boots resting on top of the desk, he rocked back and forth, his forty-something face and big bushy beard hidden behind the piece of paper that he was studying to the T.

"Well, George..." He lowered the letter. "Ya don mahnd if I call ya George, do ya? We ain gawt no lords an shit out hair."

George shook his head.

"Not at all." He sat down across from the major, crossing his legs elegantly.

"Mm-hmm. Daisy." Wicks leaned back in his chair again, rocking back and forth. "It's all in hair." He folded the letter back up. "If maah boss says ya kay-un gitty-up wherever ya want, then ya kay-un gitty-up wherever ya want with maah blessin'. Even up to them redskins."

George got up.

"Splendid. I shall waste your time no more then," he said and was about to turn when Major Wicks took a loud deep breath in to announce there was a *but* on its way.

"However..." Major Wicks pulled his feet off the table and leaned over his desk, hovering over the letter. George sat back down, sighing heavily with a pinched expression.

"This leder says squat about guh-rantin' ya supplies, eend as ya know, we gawt them marchin' orders, so all supplies in burg are now confiscated."

What the bloody hell did this guy want? George wrinkled his forehead and crossed his arms to signal this very question to Major Wicks in silence. He seemed to have gotten the message.

"All ah want is the truth about what ya really up to with them Indians up thair."

George narrowed his eyes, studying this man in front of him. Why would he even care? Was he hoping for a war? Bored to death out here? Ready for some blood? Maybe George could smooth-talk his way out of this...

He opened his mouth to say something, but the major interrupted before he got a word out.

"An don' ya be lyin' to me. Ah called out lies from me-yn beggin' for their lives. Ah sure as blazes will catch a lie from a man askin' for a horse an some beans for his journey up to them natives," he commanded wagging his finger at George. "But awf course ya don't have to tell me. Ya kay-yun always walk uhp their on them tender beetle-crushers awf yours."

George was looking at the man in front of him who was now trying to get a piece of food stuck in his tooth out with a big sharp knife. Besides George not understanding half of what Wicks was saying, this was one of the few times he had no idea where to place this man. His sharp senses were pretty much in a deep slumber. Was he trying to find out if George would rob him of an exciting opportunity to kill natives, or was Wicks simply trying to protect his men? George decided to take the risk and go with the old saying that the truth is incontrovertible.

"I bought a lot of that native land that the government sold to the miners. Now I want to offer the natives their land back and ask for permission to mine the land for gold."

Wicks stared at George for a moment as if he was waiting for him to laugh. But his face stayed as serious as that of a dead man. Suddenly the major lost it.

"That's what ya told Major General Patterson?" he was barely able to spit out, slapping his hand onto his desk before throwing his head back in uncontrollable laughter.

"More or less…"

"That's thuh dad gum craziest thang ah have evher heard!" He continued blasting away, his unkempt beard moving with his shaking head as if it was alive.

George couldn't help but roll his eyes in annoyance. Never in his life had anybody ever laughed at him like that. But then, hearing it out loud like this, it did sound pretty foolish.

"I guess you can say that." He pursed his lips.

"Oh, come awn now. Ahm just kiddin'. Ya kay-yun have whatever ya need, just as the baws wants it." He chuckled, wiping a tear away.

George raised an eyebrow. "Excuse me?"

Wicks grabbed the major general's letter and held it up.

"Ah know dung from wild honey. You never upset the major general, not me... no-no," he declared nodding his head.

"Does that...mean I get my horse and beans?" George inquired carefully.

"It shaw as blazes does."

George sat for a moment in silence, his head still wrinkled in confusion.

"So we are good?" he asked, just to make sure.

"We good," the major confirmed.

"All right?" George slowly got up, testing the waters.

"Alraahyt," the major repeated his words with a grin. All of a sudden, George remembered that he also had to find Billy. In all this chaos and horror, he'd almost completely forgotten about his old friend who also happened to own the other half of the land he wanted to present to the natives.

"One more thing, I have a friend whose name is Billy—"

"Tall, skinny fellow with a burn awn his hand?"

That was him!

"Yes! Is he here?" George stumbled a step forward in a clumsy mixture of relief and surprise. Wicks put his boots back on his desk.

"He shaw is. Owns the saloon."

"B-billy's is Billy's?" George stuttered in awe about how obvious and simple it was. It was right in front of him; how had he failed to notice? Looks like Lady Luck was looking his way again.

Wicks rolled his eyes.

"Yes. Billy's is… Billy's," he said, as if he was talking to a simple-minded child.

"It's been a looong week," George countered, a bit embarrassed.

"Mm-hmm… Teyn-dollar Stetson on a five-cent head…" Wicks mumbled to himself but loud enough for George to hear.

"I do not know what that means, but fair enough." George smiled at him, and for the first time in a while, he meant it. He opened the door and was about to leave when Wicks shouted after him.

"Oh, one more thang… Whe-yn ya git your horse, don' git them banktail, get them barn sour." He smirked. "Or ya will wawk back after all."

George tipped his hat with a nod. For some unexplainable reason, he liked this guy.

"I shall keep that in mind, not the bangtail…" George shook his head. "Whatever the bloody hell that means," he mumbled, closing the door behind him.

He couldn't help but notice that his steps felt lighter on his way to Billy's. He hadn't seen his friend in ages, and to hear him well let alone thriving as a saloon owner, was like feeling the much-welcomed sun after a long thunderstorm.

"Whiskey, and not your rotgut," George demanded in an American accent from Billy, hiding his face under his hat.

Billy was about George's age, and not too bad on the eye. He was wearing a white cotton shirt and brown pants. His dark hair was combed nicely, and he was even clean-shaven, a luxury most men in this area didn't have the time or interest to do. But none of that surprised George. Billy was one of these men who could be thrown into a pit and still find a way to make the best of it, so seeing him thriving in a town he was pretty much imprisoned in was typical for Billy.

"I don' have no rotgut, only the good stuff," Billy said with hurt pride, placing a glass in front of George.

"Splendid, as I am only used to the grandest of liquors," George jested in an overly arrogant, British accent. Billy jerked George's hat right off his head. His wide-open eyes blinked before his head finally flopped backwards and he barked out in loud laughter to catch his breath.

"I—will—be—damned!" He shouted so loudly, the whole saloon stopped for a moment to see what was going on. Billy was now storming around the bar to give George a strong, manly hug.

"I will be damned!" he repeated, slapping George on the back with a loud thump that caused George to cough a little.

"It's good to see you too, Billy." He pulled himself out of the hug to step back and take a closer look at his friend. Same old Billy with those lively brown eyes and contagious grin on his face.

"To see ME? What in the Lord's name are *you* doing here?" Billy sat down at the bar, reaching over to grab a bottle of whiskey and two glasses.

"I haven't heard from you in months, so I thought why not cross the globe to see what Billy is up to." George smiled.

Billy filled both glasses, his smile waning.

"I tried, George, I did. But the damn government pretty much cut us off the map. At first, they said only for a few days, but the days turned to weeks, and weeks to months." Billy seemed a little bitter, swigging down his whiskey only to refill it.

"So I have heard." George nodded, squeezing Billy's shoulder. "Don't blame yourself. I'm just relieved to see you so well. Owner of *Billy's*." He grinned, playfully swatting at his friend. But Billy did not return his cheerfulness.

"George…as much as I would love to spend time with you drinking and jesting like the old days, I have to talk to you about something very important first…" His head leaned down and his voice was as soft as a whisper. George knew exactly what this was all about.

"Don't trouble yourself. I know about the land, Billy." His hand was still on Billy's now tensed shoulder. Shame flickered in Billy's eyes, replacing that once happy sparkle he was so famous for.

"You do?"

George nodded his head and emptied his whiskey. "Yes."

The air filled with silence for a brief moment as both men stared onto their empty whiskey glasses.

"I'm so sorry about all of this, George. If I'd known I would have never —"

"I know, Billy, I know. Please don't blame yourself," George said, cutting him off. There was no need for his friend to beg for forgiveness or be eaten up with shame. Billy was a good man. When he'd approached George back then about this land, he did so with good intentions. Nothing more and nothing less but to help George out of his financial hardships.

Billy was still staring at his empty glass that he held with both hands. He was clearly struggling with shame, nonetheless.

"I am still deeply sorry," Billy mumbled, refilling their glasses. George squeezed his friend's shoulder one last time before he pounded the whiskey in one go and stood up.

"I'm afraid we will have to continue this conversation another time. Do you know where I have to go to get a horse and provisions?"

Billy stood up beside him. "Is everything alright?" he asked with a hint of worry.

"That my friend, I shall soon find out myself. One way or the other." George put his hat back on. "Do you think you could help me? I shall explain on the way to the stables..."

Billy waved to a man who was serving food to the tables.

"Take over," he shouted to him. The man simply nodded without any emotion and continued with his work.

"I need a barn sour." George repeated Major Wicks' words walking out of the saloon. Billy followed him.

"A barn sour?" He stopped in his tracks, and much to George's surprise, without the slightest bit of amusement.

"Please tell me you're not heading up to them Indians."

"You know what a barn sour is?" George asked, throwing Billy off.

"Of course. It's the opposite of a bangtail," he declared, as if it was the most normal thing in the world.

George frowned.

"Stop throwing me off like a wild mustang would a rabbit." Billy crossed his arms. "You are heading up to them natives; that's why you want them barn sour, don't ya?"

George nodded, dropping his gaze onto the dusty, mud-filled ground before looking right at his friend.

"I will offer to return my share of their land to them and hope they will let me mine it in exchange for a fair share."

Billy looked at George as if he was waiting for him to say that all of this was a joke, but he didn't. His eyes held Billy's gaze with an intense stare. Billy threw his arms up.

"That is the dad gum craziest thang I've ever heard!"

"So I am told." George let out a sigh.

"They'll shoot you at first sight!"

"Let's hope not."

"Has the sun burned all logic out of your head?"

"Perhaps…"

Billy let out a sharp breath and started walking again.

"Where are you going?" George wondered catching up with him.

"Getting a barn sour — for two."

"No, you are certainly not." George protested, but Billy wouldn't have it, not even wasting a second to look.

"The hell I am. I've traded with them before. I might be your only chance to get a word out before a bullet finds its way into your chest."

George tried to keep up with Billy. He didn't like the idea one bit but what he said made sense. He knew the area and if he had really managed to trade with the Apache before, Billy was indeed his best chance of coming back alive without a bullet or perhaps an arrow in his head.

"Besides, if we throw our share of the land together, they might take us seriously."

Billy turned off the main street and onto a small path. "I would be more than fine with an honest mining permit over owning land soaked in blood."

With a faint smile on his lips, George couldn't help but be grateful for a friend like Billy. Granted he'd got them into this mess in the first place, but by no means did he have to risk his life and share to get them out of it. He was not the one at the brink of ruin with a sister engaged to a monster and "one breath away from—God forbid—having to marry Emily Wayne," George unwittingly uttered the last part out loud, shaking his head in disbelief.

"Emily Wayne?" Billy wrinkled his forehead.

"I will explain on the ride up there," he replied, still shaking his head in disbelief over everything that had happened on this trip.

Billy laughed. "Sounds like your noble life of servants tying your shoes and wiping your ass has been shaken up a bit by my good old America." George couldn't help but laugh as well.

"The *blazes* it has," George joked back, "the blazes it has!"

CHAPTER 13

Peggy nipped at George every time he was in reach for her to do so. George swore by everything that was holy to him that he saw a smile on her horse mouth every time she got him, which Billy brushed off, stating it was just a darn horse.

"Ol' Peg don' like to move," An older cowboy sitting on the porch in front of *Billy's* spat onto the floor. He smirked when Peggy nipped at George again and this time sank a dull teaser bite into his lower arm.

"Stop that, Peggy!" he reprimanded her, all under the cheerful eyes of Billy, who ended up with the far better deal of their two barn sours—which turned out to be lazy horses that loved their stalls and were useless to the natives.

"She likes you," Billy said tying Susie, his lazy but easy-going mare, to the post.

"I am afraid the feeling might not be mutual," George mumbled, stepping back just in time before Peggy got him again, much to everybody's amusement.

After George had finally managed to tie Peggy to the post, which had taken four tries with him constantly jerking various body parts out of her reach, he made his way up to Jones's room to check on Esther and inform her about his plan to leave right away. He was hoping that Jones would be able to draw up some legal papers that would focus on returning the lands in return for rights to mine, splitting the profits evenly.

George leaned an ear closer, gently placing his hands on its rough timber door. There was nothing but odd silence ended by a loud thump followed by constant creaking. Taking one final breath, George gave a firm knock at his door.

"Come in!" Jones's desperate voice shouted through the door. Billy and George exchanged quick, worried looks before George tore the door open. His heart stopped, lungs failing as he gasped for air. Esther was not back in a dress happily babbling about how Jones had figured everything out, she was lying on Jones's bed soaked in sweat, tossing herself left and right, mumbling feverish prayers.

"Esther!"

George dropped his saddle bag and stormed over to her side, throwing himself on his knees next to the bed. He flinched as he grabbed her hand. Her raging fever burned into his skin. He pulled aside her shirt and vest to expose her gunshot wound, festering in puddles of yellow and red. Pus had soaked the linen that aided as a bandage. It looked absolutely awful.

"Have you called the doctor?!" George shouted at Jones, who exchanged the cold rag on her forehead with a fresh one, his eyes filled with deep sorrow and worry.

"I have telegraphed—"

"TELEGRAPHED?!" George interrupted him. "You don't have a doctor in town?"

Billy and Jones exchanged anxious looks, their eyes filled with utter fear.

"I'm afraid not. The closest doctor would be in Alamosa or Santa Fe, both about two days away." Jones sighed with grief.

George turned back to Esther, leaning close to her face, tears swelling in his eyes. Not once in his life had he experienced such pain or anxiety as he did in this very moment. The thought of losing her was like a knife stabbing into his heart.

"Esther…" he whispered, leaning his head against her hot cheek. "Esther can you hear me…?"

Nothing. No response whatsoever.

His head sagged down onto her arm, despair choking him up from the inside. This could not be it. She couldn't just leave him like this. His brave little guide, now his fragile little lover.

"Is there nobody in town who could help?" George begged. Jones and Billy threw each other searching stares again.

"A…wet nurse…healer…ANYBODY?" he cried out, holding Esther's burning hand closely against his cheek.

Billy let out a loud sigh, instantly drawing Jones and George's attention to him.

"There…is…a…a medicine man…" he carefully stated, knowing he was entering dangerous territory.

"The Apaches?" Jones clarified, his eyes and mouth wide open as if Billy had just said the unthinkable. He then wildly shook his head.

"Why not? Their knowledge of healing plants is far superior to ours. The doctor from Santa Fe said so himself when that girl was bit by the rattler, remember?"

"That might be… But Billy…where have you been over the last few months? With me here imprisoned in Chama or on the moon?" Jones barked sarcastically, clearly letting off steam as a way of dealing with his own pain. "We have mistreated the Apache for months. Stolen from them, trying to trick them into these despicable agreements. Now you want their assistance in healing our sick? Out of the question! They will never agree to this! They will rightfully shoot us on sight!"

"The natives use herbs that we don't know of. It's worth a shot." Billy pleaded his case, stepping closer to Jones who pushed him out of the way to get fresh water from the basin.

"That might be, but why the hell would they help us? We have nothing they could possibly want!"

George jumped up at Jones's statement.

"What did you just say?"

"I said we have nothing they could possibly want," Jones repeated in annoyance. But what Jones didn't know was that George happened to be in possession of the only thing they'd ever wanted—and rightfully so!

"What if I could give them their land back?" he asked Jones, who sat back down on the chair next to Esther, gently cooling her forehead with a fresh, wet rag.

"And how would you do that, unless…" Jones froze in his tracks and jerked his head from Esther to stare at George.

"But of course! You are the English nobleman who bought half of the darn mountain! Up by the big lake!" He let out a sarcastic laugh. "One of the very reasons the government is trying so hard to keep this land rather than admitting they've made a mistake and return it."

"What do you mean?" George narrowed his eyes.

"Jones…leave it be." Billy stepped in. "You know as well as I do that the white men wanted the natives gone long before these idiots found gold up there and sold the Apache land with the natives on it."

But George held his hand up in Billy's direction to signal him to stay out of this. He faced Jones again.

"What do you mean?" George repeated in a more demanding tone.

"Very well..." Jones returned to tending to Esther. "Billy is right about the white men wanting the natives gone one way or the other. So don't blame yourself too much. However, it is also true that during the endless negotiations and talks between the government and the natives, we came close to buying out most of the miners to return the land to the natives. But a few senators back in Washington refused to contact the English investor to negotiate a refund of his investment overseas. They argued that the relations to England were still fragile, the war of our independence still too fresh in everybody's memory. They believe a few 'redskin souls' wouldn't be worth the trouble of upsetting the English aristocracy, or even worse, the Queen. They feared that a lengthy court battle with England would make the US government look like the fools they were when they sold the natives' land to folks in the first place."

Jones's words settled on George like Thor's mighty hammer. The silence in the room was crushing. George had had no idea that he was not only an innocent investor in all of this, but the unknowing culprit.

It was Esther who pulled everybody out of their thoughts and back into the present. A weak sigh escaped her throat, drawing everybody's focus back onto the pressing issues at hand here.

George nodded his head in silence. None of this mattered any longer. The dice were rolled, the path determined. There would be no gold, only what was right—and her life!

"They shall have their land back. All of it. I don't want it. I just want her to live."

Jones threw him a look as if he wanted to apologize for his harsh words. Billy now stepped forward as well.

"They can have my share back too. It's not as big as yours, but still… I should never have talked you into buying this land without knowing all the details. Besides," he said, lifting his chin in pride, "under all the whiskey and cards, I am a God-fearing man, and I doubt the boss above would like me getting rich by stealing land from women and children."

George was deeply moved. This was by any measure absolutely the worst time of his life, but at the same time he'd also got to experience true love. He nodded over to Billy, his eyes filled with tears and gratefulness. If he were ever to possess a single dime to his name again, he would repay his loyal friend, with everything he had to offer.

"Is there a way we can stop the government from re-claiming the land once we hand it back to the natives?" George asked Jones, gently running his hand over Esther's cheek. Jones tilted his head, deep in thought for a moment as if he was trying to pull a rabbit from a magic hat.

"We could write up an agreement. If we keep you as the owner only by name, the government would have a very hard time taking the land from you to remove the natives for the miners with claims around your land. We can include a clause that shall grant the natives the sole use of the land for eternity or until they sell it. There is a law —"

"Yeah, yeah," Billy interrupted him, with a dismissive wave of his hand while rushing to the door. Judging by both men's body language, this seemed to occur quite often between the two men during their confinement here—Jones talking legal jargon, and Billy cutting him off.

"I will get a cart so we can leave immediately," Billy declared, shutting the door behind him. Things started moving again—quickly. Jones jumped up and started packing a leather bag with documents and ink in a great hurry.

"I'm coming with you," he announced.

George eyed him, measuring the man behind the lawyer. Of course, he would not tell Jones that he couldn't, he had no right to do so, but just by the looks of him it was obvious that Jones had never fired a gun in his life before. The least he could do was to warn him of the dangers.

"It might be a one-way trip."

Jones grabbed another paper off his desk, dismissing George's warning with a simple shrug.

"Cliff, her father, was my best friend. The Lord has never blessed me with children, but that girl whose hand you're holding is not far from being my own. I'm coming with you and that's the end of it."

George nodded as a silent sign of respect.

"G-George...," Esther suddenly whispered, throwing her head to the side in pain. She was still deep in her fevers, eyes closed shut.

"I'm here," he whispered back, gently squeezing her hand. "Don't worry, you'll get better soon. I promise it on my life, my love. I won't let you leave on the next adventure without me."

It must have been around noon as the sun was towering high above them, unleashing its hot shine onto the mighty mountains and plains, and tiny travelers alike. Under different circumstances, George would have marveled at the breathtaking beauty of this land: golden fields as far as the eyes could see, always accompanied by the breathtaking Rockies behind. George had never seen brighter and thicker clouds before, their white beauty swirling up in artful formations high into the sky.

The Jicarilla Apache's land was only two hours from Chama. Billy had managed to return with a wagon he'd borrowed from the military, so they wasted no time heading out on nothing short of a suicide mission. Nobody wanted to say it, but there was that universal worry thickening the air, making it barely breathable. The natives would not trust them. And why should they? An army was at their front door with marching orders to take their land from them like thieves.

George was sitting in the wooden cart next to Esther, one hand holding hers, the other ready to draw his pistol. Billy was driving the cart, with Jones seated next to him, both nervously jerking toward every sound the Rocky Mountain landscape could produce. But Esther's wheezing breath was most audible to all of them, sucking up her last bit of energy, making her even too weak to whisper George's name again, something she had done a few times earlier. George was unblinking, anxiously staring down at her for the slightest signs that things might get worse, something he feared could happen every second. He'd held Esther's hand close to his heart since they had left. She was soaked in sweat, her cheeks bright red from fever. The sight of her chipped away at his already fragile heart, falling into a thousand tiny little pieces, each piece heavier than the next. He leaned closer to listen to her breath as they made their race against time.

"Faster," he shouted up front to Billy who was giving Peggy another urgent wiggle on the reins. She understood this command perfectly well and picked up speed with a little neigh, pushing the wooden cart to its limit on the bumpy grounds of the seemingly endless golden fields. If the natives could see Peggy like this, they might still think her a bangtail after all.

Suddenly Billy jerked back drastically, pulling on the reins as they came to a complete halt.

George let go of Esther's hand, scouting the area with nervous, jerky movements.

"What is it?"

"There." Billy pointed straight ahead to a tall, red rock formation with a wide opening in it.

"Lord give us strength," Jones prayed. George now focused his gaze on the rock formation ahead of them. It almost looked as if there were wagon wheels hanging off its cliffs.

"Are those…"

"Wagon wheels," Billy confirmed, shooting glances at the wall as if he were trying to tear it down with his eyes.

"It's a warning. As ya know, we whites have a bit of an issue with respecting their boundaries." Billy gave Peggy a soft wiggle with the reins. She understood and trod slower than before. It almost seemed as though even she didn't want to give off the wrong intentions, let alone come as a threat.

George pressed his lips flat as the cart slowly made its way past the wagon wheels and into the canyon.

He looked up to the edge of the rocks, and for a brief moment he thought he had seen something move. But once he narrowed his eyes to escape the blinding rays of the sun and focus his view on the very spot again, it was gone.

"Did you see that?" He leaned over to Billy, almost whispering. All three men now scouted the upper edges of the canyon, slowly turning heads and eyes with their hands in plain sight and away from their weapons.

"I think so," Billy whispered back, clearly nervous.

"Why aren't they showing themselves?" Jones asked, crossing and uncrossing his arms and legs anxiously.

"They are observing us, to see what we want," George guessed, scouting the area left and right of their cart. This was nerve-wracking. He needed to calm himself, find his usual composed self. He took a deep breath, forcing his heart to slow down, going from wildly pounding to a rhythmic, calm beat.

All of a sudden, out of nowhere, a shadow rushed right in front of Peggy, who abruptly jerked back a step with a startled neigh, giving everybody a good shake. And as the shadow in front of them now became flesh and blood, it was clear that they were no longer alone in the canyon.

Stepping out of the corners of their vision, there they were. In their full glory — the Jicarilla Apache were here!

Several of their men lined up on top of the canyon. The man in front of Peggy was now joined by several other warriors, all of them holding rifles to their chest. George had seen paintings of natives before, but not in his wildest dreams did he imagine to ever stand right in front of them one day. Most of the men were wearing leather war shirts and breeches with fringes along the shoulders and sleeves. Their long, black hair was either loosely moving with the wind, or tied together hanging on the sides of their faces, tamed by red cloth headbands on their foreheads. Some of the warriors were wearing military hats or jackets and for some reason, there was one woman amongst them as well, towering high above George on top of the canyon. She was dressed very similarly to the men, but was wearing a skirt instead of breeches, heavily decorated with different colored beads that shimmered like a rainbow under the scorching sun. Nobody was moving. The Apache did an excellent job at staring down their intruders, making it impossible to read their faces. George slowly lifted his hands to show that he meant no harm.

"We are here to trade." His own voice echoed through the canyon as if someone else had spoken the words. And as his voice was swallowed in the far distance, time just kept passing, but the Apache didn't move an inch, nor even blink once. Billy, George, and Jones exchanged edgy looks.

"Trade," Billy repeated cautiously, placing his hand on his chest and then stretching it out toward the young native closest to the cart, the one who'd startled Peggy. But the young warrior who was distinguished from the others by having white face paint run from his lower eyelids down his cheeks, only gave him an icy stare in return.

George now hesitantly moved his foot a few inches to test the waters, see if the natives would allow him to do so. And they did, none of them even flinching in the slightest. So, George slowly started to climb out of the cart, almost in slow motion, careful not to misstep. He was hanging over the edge of the cart, one of his feet already safely on the ground, when his pants got caught on a nail and he lost his balance, falling onto his knees, dust forcefully swirling into his mouth and eyes. In a matter of seconds, accompanied by metallic clicks, every darn rifle in this canyon was now pointing at them.

George didn't dare to move or get back up on his feet but instead stretched his hands up high into the sky. Billy and Jones followed suit, slowly elevating their hands high up above their ears. For how long they stood there like that, listening to the desert winds move dust from one place to another, nobody knew, but out of nowhere, interrupting the deadening silence and singing winds, Esther let out a loud, painful moan. It instantly caught the attention of the young warrior with the white facial marks, stretching his neck over the barrel of his rifle to catch a glimpse of her. He slowly lowered it and stepped closer toward the cart. George was about to jump up to stop him, but Billy wildly shook his head to signal him to let it happen. The Apache man now peeked into the cart, narrowing his eyes in curiosity.

"Dide," he suddenly said, looking straight at George, then at Billy and Jones.

"Dide," he repeated as if saying it a second time would help them understand. But George, Jones, and Billy simply exchanged lost glances.

"Dide 'izdzanii." The young warrior now turned toward his people, shouting all the way up to his backup towering on top. Another warrior, who was around George's age and was wearing a blue soldier hat, now lowered his weapon and walked up to the cart to see for himself. George got a better glimpse of him. He had long hair that was tied up in the back. His artfully crafted leather shirt looked soft and comfortable. A beautiful necklace decorated with beads hung loosely from his neck in the form of a big 'T.'

"Your native woman is sick," he said to George, waving at the others to lower their guns.

For a moment George just stood there, his eyes blinking rapidly in the sun, confused by the fact that this warrior not only spoke English, but had also called Esther a native.

"Native woman?" George carefully asked. Jones now jumped off the cart and rushed over to George and the native man.

"Cherokee." He pointed at Esther. "Her mother was Cherokee," he said hastily while opening his leather bag.

"We are here to trade. Land for medicine." Jones pulled out a piece of parchment with something written on it, stretching it in front of the man. But the Jicarilla Apache warrior simply stared at him with a wary look before turning around and walking past Jones and the cart and back to where he'd come from.

George managed to squeeze a breath and turned to Jones with a searching gaze.

"Esther is half native?"

What else did he not know about the woman he loved, he thought to himself with a feeling of resentment.

"Yes," Jones mumbled at the sight of the native man walking off, leaving him disheartened, his head bowing down to the dirt. This man seemed to have a say around here as the other natives followed his example and also started to leave the canyon.

George ripped the paper out of Jones's hand and rushed after the warrior. It couldn't just end like this!

"We can give you back your land. A lot of it." He desperately tried to convince the man, blocking his way to hold the parchment up in front of his face. The man seemed to read the paper, a gesture that filled George with hope, but then he simply walked around George, ignoring him again as if he was air. Panic assailed George as the worry of losing Esther started to creep through him like poison. He peered over his shoulder to Billy and Jones who seemed just as lost as he was, with Billy kicking a rock in frustration and Jones falling on his back against the cart, staring onto the dirt with dead eyes. Everyone was lost. George crumbled to his knees.

"Please, help us. I beg you!" He was ready to slave his life away if that would help, ready to do anything they asked of him, if it would only save her. Suddenly, the warrior turned around again. George shot back up onto his feet.

"All of you…" His deep voice boomed across the mountains like it was part of the air around it. "Come speak to my father."

George felt an electric current rushing through him.

"YES!" he enthusiastically yelled after the man as he sprinted back to the cart. Billy and Jones were already pulling themselves back up onto the driver's bench.

"Come on Peg," Billy hollered, signaling the lady in front to get going.

The cart started moving, picking up George, who swung himself over into the back next to Esther, along the way.

"Can we trust them?" Jones asked out loud to whoever of the two wanted to answer his question. Billy stayed quiet, which wasn't a good sign.

"It would only matter if we had a choice..." George said, holding Esther's hand close to his heart with his one hand while using his other hand to wave cool air toward her with his hat. She didn't look like she had much of a fight left in her. Up until about an hour ago she would hold on to his hand, but now, it limped lifeless as a rock.

It took another hour to get to the Apache's campsite. They had to abandon the cart and carry Esther the last twenty minutes or so as the path to the camp led through rocky terrain before opening into vast, grassy plains. Before entering the campsite, the man who spoke their language made some sounds that seemed to signal the others to let them pass.

The campsite itself was made of hundreds of teepees set up closely together. People were going about their business when George, followed by Billy and Jones, entered their campsite carrying Esther. They passed women and children weaving baskets and scraping hides staked to the ground, when suddenly everybody stopped with their work to nudge the intruders forward into an open place within the heart of their nation, surrounding them while talking in their native language. Billy and Jones exchanged anxious glances, unsure of the notion of what this all meant. George maneuvered Esther's motionless body as well as he could to avoid the constant grabbing of her arms and hands by tribal women.

An older man wearing a full eagle-feathered warbonnet now stepped into the circle, followed by the native man who was wearing the soldier hat. The older Apache raised his hand, causing the loud chatter to drop into dead silence. He crossed his arms, his eagle eyes running up and down over the four of them, but mostly lingering on George and Esther. This man hadn't even said a word, yet he had that energy around him that made others feel as if he held the wisdom and secrets of the world inside him. The younger Apache now leaned closer to the Chief and said something in their native tongue. After he was done, nobody spoke again, respectfully waiting for the Chief to take all the time in the world to do whatever he saw fit. Then the Chief spoke in their language for all to hear. The man in the soldier hat translated.

"My father asks what you have to offer for the life of this woman."

George stepped closer to the Chief, squeezing Esther tightly against his chest.

"Land."

He stopped, thinking about his next words. He had to speak wisely as there was not much time to explain a complex legal situation and more importantly, not say something foolish that would ruin everything.

"The land that was stolen from you. I will give the parts back that were given to me and my friend." At this point, George wouldn't even dare to add mining rights for him to the agreement. That train was long gone, a different time and deal. Now all that mattered was to save the woman he loved.

The Chief's son translated what had just been said for everybody to hear, but mainly for his father. At least that is what George was hoping. But after the translation was finished, the Chief just stared at George in silence.

"It's a lot of land. The whole mountain." George tried to push his case. He was sounding desperate, and rightfully so as Esther's situation was taking a sharp decline, getting worse by the minute.

"We even brought a lawyer." Billy jumped in to aid his friend. He gave Jones a little push forward into the spotlight while at the same time tearing him out of his state of frozen fear. It worked. Jones shook his head and opened his bag.

"Y-yes. I-I'm the lawyer, remember? I already wrote up the agreement for all the parties involved," he stuttered, holding the parchment up to the Chief, who, unlike his son earlier, accepted it with a long, frowning stare. He said something to his son while he held the paper up against the sun as if he wanted to see if the parchment would catch on fire and burn away the lies their people had had to endure for generations.

"My father wants to know if this will keep the white men away and approve the application for land he had sent out to your government over ten years ago. We are one of the last tribes without legal rights to our land."

George and Billy were completely lost, but Jones on the other hand seemed to know what application the Jicarilla Apache Chief was referring to. He took a deep breath to calm his nerves and stepped closer.

"I can't promise that," Jones answered honestly, shaking his head. This answer might not please the tribe but George understood why he hadn't lied. These people had been robbed of their land, killed, sold as slaves by the Spanish, forcefully relocated by the army, lied to over and over again. They deserved every bit of honesty the world had to offer.

"But…" Jones pressed his palms together as if he was saying a desperate prayer. "I swear to everything that is holy to me, I shall do whatever is in my power to help you with your petition. And this paper," he said, pointing at the paper the Chief was holding, "will give us a fighting chance in court."

The Chief leaned over to his son to receive his translation. Just like before, he stood there staring down at all of them, before lifting his arms up to the sky.

"Li yeedondi isdzan," was all he said before he turned around, splitting the crowd, and faded through them. The silence was broken by the start of one chant that turned into dozens, their mesmerizing voices rippling across the plains under the vast clear skies. The women closed in on George and started pulling Esther, tearing her out of George's arms. He wanted to stop them, fight them if he must, but the Chief's son grabbed him by his arm.

"They will heal her," he informed George. "Come. We will now smoke the sacred pipe to sign the agreement."

The relief that swept through George was so powerful, his legs almost gave in. The Jicarilla Apache had accepted his offer. Billy let out a huge breath, while Jones on the other hand, wiped away sweat off his forehead with a trembling hand.

"I'll be damned! You did it!" Billy swatted George on his shoulder.

"Maybe I'm not so foolish after all." George now also let out a huge breath.

"Let's not go that far," Billy joked.

They followed the Chief and his son past the gathered crowd and into the shadows and coolness of a large, distinguishable teepee tent, muffling the endless chanting from the other side. None of this guaranteed that Esther would recover, but at least she had a fair chance now. The natives were famous for their natural remedies. If anybody could help her now, it was them.

George and the others sat down on soft pelts in front of a little fire. The teepee had several ornaments hanging from its walls. Some of them were round with feathers braided into them.

"Sacred hoops. My children like to sleep here, and it catches their bad dreams," the Chief's son explained as he noticed George staring at the dreamcatchers.

"It's beautiful."

"Ka-e-te-nay." The Chief's son now pointed to his father. "It means Warrior and Chief."

George nodded humbly toward the Chief.

"George," he replied touching his hand to his chest before pointing at Billy and Jones to introduce them as well. The chief nodded in response.

"Itza-chu." The chief's son pointed at himself. "It means great hawk," he explained, proudly picking up a pipe that was heavily decorated with eagle feathers. "When the white men took me away from my father, I was still a small boy, forced to speak their language and read their words. They re-named me John," Itza-chu told

George, putting some sort of dried herbs into the pipe. "But when my father rescued me, John stayed with the white men and Itza-chu returned to his father."

George nodded respectfully. He couldn't even begin to imagine the hardships these people had had to endure and were still going through.

One of the others who had joined them handed George a pipe heavily decorated with feathers. It was the most remarkable pipe he had ever seen. But something warned George that this was not like the usual cigars he sometimes smoked in the library after dinner. He suppressed a grimace at the sight of it, wondering what magical powders and herbs were placed in this pipe. But nothing mattered at this point, except Esther. He would do whatever it took to be by Esther's side again soon. Besides, he thought to himself trying to be optimistic, this might be the greatest honor ever bestowed on a man like him.

George leaned in, wrapping his lips around the pipe, taking one deep breath that seemed to have kicked him straight in his throat, instantly coughing his brains out, which united everybody—natives and whites alike—to burst into loud laughter.

The whole ceremony of the agreement lasted less than thirty minutes, at least for George and the others. The natives seemed to prepare for a big celebration, the whole campsite shouting and moving, swirling around like busy bees.

Jones and Billy had left for Chama the moment the Chief had put his signature on that piece of paper that would hopefully not only delay the march on the Jicarilla Apache, but maybe even save them for good. Jones had to get the document in front of Major Wicks without delay so they could telegraph Major General Patterson right away. At first, Billy wanted to stay behind, but George had convinced him that it was more important to make sure Jones got back safely. It came as no surprise that George felt safer here with the natives than he did around the cowboys who actually did try to rob and shoot him. They were peaceful and honorable people and only showed their warrior side when they were forced to do so.

George entered the teepee where Esther was being cared for and found her naked from the waist up and wet cloths covering her bare chest. Several women were tending to her different needs. One of the older women was rubbing herbs into her wound while another woman was singing, rocking back and forth next to a fire which made shadows dance across the tent. She was most likely singing prayers. His throat tightened seeing Esther like this. That heavy weight that seemed to have been lifted when the Chief had agreed to help her was back again, clinging to his chest as his heart sunk into dark, murky waters.

Grabbing her weak hand, he sat down on a pelt next to her. He would not leave her side again, no matter what. Even if the world itself broke apart, he would stay here by her side and die holding her in his arms. This woman in front of him was his world now. She'd swept him off his feet long before he even knew who she really was. She made him laugh and filled the deepest corners of his soul with love. She had even risked her life for him. Not once, but twice.

"I love you," he whispered against her hand, kissing it. "I love you more than you will ever know…"

CHAPTER 14

orris sat down in front of Major Wicks. There was only one chair, so Morris took the freedom to take it and let Mr. Gorsh stand next to him. This dusty, little New Mexican town had already thinned his patience. He hated it here.

"So that sick boy that went awn to them Indians is a girl that ran away?" Major Wicks repeated Morris's words, rocking back and forth in his chair.

"Yes. She is my ward."

Morris placed Cliff's will along with the wanted poster in front of him. Major Wicks curiously picked them both up.

"I have been turning every stone to find her. She is confused and all alone out there. She needs me," Morris sighed, trying to look depressed. The major raised an eyebrow.

"Alive or...*dead*?" He narrowed his eyes, locking them in on the questionable man in front of him. The major was a simple man, but no fool.

Morris slapped his hand against his breastbone in a loud thump, playing a theater act that was supposed to look like shock and horror.

"A mistake! These savage bounty hunters changed the poster, I guess to make it easier for them to catch her and get the reward." He shook his head looking down at the floor with a frown. "I was worried sick something might have happened to the dear child."

The major lit a cigar. "Mm-hmm...," he mumbled.

"I am so relieved to hear she is unharmed." Morris added to his performance as the major was clearly not taken with it.

"Mm-hmm...," the major mumbled again, putting his feet on the table while puffing a mist of fumes that suffocated the room in a heavy fog of blurry smoke.

"So why are you tryin' to may-uk that maah problem? Ah'm a soldier, not a nanny."

Morris signaled Gorsh to hand him a small leather pouch.

"I am not here to cause any problems. But as you know, the civil war is over and if there is any truth to the conversation amongst your soldiers in the streets, then it seems like whatever conflict you had going on here with the Apache savages has just been resolved by coming to an agreement."

The major took a puff of his cigar in silence.

"With the military's glorious days now behind us and thousands of men begging for work...wouldn't ten thousand dollars help a soldier get back on his feet?"

Morris placed the leather pouch on the major's desk.

"Mm-hmm...," the major muttered, still rocking back and forth in his chair. "Te-yn thousand bucks mean squat with a rope aroun' maah neck. Ah can't just raahd to them Indians and kill a bunch of them for some missing gal. Thuh big bosses will have maah head for that."

Morris pushed the pouch further over the table.

"No killing. I would never ask that of you. All I am asking for is a few men for my safety. Maybe let them growl a little to make a statement when we get there. That's it. The girl will come without bloodshed. I promise."

Major Wicks eyeballed the pouch, spewing another mist of heavy fog into the air.

"One morning of your time." Morris kept hammering the major, noticing a crack in his defense. "In and out, nothing more..." His voice sounded almost hypnotizing.

"In and out...," Mr. Gorsh's slimy voice parroted after Morris. The major relished the last remaining puff of smoke, spewing it all out onto Morris's flinching and coughing face, staring back at him with suspiciously narrowed eyes. He crushed the embers on an ashtray before leaning forward to grab the weighty pouch with his hairy hand.

"In and out, nothing more," the major repeated, almost like a warning.

Esther felt cold and grabbed down to her waist to pull her blanket up, but instead of the expected wool of a blanket, she felt the soft plush of pelt in her hand. Panic made way to her sleepiness, and she shot up just to fall right back into a daze. In front of her was an old native woman tending to a fire in the hearth of what seemed to be a teepee. Esther rubbed her eyes as hard as she could, but the scene in front of her stayed the same. She was indeed inside a teepee! Her gaze wandered around, searching and discerning the space around her, only to freeze upon the sight of George soundly asleep next to her bed, his face buried into her hand. A warm, fuzzy feeling spread through her aching body and she couldn't help but smile. Seeing the man, she loved so dearly by her side…it meant everything to her.

"Dataa," the native woman said with a smile that broke through the wrinkles on her face. She was pointing a finger at George then both of them. Esther surmised it meant something like 'husband,' or 'lover,' as her cheeks flushed red.

Slowly, the bits and pieces of her last moments before she'd passed out came crashing back to her. The pale wooden room at Billy's in Chama, George's voice in the unreachable distance calling for her, and now she was here within the shade of an unknown teepee filled with indistinguishable scents and the dancing flames of a warm fire. But how?

"Iya."

The woman handed her a bowl with some sort of mushed berries and plants in it. "Iya," she repeated in a friendly but somewhat demanding tone.

George slowly opened his eyes, staring right at Esther who was not only alive, but sitting upright and holding a bowl.

"ESTHER!" he cried out, pulling her into his arms.

"You are alive!" He squeezed her so tightly, she coughed a little. Her bowl dropped right out of her hand and spilled its contents onto the floor.

"Did you think I would just let you have all the fun without me?" she teased him and nestled her head against his warm, muscular chest. It felt wonderful.

"Impossible! You *are* the adventure," his voice touted with happiness, uplifted to new heights.

"Iya," the woman now commanded as she picked up the bowl from the floor and filled it with food again. George released Esther from his grip of loving death so she could start eating like a good girl. But one bite of the bowl's contents was enough to twitch her whole face into a grimace.

"It tastes like a thousand lemons," she cringed. The native woman giggled while George threw his head back in laughter.

"Wait until you smoke their sacred pipe—I hallucinated for hours. For a moment I thought old Peggy was a bangtail."

Esther smiled back at him. "Old Peggy?"

George laughed again. "The most stubborn bloody horse in the West."

It was such a blessing to not only still be alive but to get to see George laugh again. She could shed tears of happiness.

"I assume your agreement with the natives was accepted?" She carefully took another tiny sip from the bowl, shivering just at the thought that she had to get that down again. But George didn't answer. He just looked at her with a faint smile on his lips.

"It was, wasn't it?" Esther placed the bowl aside, drawing her brows tighter in worry. This agreement meant so much more for George than money. His family depended on it, and so did the natives.

"…More or less."

He tilted his head with a cheeky grin to distract her. But she cared for this man too much to be put off so easily. George picked the bowl back up and handed it back to her.

"You should eat. I will explain everything later."

Esther was about to inquire more about this horse Peggy when a loud voice coming from outside startled her.

"George!" Jones's voice echoed into the teepee from not far away. She and George exchanged worried looks and she was about to try to get up on her feet by maneuvering all her weight onto her arms, when George grabbed her arm, stopping her in her tracks.

"Wait here," he said in a gentle but firm tone. "I'm certain it is nothing…"

Just like that he kissed her on her forehead and left.

Esther exchanged a confused glance with the native woman. Something felt off here. George acted strangely enough when she asked about his agreement to mine the land for the natives, but now Jones added a new level of concern to the whole matter by shouting about like that.

Esther pushed herself onto her knees and tried to get up at once, but her body couldn't find the energy for it and she fell back onto her buttocks. The native woman now walked over to her.

"Yidiits'e," she said, touching her ear.

Was she telling her to wait here and listen? But Esther tried to get back up again, this time almost making it before flopping back onto her buttocks once more.

"Yidiits'e." The woman tried one more time before she rolled her eyes and grabbed Esther under her arm to lift her up back onto her feet. Esther now realized that she wasn't wearing anything waist up but a wet cloth of some sort. She looked around for her clothes but the Apache woman grabbed a leather shirt from the floor instead and pulled it over Esther's head, carefully helping her with her arm to avoid touching the still very painful wound on her shoulder. Esther now took a more detailed glance at her savior. The woman had silver strains running through her coal-black hair. Her leather shirt and skirt were beautifully decorated with beadwork and she was wearing jewelry made of turquoise. She couldn't help but wonder if this was what her mother would have looked like before she was forced into the white man's world.

Esther grabbed the woman's hands.

"Thank you, from the bottom of my heart," she said with tears in her eyes. The woman nodded understanding perfectly well — not the words, but the meaning.

"Dataa," she whispered in a motherly voice, throwing her head into George's direction. Esther nodded back at her.

"Yes, dataa…"

She then left the teepee on wobbly legs, staring onto the Jicarilla Apache campsite that was surrounded by vast plains and the misty air and sun rising beyond it.

The cold air wafted onto Jones's shivering face as he dismounted from Peggy in one swift motion, quite impressive for a man who enjoyed food that much. Billy was right behind him on Susie and dismounting as well. Some of the Apache stared over to them before continuing with their usual business.

"George," Jones yelled rushing toward him.

"What is it?"

"It's Morris." Jones tried to catch his breath. "He is on his way here with Major Wicks."

George's body locked up with rage. Morris…The very man who'd tried to rob Esther of her father's company, hunted her like an animal, and put a price on her head that sentenced her to death… He was coming.

George's fists clenched and unclenched in anger, ready to face this man and put an end to this farce—and him if need be.

"We have to hide Esther, or he will take her before I can challenge him in court."

"Let him come," George growled, drawing his pistol to count the rounds in it. Billy and Jones exchanged concerned looks.

"George." Billy stepped closer, trying to talk sense into him. "We can't take the military on. Not here. Not like this."

What Billy said made sense, and yet George had the hardest time controlling his boiling hatred. His heart was nothing but pitch black for the man they called Morris. Everything the woman he loved had been through, it was all his fault.

"Billy is right," Jones pleaded. "We have to get her out of here or hide her. We can't just shoot at the military."

As much as he hated it, they were right. Engaging the military like this would be a suicide mission—the opposite of saving Esther.

George tried to take a deep breath to calm himself, find his usual composed nature. He placed his gun back in his holster.

"Very well, let us hide her. I shall go and—"

"We will do no such thing." Esther interrupted him as she teetered toward them.

For a moment, Jones forgot everybody and everything and ran over to her, pulling her into his arms.

"My child! You are saved!" he sobbed, heavy tears running down his face. Esther gave him a loving squeeze.

"I am," she said in a gentle tone to calm his nerves before tearing herself free from his hug. "But I won't hide. And I won't run," she declared, not leaving even the slightest room for negotiations.

"What do you mean?" George grabbed her arm in utter shock. But Esther faced him all the same, her gaze steady as her heart.

"The people here have saved my life. I won't endanger them in any way. It's me they want."

"We made an agreement to save you and we shall honor it," Itza-chu said, entering the conversation out of nowhere. "You can stay, and we will fight."

"No," Esther urged in a loud breaking voice. "No," she repeated in a softer but still determined tone. "I could never forgive myself if anything were to happen to your people. I have made up my mind. I will ride up to them before they can get here and start their slaughtering."

Esther tried to break her arm free of George's grip, but he tightened it.

"I can't let you do that, Esther." And he wouldn't. He'd almost lost his love before; he would not let that happen again. She could fight him all she wanted, he would carry her out of the camp on his feet if he had to. But much to his surprise, she didn't fight him. Instead, she looked him deep in his eyes with a faint smile on her lips. She then gently grabbed his hand, softly rubbing her thumb over the back of it.

386

"It will be alright. I shall break free again and come find you," she lovingly whispered to him, tears forming in her eyes. But something in her voice told George that she did not believe one word she had just promised him.

No, it couldn't end like this. He couldn't just let Morris take her. Not after everything they have been through together. Think, George. Think, God damn it. This is the woman you love! You wish to marry! Bloody hell…THINK!

Esther leaned forward and gave him a soft goodbye kiss. And just when it seemed like this was really it, that Morris would take her from him as if she had never existed, right there and then, it hit George like an enormous, bright bolt of lightning! How had he not thought of it sooner? The answer to saving his love was here right in front of him! He would end up as poor as a church mouse as it would also ruin his options of marrying a rich heiress, but to hell with it! He would find a way, manage somehow. This was the woman he loved, and he would be damned if he would see her go — or taken.

"Marriage," he now announced out loud to share his ingenious idea with the world.

"Excuse me?" Esther wondered, exchanging looks with Billy and Jones as if George had lost his mind.

But he didn't seem fazed by any of this and out of nowhere, just as if he truly had lost his marbles, he kneeled in front of her, taking her hand firmly into his once again.

"Will you marry me, my love?" he asked on his knees. If his eyes hadn't been so serious, one might think he was jesting, that the strong New Mexican sun had done him damage.

"I can't." She pulled away, turning so George would not see the pain in her face.

"Don't you remember? I can't legally marry without Morris's consent until I'm twenty-one, and I doubt I will live until—" She stopped abruptly mid-sentence, her eyes filled with tears. But George was not deterred by any of her words.

"Jones!" he shouted enthusiastically for the lawyer.

"...Y-Yes?" he answered, more confused than ever.

"In the canyon... Didn't you say Esther is half native?"

Jones scratched his head, still bewildered. "Yes, I did say that. But I don't see how—" He stopped talking with an inquisitive gaze at George, his mouth dropping to the floor.

"YES, OF COURSE!" he now yelled, looking just as euphoric as George did.

"Can somebody help the slow fellow out?" Billy now stepped in, a bit annoyed.

"Yes, please," Esther agreed, a hint of anger in her voice.

Jones wildly grabbed both of Esther's hands, looking straight into her still muddled eyes.

"Don't you understand? You are half Cherokee. You can be married on native land at any age you want."

Esther's eyes tore wide open in shock and she almost lost her balance, but George was there just in time to catch her.

"If that is what you want, of course," he said with a sweet smile. "Although I would take it rather personally if you would prefer to leave with Morris than marry me," he joked.

But Esther paid him no mind.

"Of course I want to marry you!" she beamed, throwing herself around his neck.

Watching the happy couple and with a fatherly smile on his face, Jones turned to Itza-chu.

"Would the Chief be able to marry them?"

"The Chief has left to meet with the other Apache tribes, but I am Itza-chu, his son," he said with pride. George gave Esther another quick kiss before he respectfully walked up to Itza-chu.

"I know we ask a lot, and I have nothing to give you but the fact that this marriage will upset a man who is a thief and murderer. And I can give you Peggy here." He nodded over to the horse, almost ashamed to even bring her up. "But will you please marry us?"

Itza-chu narrowed his eyes, looking at Peggy.

"This horse is Peggy. She bites and hates to move." He crossed his arms. "But it will happen to help you... And to upset the white thief." He smirked.

George picked Esther up with the biggest smile she had ever seen. He felt light on his feet, wanted to swirl her around — and managed just in time to stop, reminding himself of her wound — when the harsh reality of his dire financial situation struck him hard. His sparkling eyes turned dull, which everybody, including Esther, noticed right away.

"What is it?"

George looked deep into her beautiful eyes.

"The deal with the natives... I didn't get the mining rights. If you marry me, I will have nothing to give you or the children. Not a penny, not a dime."

Esther gasped, taking a step back and staring at him as if she had seen a ghost. George feared for the worst, that she would reject him. But instead, she burst into laughter.

"You didn't tell him?" she asked Jones with a huge smile.

Jones shook his head. "Why would I? I thought he knew."

"Knew what?" George frowned, more confused than ever.

Jones stepped closer with ease. "Have you ever heard of the Silvertons?"

George scratched his head trying to reach further into his mind until it rang a bell. Yes, he remembered. It was the talk of New York; next to his own arrival, that was all society gossiped about. The disappearance of the Silverton heiress, next in line to one of the most powerful fortunes in the nation—no, the world!

"Well, my boy, the heiress herself is standing right in front of you."

Esther was able to grab George's hand before he tumbled backwards.

"You…are…a…Silverton?" He was barely able to get out. She grinned.

"The one and only."

Suddenly it came to her. At the saloon in Antonito, was money the reason why he'd acted strangely?

"At the saloon…" she whispered, her cheeks turning fire red, "were finances the reason for… I mean after…" She looked away, too shy to speak further in front of the others. But she didn't have to. George understood perfectly well and pulled her into his arms, holding her tightly.

"I thought I could not provide you the life you deserve, that I would drag you down with me."

"How foolish..." she whispered back with an uncontainable smile. "I would rather be penniless with you and the children than have all the wealth in the world without you."

George kissed her on her head. Being so close to him gave her the tingles all over again. She would have loved to bury her face in his warm neck a bit longer, but their celebration came to an abrupt halt as an Apache man came riding wildly into the camp, shouting over to Itza-chu in loud urgency. Itza-chu faced them with a burden of worry painted across his face, weighing down his body.

"We have to start. They are close," he announced in a grave tone.

George and Esther nodded.

"What do we have to do? Do we need rings?"

Itza-chu shook his head. He pointed at the big fire in the middle of the camp.

"To become one, the man and woman have to take seven steps around the sacred fire." He started walking toward the fire. "Each step followed by a sacred vow."

Esther and George followed him. The fire burned strong and high with scorching heat dancing in the wind, reaching to the sky. Itza-chu shouted something in a great voice to gather everyone's attention. Different shapes and sizes joined in droves to heed the call, forming a circle around the sacred flame. George and Esther stood in the middle, watched by a hundred faces, gazing in joy and harmony.

"Haskiiyii izdzanii data," his voice boomed, followed by loud singing and ululation, merged by the sounds of a dozen beating drums as the rest started dancing around the edges of the great hearth. It was stunning. Breathtaking. Utterly incredible. Their beautiful voices sang up into the sky, their decorated heads rhythmically moving with their feet that now seemed as light as feathers. Esther and George were held captive by their chants, drowned in speechlessness. She almost had to thank Morris for this beautiful wedding.

Esther threw her head back to look at the brightening sky bursting in violets, and oranges, and reds. A deep thought uncurled beneath her heart and came rising into the air above. Were her parents watching?

Itza-chu placed a hand on George's shoulder.

"You make the first step and say a vow." Then turned to Esther. "Then you do the same. Seven each and you will be one under the great sky."

George squeezed Esther's hand and took the first step, not once moving his gaze away from hers.

"I promise to always be at your side."

Esther took her first step.

"I promise to fight the world for you."

George took his second step and vowed to always honor and respect her. Esther did the same.

"I shall love you in good times as well as bad, in sickness and in health," George promised her.

"For richer or without a gold mine," Esther lovingly teased him with tears of joy in her eyes.

They both took step after step, vow after vow, until George took his seventh and final step.

"I will love you and honor you until my dying breath."

The dancing and drumming raged on as they felt the heat of the people drawn in the great flame. Esther felt weightless as the chant grew louder. Wondering whether anyone has ever died of happiness, she took her seventh and final step.

"I will love you and honor you for all the days of my life."

George pulled her closer, leaving almost no distance between their lips. Esther was about to forget all the pain and loss, the burden she'd had to carry, and even Morris himself, when all of a sudden the singing had died and the dancing was replaced by a hundred men and women standing still. The whole wedding had turned into complete silence as the crowd started splitting only to reveal the devil himself—Morris.

The air felt thick as morning fog, drawing a hundred gasping breaths into endless chattering voices. Morris rode closer, a smirk on his face that made Esther gag. In his mind, there was no doubt that he had finally won, had found her. His victorious grin suggested that he was playing all the twisted little thoughts his black-painted brain had planned for her. A riding accident? Falling down the stairs? Choking on food? He might as well choke her himself in the middle of the night. Who would know?

Major Wicks and Mr. Gorsh were right next to him. On a hilltop in their backdrop was an army of soldiers, awaiting the major's command to attack if need be.

She suppressed a shudder as bitterness filled her mouth. She remembered all the nights she'd lain awake, her belly growling with hunger as she shivered in the freezing cold. She recalled every moment when she'd feared for her life, peeking over her shoulder to see if Morris had finally found her. If it was up to her, if it was only her and Morris here, she would do all sorts of terrible things to this man.

George must have felt the same way as he suddenly took a step toward Morris, both fists clenched in hatred. But Esther pulled him back. He could not harm him. She could not harm him. As monstrous as Morris was, the law was on his side—but not her fortune.

Esther closed her eyes for a moment, praying for strength to calm herself. *You are a Silverton, born of a warrior mother and strong father, now give this piece of horse droppings what he deserves.*

Jones, who was too far away from her to grab and hold back, made his first few steps with trembling, clenched fists. She had to act, now.

"Morris my dear friend!" Esther shouted in the happiest tone she was able to produce. George,

Jones, and Billy jerked their heads to her in utter puzzlement, but she kept smiling, throwing George a cheeky wink. He understood and parted his lips to a grin.

"How thoughtful of you to come all this way!" Esther sparkled at Morris who found none of this comical.

"You must have lost your mind living with these savages!" he condemned her, shaking his fist in rage.

"I AM HERE TO TAKE YOU BACK! NOW!"

"To New York? What for?" she giggled nonchalantly, enjoying every bit of his outrage. He had always been such a drama king; perhaps he could find work in a theater after this?

"What for? WHAT FOR? I am your guardian, and I demand you come with me now!" His temper boiled with skin as red as the morning sky.

"Oh… I thought you'd come to attend my wedding," she rejoiced, grabbing George's arm.

"Your what?" Morris was taken aback, now speechless.

"Absolutely absurd. You are not of age to marry without your guardian's consent," Mr. Gorsh hissed from behind.

Jones now stepped in, raising his chin. "Well, legally speaking, whoever you are, her mother was Cherokee, so I can assure you that this is very much a marriage in the eyes of the law."

Mr. Gorsh's face now looked as if an elephant had just stomped on his foot.

"N-n-native wedding?" he stuttered, wiping his sweaty forehead with a handkerchief. Morris on the other hand seemed as if he was close to a heart attack. His eyes were shot wide open and an expression that could only be described as pure terror had taken over his entire body. He jerked his horse toward Mr. Gorsh to grab him by his coat. "That can't be true! She can't just marry here!"

But Mr. Gorsh threw his face into his hands and cried. "Dear God! What now?"

"God has nothing to do with this," George stated arrogantly. "But while we are getting so comfortable with one another... you wouldn't happen to know more about this wanted poster, would you? Alive or...*dead*, was it?"

He pulled his coat back to reveal his pistol.

"I mean," he said, narrowing his eyes, "that would almost seem as if you were trying to kill my wife, wouldn't it?"

Billy now stepped closer, revealing his gun as well.

"It sure as blazes would." He spat onto the floor.

Morris's red face turned white as ashes. He turned his horse toward Major Wicks.

"Do something! I paid you well for this!" he yelled in a mixture of fear and anger.

Major Wicks rolled his eyes in annoyance and calmly gave his horse the spurs to ride up to George.

"Is this yo-wr wife, Sir?"

"She certainly is."

Major Wicks threw Esther a nod with his hat. "Congratulations, Ma'm."

She nodded back at him, crossing her arms.

"I won't bother ya'll no more. He's all yours."

Those were the major's last words before he turned his horse around, leaving what was left of Morris and his band of two to fend for themselves. Morris almost fell off his horse.

"How dare you! Wait!" He screamed like a child having a tantrum as he watched Mr. Gorsh turn his horse around to follow the major.

"Gorsh, you snake! I won't hang alone! I swear it!"

Morris had a sheer look of madness on his face.

"COME BACK HERE RIGHT NOW!" he cried out, whipping his horse with its reins to ride after them, leaving a trail of dust and dirt of who he was, and who he will remain to be, for better or for worse.

Billy and Jones stood next to Esther and George, as they all watched in silent victory, Morris getting smaller and smaller in the distance.

"Should I go after him?" Billy asked with his hand on his pistol. He meant it just as it sounded. But right after the words had left his mouth, several Jicarilla Apache warriors rode by them like a thunderstorm, shaking the earth underneath them.

"Where are they going?" George asked Itza-chu.

"Trade. The thief's horse for his insult of calling them savages."

"Will he survive walking back home?" Esther asked.

"If he's lucky, no." Jones crossed his arms. "I will have him charged in New York with attempted murder and forgery as soon as I get back."

Esther stared at the man in the far distance. A man who had almost destroyed her and everything she loved. For a while, it felt like a long lingering gaze. Like a mirage fading in the desert, a far-off nightmare that was never even real. And finally, with a feeling of great relief, she directed her gaze to her husband. Stunning and brave. Strong yet sincere. In every single way he was a man a woman could only dream of. He now faced her too, glimpsing deep into her eyes. That beautiful tingling she always felt around him spread throughout her whole body all the way to her fingertips.

George leaned closer. "I love you," he whispered softly brushing his lips against hers.

"I love you, too," she whispered back, pressing her lips onto his.

And as the drums picked up their rhythmic beats again, accompanied by beautiful songs in a mystic language, Esther thanked her God and theirs for everything that had happened. The good, the bad — it all was part of a greater plan that had led her right into her husband's arms — George Astley, the love of her life.

EPILOGUE

"**M**ama!" Miki shouted, storming past Helga and little Cliff onto the street to throw herself right into Esther's arms. Jeff and Tom followed suit.

"Miki! Jeff! Tom!" Esther cried, tears of joy running down her face. She had missed them so terribly.

Little Cliff now stretched his arms toward Esther, his face ready to cry if he wasn't held by her that very second. Esther took him into her arms and squeezed him tightly, feeling the warm joy in her heart that only a mother could feel.

"She is a woman again!" Miki blurted at Milton who was rubbing the children's heads to tell them in his own way that he was happy to be back.

"Yes, just like you," Milton replied, nodding at the cute, pink dress Miki was wearing. Esther took a step back to look at the kids. They looked fantastic. Going to school and living in a good neighborhood had turned them into children that were allowed to be just that—children.

"You also brought a man!" Jeff shouted happily.

George threw his head back in laughter before he leaned over. "Yes, she did."

"Are you going to stay with us?" Tom asked, raising an eyebrow.

"If that is all right with you." He rubbed Tom's head.

"I guess so, but it would have been better if you had brought a gift, you know." Tom grinned.

"To buy our love faster," Miki clarified.

George laughed heartily and turned toward Esther.

"I love them already!" He turned back to the kids. "Well, fortunately for me, I did not come empty handed."

"A present?!" All three gushed over George with eyes sparkling like stars. George nodded and stepped aside to reveal Peggy, who was standing a few feet away tied to the back of their carriage.

"A HORSIE!" Miki gave a high-pitched squeak, launching toward Peggy closely followed by Tom and Jeff.

"Wait!" George called after them to warn them of the famous Peggy nips, but it was too late. Miki, Jeff, and Tom had already thrown their arms around Peggy's chest, rubbing their faces against her soft fur like this was the greatest moment of their lives. George and Esther's mouths fell to the floor. Peggy, the horse notoriously famous in the whole West for her grumpiness, stood as still as a statue, letting Miki, Tom, and Jeff do with her as they pleased.

"I love her!" Miki shouted to George who was now walking over to them. Maybe she wasn't a barn sour after all? Maybe she just didn't like the dry West? But the moment George stepped into her reach, Peggy nipped at him, almost getting him in his arm. Esther and the kids burst into loud laughter.

"Bloody horse..." George growled to Peggy, but his heart was filled with joy. He looked over to Esther who was holding Cliff tight to her chest. She caught his gaze with a smile that swept him off his feet.

"We are very lucky," he mumbled to Peggy who was clearly enjoying the kids' attention and love.

"Very, very lucky…"

Several Months Later

The carriage stopped on top of a hill, looking down onto the enormous complex of Aberdeen Park. Its façade shimmered golden in the sun, ready to welcome back its Duke and Duchess with all the elegance and bling they deserved, nothing less.

Esther and the kids were speechless. Never had they seen anything like it.

"Is this the town hall, Papa?" Miki squeaked under wide eyes and gasping breath.

George laughed. "No, my princess, this is your new home."

Miki let out another happy squeak, throwing her arms around George. "I am so happy I could scream."

"You just did." Milton rolled his eyes, still staring at the castle that would now be his home and someday, as the oldest son, his.

"Can we run down?" Tom begged.

"Pleeeeeeeeeease." Jeff threw in his support for the idea.

"If your mother doesn't mind your new clothes getting dirty again." George smiled at Esther. She let out a deep breath.

"You totally ruined your other clothes this morning when you tried to bathe Peggy." She tested the waters for a no. But the kids all fired back at her with big, droopy eyes, their little mouths frowning all the way to the floor. Esther let out an audible sigh.

"Fine..." She gave up.

"Yeay!" Miki, Tom, and Jeff shouted, jumping off the carriage, giving it a good shake. Tom and Jeff had already stormed down the hill, but Miki ran to the back of the carriage instead.

George turned to see what she was doing. She had freed Peggy, who was tied to the back of the carriage.

"Peggy has to come with us," she said in her cute little girl voice.

George frowned. Poor Miki didn't know that Peggy was a barn sour. It had literally taken four bloody men this morning to push Peggy out of her barn before they could tie her up to the back of the carriage. It took another two men to push her into motion to let the carriage start its journey. This whole drama had taken so long, Helga had had to take another carriage ahead of them to inform the staff that their late arrival was nothing to worry about.

"That's so nice of you, princess, but you know that Peggy doesn't like to move much." But George had barely spoken his words, when old, lazy Peggy flew down the hill like Pegasus! George jerked up in his seat to make sure his eyes weren't playing tricks on him. He even rubbed them once just to be absolutely certain that this was really happening. But Esther's beautiful laugh that always warmed his heart confirmed that this in fact was real.

And if that wasn't enough, all of a sudden, out of nowhere, little Cliff opened his mouth and pointed down the hill:

"Peggy," he announced, his first word ever spoken, loud and clear. "Peggy, Peggy!" he now yelled down to the horse that was running up and down the hill to entertain the kids, her long legs galloping pridefully like a wild mustang. George fell backwards into his seat.

"This bloody horse," he growled with a smile on his face that was as bright as the sun above them. "This bloody horse…"

A Few Notes of Interest

(Jicarilla Maiden, Curtis Edward S., 1905)

THE JICARILLA APACHE

Struggles Both Past and Present

The story of the Jicarilla Apache began hundreds of years ago during the Canada to Southwestern migratory period. This nomadic group ranged across what is now New Mexico and the southern edge of Colorado. As with most other Native American nations, they gradually settled in one place as agriculture took hold as a prominent practice. Unfortunately, similar to other indigenous groups, the arrival of European explorers and the eventual practice of Manifest Destiny pushed them away from their chosen home.

This oft-repeated story of the clash between Native Americans and Europeans echoed through the centuries as the Jicarilla Apache fought to protect themselves and their culture and claim a reservation for their own.

A History of Displacement

The earliest movements of the Jicarilla Apache involved the natural travel associated with a hunting and seasonal farming group. It was not until the Spanish arrived that they began to feel real pressure to abandon their normal territory. Although prior to forced relocation the Jicarilla were not completely peaceful and regularly raided other Apache groups, they were not threatened with obliteration until the Europeans showed up.

The American Indian wars around 1850 forced the Jicarilla Apache to become one of the most feared groups in the Southwest. Subsequent US military actions were met with a fierce defense. Ultimately, however, the group was killed, died due to disease, starvation, or exposure, or dispersed to other areas.

The Long Journey to a Reservation

After the battles, broken treaties, and other efforts to destroy the Jicarilla Apache completely, the group was left without any land to call their own. Representatives arrived in Washington DC in 1873 for the first request but were not granted reservation land until 1887. The area did not include traditional sacred lands or areas suitable for agriculture. Twenty years later, additional acreage was added so that the people could start farming sheep.

While the long struggle to get a reservation was over, it did very little to provide a bright future for the Jicarilla Apache. Natural gas and oil were discovered in the late 1940s and improved the economic standing of the tribe. A 1971 monetary payment for loss of sacred lands for $9.15 million was awarded as part of the Indian Claims Commission.

The Jicarilla Apache Today

While, like many other Native Americans across the United States, large numbers of the Jicarilla Apache have assimilated into modern culture, the reservation remains a focal point in their lives. Tribal children go to school there, many members work at the tribe-owned casinos and natural gas and oil wells, both sheep and cattle ranching are prominent moneymakers, and they generally welcome all modern amenities into their lives.

The fight to get the Jicarilla Apache Reservation in the late 19th century has provided many of them with a place to call home. However, it comes with many of the common issues that plague reservations across the country: unemployment, poverty, crime, and alcohol abuse.

The continuing effort for the preservation of the Jicarilla Apache culture exists in many of the same ways as it has for hundreds of years. Although they no longer have to defend their people from European invasion or tribal battles, their way of life still involves struggles that affect their well-being and success.

STREET ARABS OF NEW YORK

Poverty in Victorian NYC

Street Arabs in sleeping quarters.

Three children curled up on a metal grate in a below-grade areaway.

New York, cs. 1890,

While many modern people think of opulent furnishings, clothing, and industry in the Victorian era, things were much different for the lower classes in New York City and beyond. For those who could not afford velvet draperies and carriage rides, the mid-to-late 1800s were defined by squalor, hard living conditions, and often a complete disconnect from society at large.

The so-called Street Arabs of New York were a vast population of tens of thousands of homeless children and youth. Most of those captured in early photographs and written about were boys.

The Truth About Poverty in Victorian Times

The Industrial Revolution may have heralded a new age of products and possibility, but it also boosted US immigration numbers by a lot and flooded New York City. All of these people needed places to live and jobs so they could support themselves and their families. These conditions simply did not exist for many.

With limited or no regulation, tenement homes sprouted up everywhere. Families got barely enough floorspace to lie down at night, had no access to hygienic amenities, and simply could not afford to care for all their children. Of course, in those times, many children went to work in the factories or elsewhere by the time they were ten or twelve years old.

Those who could not get a position or were otherwise unsupportable ended up on the streets in the Street Arab population that was first brought to life in 1888 with Jacob Riis' iconic photograph of three small boys sleeping on a heater vent in an alley.

Who Were the Street Arabs of New York?

The term "Arab" in the Street Arab moniker referred to the nomadic lifestyle of these children and has nothing to do with the Middle East or Arabic ancestry or culture. They were also called urchins, gamins, or simply homeless. They existed throughout New York City in both poorer and more established areas where they begged or performed simple jobs like shoe shining, selling newspapers, and one-time jobs to fetch and carry items and similar tasks.

The initial story and photographs that brought attention from the middle classes revealed that these Street Arabs were not all orphans as some might expect. Some were turned out by their families because they could not afford to keep them while others chose the life of a street nomad because conditions in the tenements were so dismal. They formed their own gangs or pseudo-families, cared for each other or squabbled over the slim pickings in the city, and grew up mostly forgotten if they got the chance to grow up at all.

THE BRUNOT AGREEMENT

Severe Limits on the Ute Nations

Six tribal leaders (l to r) Little Plume (Piegan), Buckskin Charley (Ute), Geronimo (Chiricahua Apache), Quanah Parker (Comanche), Hollow Horn Bear (Brulé Sioux), and American Horse (Oglala Sioux) on horseback in ceremonial attire

The United States government created the Brunot Agreement in 1873 so they could take advantage of the high presence of gold and other precious metals in the San Juan Mountains of Colorado. This so-called agreement is just one example of the continuing powers of the federal government over what was designated as Native American land.

At that time, the Utes already had control of approximately 15 million acres of land given to them in the Treaty of 1868. Their reservation covered approximately 30% of Colorado and did not allow any use or specifically mining activity by non-tribal people. Unfortunately, as things frequently go for the Native American people, their claim to land was ignored and eventually turned over officially with the Brunot Agreement.

Initial Negotiations Are Met with Failure

As soon as the minerals were discovered in the San Juan Mountains around 1869, the European Americans and especially the federal government took notice. By this time in history, it was standard operating procedure to remove control of anything of value from Native American people no matter where they had settled. Creating reservations outside of sacred or traditional lands was a part of this.

When the development of mines by the Ute people began, the US government launched their efforts to have the profitable mountain regions removed from the reservation. The Utes and other groups such as the Jicarilla Apache were there to strengthen the refusal to sell the land and attempt to enforce the removal of trespassers as promised by the original treaty.

The Brunot Agreement — A Matter of Delay and Deceit

Despite the refusal of the Ute and other first Nations people to allow their mining land under the control of the government, they did not have the power to keep non-native miners off their reservation lands. Throughout the early 1870s, the incursions to gather up as much lucrative minerals as possible occurred on a regular basis. Despite the treaty that stated the US would remove them, nothing was done.

It was this type of external pressure combined with more deceitful negotiations that led to the Brunot Agreement in 1873. Felix R. Brunot, who was at the time the Chairman of the Board of Indian Commissioners, orchestrated forced negotiations that were defined more by delays, misdirection, and deceit than by any sense of fairness. He used promises for a return of a kidnapped son as leverage but did not deliver. He ultimately presented a choice of a lesser of two evils to the Ute people. Either sign the Brunot Agreement and get compensated for the land or lose it by force.

The acceptance of the Brunot Agreement lost the Ute people a large percentage of their existing reservation, rights to many of the mineral mines in the mountains, and some of their prime hunting land. The American towns that sprung up near the mines grew quickly and expanded into land still owned by the tribe. Ultimately, the same thing that had happened to so many other Native American peoples happened in western Colorado. The march of so-called progress through the west took over and the Utes could no longer remain on their traditional lands.

THANK YOU!

First of all, thank you for purchasing An Outlawed Heiress and Her Duke. I know you could have picked any number of books to read, but you picked this book, and for that I am extremely grateful. As a small-time author and full-time mom, my readers mean a lot to me.

If you enjoyed this book, it would be really nice if you could leave a review for it on Amazon.

You can review the book here:

https://www.amazon.com/dp/B0867QCBXF

Your feedback and support will help me to continue writing novels.

Also, don't forget to sign up for our newsletter to stay up to date on new releases and get FREE books!

www.timelesspapers.com

Thank you!

New!!!

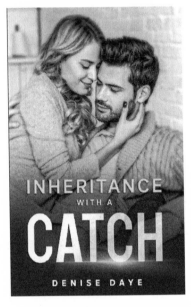

Don't forget to check out Denise's newest novel, *Inheritance With a Catch*!

https://www.amazon.com/dp/B08967Q8X8

To save his inheritance, a compelling billionaire must marry his gardener's daughter.

Is she his salvation... or his undoing?

ABOUT THE AUTHOR

Denise graduated with a master's in Social Work from an ivy league school and has dedicated many years of her life helping families and individuals in need of assistance. She has always had a passion for writing, but it wasn't until her own baby boy was born that Denise turned her passion into her profession. Whenever Denise is not typing away on one of her books, you can find her caring for her son (a.k.a. one of the toughest jobs in the world), bingeing Netflix with her beloved husband, or chasing after her puppy (who should technically be an adult dog by now).

Copyright 2020 by Timeless Papers

All rights reserved. This book or any portion thereof may not be reproduced or used in any manner whatsoever without the express written permission of the author except for the use of brief quotations in reviews.